Cammy Sitting Shiva

Cammy Sitting Shiva

♦ *A NOVEL* ♦

CARY GITTER

alcove
press

Books should be disposed of and recycled according to local requirements. All paper materials used are FSC compliant.

This is a work of fiction. All of the names, characters, organizations, places, and events portrayed in this novel are either products of the author's imagination or are used fictitiously. Any resemblance to real or actual events, locales, or persons, living or dead, is entirely coincidental.

Copyright © 2025 by Cary Robert Gitter

All rights reserved.

Published in the United States by Alcove Press, an imprint of The Quick Brown Fox & Company LLC.

Alcove Press and its logo are trademarks of The Quick Brown Fox & Company LLC.

Library of Congress Catalog-in-Publication data available upon request.

ISBN (hardcover): 979-8-89242-254-3
ISBN (paperback): 979-8-89242-278-9
ISBN (ebook): 979-8-89242-255-0

Cover design by Chelsy Escalona

Printed in the United States.

www.alcovepress.com

Alcove Press
34 West 27th St., 10th Floor
New York, NY 10001

First Edition: August 2025

The authorized representative in the EU for product safety and compliance is eucomply OÜ Pärnu mnt 139b-14, 11317 Tallinn, Estonia, hello@eucompliancepartner.com, +33757690241

10 9 8 7 6 5 4 3 2 1

For Meghan

So they sat down with him on the ground seven days and seven nights, and no one spoke a word to him, for they saw that his grief was very great.

—The Book of Job

Heaven looks a lot like New Jersey.

—Jon Bon Jovi

PROLOGUE

Saturday

CAMMY WAS ADRIFT AT a party the night her dad died. Her theater friend Gretchen had thrown herself a thirtieth-birthday bash at a German beer hall in the wilds of Williamsburg. The venue made Cammy a tad uneasy, given her Polish Jewish ancestors' unfortunate history with the German nation. What would she say to her grandma Ruth if she were still around? "Sorry, *Bubbe*. I know the Nazis killed your whole family, but the draft selection here is really amazing." Then again, she was probably overthinking it.

This is why Cammy was weird at parties.

Brooklyn always felt a bit like outer space to her. Unlike her hipper acquaintances who called the borough home, Cammy lived in a tiny, semilegal basement apartment off the last N stop in Astoria, Queens—an outlier among her New York peers. But here she was in bohemian BK on a crisp Saturday night in October, mixing it up with the cool theater kids at the cavernous beer hall. Raise a stein, pass the schnitzel.

To be clear, Cammy wasn't exactly a theater kid herself. Again: an interloper. She'd recently joined a group called the Drama Collective, which sounded like a histrionic communist cell but wasn't. Rather, it was an assortment of young actors, directors, and writers who gathered every Wednesday evening at a dilapidated playhouse above a porn shop in a seedy part of Midtown to "workshop" new material together. And also to drink cheap wine and commiserate about their struggles as artists in a cold, cruel world that refused to recognize their obvious talent. And also to hook up with each other. A multifaceted mission.

Cammy was one of the writers, or, at least, she was attempting to be. Since graduating from criminally overpriced NYU with an English degree—how prudent and wise—she'd spent her twenties trying her hand at various literary forms, to little avail. She'd taken fiction classes, screenwriting classes, even an ill-advised poetry class, despite the fact that she had less than zero aptitude for poetry. What did she have to show for all these costly courses? An unfinished novel, a pair of underbaked screenplays, and some embarrassing poems she'd deleted from her computer and released into the cyber ether, where they belonged. Now, at twenty-nine, she was giving playwriting a shot. She had a decent ear for dialogue. If at first you don't succeed . . .

She wasn't used to theater people, though. They were a different breed, nothing like the timid scribes from her previous seminars. These folks were loud, extroverted, *on*. Not only the actors, who were performative by nature, but the directors and writers too. They gushed when they spoke, roared with laughter, gesticulated. It was a lot for a dry, wry soul like Cammy to take. She'd been part of the Drama Collective for a few months now, and, to be honest, she still wasn't sure if she even liked her fellow members.

Nevertheless, she craved their boisterous company tonight. Cammy's boyfriend of the past year, David, a sweet, clean-cut, serious-minded New York City librarian, had broken up with her a couple of weeks ago. The split had been her fault: She'd screwed up by drunkenly fucking a brooding actor she'd met at one of the group's meetings. Oops. She didn't know why she'd done it. But in a moment of conscience, or Jewish guilt, she'd confessed her sin to David, and that was that. Then the self-loathing set in.

Happily, Gretchen, a whimsical director who aspired to be the next Julie Taymor—the avant-garde visionary behind the Broadway smash *The Lion King*—had come to the rescue with this welcome distraction: a party. Just what Cammy needed to take her mind off things. Right?

At present, she was sandwiched between strangers at one of the beer hall's long tables, her back to the brick wall, her butt aching from the hard wooden bench. She'd almost finished the great big stein that sat before her, which contained some amber-hued German lager with a harsh-sounding, guttural name. She found herself staring up at the vaulted, retractable roof—in the summer this room became a garden—as the voices around her carried on an animated conversation about the sorry state of the American theater.

"The problem is, there's no adventure. No one wants to take any chances."

"Well, it's all about money. It's economics."

"In Europe, the government subsidizes theater. They value the arts."

"Exactly. But this is America. Artists are expendable here."

"Excuse me," Cammy said, but nobody seemed to notice. She had to pee. She'd been holding it in for the past hour so as not to "break the seal," as Francesca, her best friend back in Jersey, liked to say. Was there any truth to that? she wondered. When you've been drinking and you pee for the first time, does it in fact open the floodgates for further, more frequent peeing for the rest of the night? If so, what was the biological explanation?

Musing on this profound inquiry, Cammy got up, though not before executing an awkward feat of acrobatics to free her legs from under the table. Benches were impractical. She felt relieved to escape the litany of complaints she'd been listening to, which, far from cheering her up, were actually making her more depressed.

On the way to the bathroom, she was intercepted by the birthday girl. Willowy Gretchen had wild, frizzy hair and was decked out in a 1920s flapper dress and a tiara. She was, to put it charitably, drunk off her ass. "Are you having fun?!" she chirped, grabbing Cammy by the shoulders.

They had to yell in each other's faces to be heard above the din of the echoey hall.

"Yes. So much fun. Thanks for inviting me."

"Oh my God, of course. I'm so glad you joined the Collective. You're the coolest, Cammy."

"I'm not that cool."

"And you're so funny."

"I am?"

"Uh-huh. Not in a laugh-out-loud way. In a like deadpan Daria way."

"Daria?"

"Don't you remember that cartoon show on MTV in the nineties? The super deadpan girl with glasses?" Cammy did, vaguely. "That's you."

"I'll have to YouTube it."

Gretchen gave Cammy's shoulders a final playful squeeze before letting them go. "All right. I've gotta go mingle with my peoples."

"Happy birthday, Gretchen."

"Thank you!" she sang out, stepping backward into the beer-swilling crowd, teetering on high heels. And then, with a mixture of wonder and morbid glee: "I'm thirty—I'm almost dead!"

Cammy went to the bathroom, broke the seal in a stall with a broken lock, and washed her hands in an automatic sink whose water flow was a game of chance. She eyed herself in the mirror. There was a yellowish light directly above her that she imagined as a spotlight. The rest of the restroom seemed to fade to darkness.

Ladies and gentlemen, we bring you Cammy Adler, alone on the stage of life.

What did she see in the revealing glow of that spotlight? She saw, of course, her familiar features: the olive complexion that prompted prying randos to ask if she were Greek or Italian (no, dummies—Jewish); the prominent nose she still felt self-conscious about, although men said it was cute; the shoulder-length brown hair that somehow never had quite enough volume; the same brand of black-rimmed glasses she'd been sporting since the fifth grade, save for an ill-fated dalliance with contact lenses in high school. (It's embarrassing when a lens falls out in the cafeteria and lands in your lunch food.)

More importantly, Cammy saw someone who didn't know what the hell she was doing. Twenty-nine years old, almost thirty—"almost dead," according to tiaraed Queen Gretchen. An unfaithful girlfriend. A dabbler, a dilettante, with writerly pretensions but no evidence that she possessed the skill or commitment to fulfill them. The product of a middle-class suburban upbringing and an expensive college education, she now resided in a glorified underground bunker and made a living temping as a copywriter in the most shallow of industries: marketing. Unmoored, directionless. And yet whom did she have to blame for this mess, this malaise, but herself and her own mysterious character flaws?

She even looked out of focus in the mirror. Or was it just smudged?

"Sorry, can I use that?" an irritated woman's voice asked.

Cammy was hogging the sink, another failing. "Oh. Yeah. Sorry."

Exiting the bathroom, she surveyed the bustling scene in the beer hall. Everyone appeared to be having a grand old time. It reminded her of one of those Bruegel paintings of sixteenth-century Dutch peasants soaking themselves in alcohol and dancing a merry jig. Dutch, German, same difference. Well, not really, but whatever.

Cammy realized at this point that (a) she was buzzed from the vat of lager she'd imbibed, and (b) she didn't feel like returning to the long table with the hard bench and the theater people.

No, what she wanted to do was drunk-dial David.

Good idea? Absolutely not. Was she going to do it anyway? You bet.

She wove her way through the Bruegelian revelers, careful not to get any ale sloshed on her, and made it out the door into the chilly autumn night. The usual suspects dotted the sidewalk outside the place: the anxious smokers; the pilgrims waiting for an Uber to take them home or, more likely, to the next phase of their Saturday evening; and, naturally, those, like Cammy, making reckless, tipsy phone calls.

A sidewalk outside a bar is truly some kind of holy way station, she thought. *I have to make a note of that; I have to write that down.* But she knew she'd forget to.

Shivering—she'd sacrificed warmth for style by wearing just a light jacket over a black jumpsuit—she pulled her phone out of her purse and checked the time. A few minutes past eleven. What was David doing now? He was probably in bed with a book, one of those thick Russian doorstops he'd been reading lately, or already asleep. What a good, gentle guy. And had Cammy not committed her senseless infidelity, she could've been tucked in next to him, cozy beneath his flannel covers, instead of out here in the void, lost among the Brooklynites.

She called and paced as the phone rang. Awake or asleep, he wasn't going to answer. Then she heard his soft-spoken recorded voice. She missed that voice. "Hi. You've reached David. Please leave a message, and I'll get back to you. Thanks."

Beep. That's your cue, Cammy.

"Hey," she began, with no clear idea of what to say next. That was the thing about drunk dials: They weren't typically well thought out. "I know it's late and I, like, shouldn't be calling you, but, uh, I'm at this party in Williamsburg and it sucks and . . ." Don't complain about the party. Talk to him. "Anyway, I've been thinking about you a lot?" Okay, don't sound desperate. Cool it down. "You know, I realized one thing we said we were gonna do this fall is go for a hike, and we never did. And I know it's kind of cold out now, but what if we just did that?" A hike? What was she babbling about? Too late. Go with it. "Yeah, what if we like took a train upstate to some beautiful place and went for a hike together, with no expectations? I just think—"

The insistent beep of an incoming call interrupted Cammy's rambling. Was it David having a change of heart? A quick glance at her phone dashed this drunken hope. She saw an unfamiliar number with the 201 area code native to New Jersey and, below it, the name "WIENER." Who?

"Fuck. Someone's calling me. I'm sorry for—Yeah. Bye, David."

Nicely done.

Leaning her body against the beer hall's brick exterior, she took the call. If this were a telemarketer, she was ready to heap all her pent-up frustrations on the unlucky bastard. "Hello?"

"Cammy?" The voice was serious, sonorous, middle-aged.

"Yeah? Who is this?"

"It's Rabbi Wiener."

Oh, *that* Wiener. In her inebriated state, she hadn't made the connection. Gary Wiener was the rabbi at her hometown synagogue back in Jersey.

Honestly, she'd never been crazy about the guy. He had a bald head, capped by a colorful knit yarmulke, and a graying goatee that lent him a gurulike air, which complemented his sagely, self-important affect. She and the other kids in religious school used to make fun of his name, with its homonymic echoes of hot dogs and penises. Anyhow, he was fine; maybe she was being too hard on him. She tended to do that.

But why on earth was Rabbi Wiener calling her at eleven o'clock on a Saturday night? Come to think of it, he'd never called her directly before. How did he get her number?

"Cammy . . . I have some terrible news."

That's when she became aware of a sound in the background: crying. No, not crying. Sobbing. Wailing. The sort of primal lament she'd witnessed only in the movies, when a battle-scarred soldier kneels over the body of his wounded buddy, weeping to the heavens. This wasn't *Saving Private Ryan*, though; this was real life.

"What? What's going on?"

"Your father . . ."

"My father? What about him? Is he okay?"

"Your father . . ." he repeated like a broken rabbinical record. And then, "He passed."

Cammy heard the words but didn't comprehend them, as if the rabbi had spoken in Hebrew or some other foreign tongue. "Your father. He passed." What did they mean? He passed what? The verb was missing its object.

"I'm here with your mother. She's very upset. She asked me to call you."

"I—I don't understand . . ."

"Your father passed away, Cammy. I'm so sorry."

There was the missing word: "away." Not an object, but an adverb. What Rabbi Wiener was saying, in his euphemistic clerical fashion, was that's Cammy's dad, Cy Adler, had died.

Which, of course, couldn't be right. Her dad was sixty-eight years old. He was healthy.

Yes, he'd recently had some minor medical stuff—namely, an elective, minimally invasive laparoscopic surgery to remove a small growth from his kidney that turned out to be benign. No big deal, the doctors had said; better to be proactive and get it taken care of.

There had been one annoying postoperative complication, a mild case of "hospital-acquired pneumonia," apparently not uncommon in such settings. So instead of coming straight home last week as planned, her father had been moved to a nearby rehab facility, where, with the help of antibiotics, fluids, and rest, he was supposed to quickly recover and regain his strength. Then he'd be as good as new.

This was what the doctors had told Cammy's mom, Beth, and what she had relayed to Cammy over the phone. Calm reassurances all around.

He couldn't possibly have died. It was absurd. Why was the rabbi playing this cruel practical joke on her? As petty revenge for those juvenile Wiener puns?

"Here's your mother," he said.

Cammy heard a flurry of noise as the phone was handed to her mom. But the hysterical woman on the other end of the line sounded nothing like any version of her mother she'd ever encountered. No, this woman was the grieving soldier on the battlefield, the source of the desperate wailing. Had the rabbi hired an impostor to prop up his hoax?

"Mom?"

"He's gone," Beth slurred between heaving sobs.

"What? How? I don't—"

"Come home, babe. Just please come home." This plea seemed to be all her mom could muster. It was followed by a chaotic sonic mash-up of phone juggling, crying, muffled voices, more static: an electronic symphony of trauma.

Rabbi Wiener came back on, intoning words like "sudden" and "unexpected" in his grave, pulpit-patented timbre, but Cammy had stopped listening. She was, to use a therapeutic term she hated, "processing." Either the rabbi was hosting a psychopathic reboot of that early-aughts MTV prank show, *Punk'd*, or this was all legit: Her dad was indeed dead.

In which case, why wasn't she crying too? Glancing around the Williamsburg street teeming with weekend life, she felt only a shocked numbness. She told the rabbi she'd be there soon, hung up, opened Lyft, and typed in her old address in River Hill, New Jersey. It would cost $83.89 to get home. Did Lyft offer a special parental-death discount? Doubtful. She requested the ride. Her driver, Sergei, and his red Hyundai Sonata were two minutes away.

Cammy spotted a huddle of hipsters smoking on the corner. Although she'd never been a smoker herself, except for the occasional intoxicated indulgence, now seemed like a wonderful time for a cigarette. She went over and asked to bum one. An ethereal person with long, dyed-white hair in a fabulous faux-fur coat lit it for her. Wandering away from the group, she took a drag and exhaled a cloud of smoke. Maybe the smoke contained the secrets of how she should feel and how she should act and what it meant to be newly fatherless. De-fathered. But before she could perceive them, the cloud dissolved into the night air.

The red Hyundai pulled up to the curb, right on time. Sergei rolled down the passenger window. A burly man in a green Adidas tracksuit, he looked too big for his car, like one of those driving bears in the circus. "You are Cammy?" he barked in a thick Russian accent.

"Yeah," she said, strangely unsure.

"You going to Jersey?"

"Yeah."

He gave her a knowing smile, displaying a row of tobacco-stained teeth. "Going home, huh?"

"Yes." She flung the cigarette to the ground, steeling herself for everything that was to come. "I am."

★ ★ ★

The front door was unlocked. Cammy pushed it open, stepped inside, and found her mother standing alone, dimly lit, in the middle of the modest living room she'd decorated in her beloved Arts and Crafts style. It appeared as if she couldn't move, as if she didn't know whether to go left or right, as if she'd lost her basic powers of decision-making along with losing her husband.

Beth was sixty-five, dark-haired like her daughter, still active and attractive but forever striving to shed the few extra pounds that were her eternal bête noire. At this moment, though, she looked like an entirely different person, crumpled, tear-streaked, quivering even with a burnt-orange fleece blanket draped over her hunched shoulders. Cammy marveled at how swiftly a tragedy could alter one's physical form. It was frightening.

With her mom rendered temporarily immobile, Cammy came to her. She expected a heavy hug, but instead Beth tumbled into her arms, no longer able to support herself. Holding her mother up, keeping her from collapsing in a heap on the floor, was one of the most disconcerting sensations of Cammy's life. Wasn't this pietà tableau supposed to be the other way around?

Then Beth said the only thing that really could be said, in the same shattered voice Cammy had heard on the phone. "What are we gonna do without him?"

A simple, unfathomably huge question.

"I don't know, Mom." Her own cracked voice sounded alien to her. "I don't know."

Day One: Monday

♦ 1 ♦

Cammy woke up early Monday, the morning of the burial, in her childhood room.

Sunday had gone by in a blur. Toby Goldfarb, Beth's close friend and fellow synagogue member—a short, sandy-haired woman who talked fast and buzzed about like a bee—had come over around noon to help with the "arrangements." For nourishment, she'd brought a homemade kugel, her specialty, a dense Jewish casserole made with egg noodles, sour cream, and cottage cheese. Cammy sat, spaced out, at the dining room table, picking at crunchy bits of baked noodle, while Toby assisted her mother in calling the funeral home, the cemetery, stunned friends and family. All the efficient business that accompanies a death.

Since Cammy had hardly any stuff at the house, she'd excused herself at one point to take a quick, exorbitant round-trip Lyft to her basement lair in Astoria, where she shoved clothes, toiletries, and her beat-up old college-era MacBook into an oversize graphite JanSport backpack. When she returned an hour and a half later, Toby departed, leaving her and her mom to spend an eerily catatonic evening together. They reheated the remaining kugel, ate what they could without saying very much, and went to sleep before ten, saving up their energy for today.

Now she lay awake in her narrow twin bed in her little room in Jersey.

Joisey. Dirty Jerz. The state, the myth, the legend. Butt of a million mocking jokes.

Cammy had a love-hate relationship with the place that definitely skewed more toward hate. She'd grown up in River Hill, a one-square-mile town—er, borough, whatever that meant—sardined among dozens of other similarly sized towns in Bergen County, which lay just across the Hudson River from glittering New York City. North Jersey was a bucolic land of highways and factories, strip clubs and smokestacks—a pastoral paradise whose natural wonders included the swampy Meadowlands, where the Mafia had once dumped bullet-ridden bodies. *The Sopranos* captured the vibe pretty vividly. And if you ventured south, you wound up in the famed seaside idyll known as the Jersey Shore, a region made glorious by Bruce Springsteen and grotesque by Snooki and the rest of her caricatural reality-TV crew.

Ever since she was a kid, Cammy had wanted to get the hell out of here. To her, River Hill represented an unholy trinity of boredom, mediocrity, and small-mindedness. Seriously, the cultural landmarks on Main Street were a Dunkin' Donuts and a CVS. But on the other side of the polluted water, over the traffic-clogged George Washington Bridge, magical Manhattan beckoned. The sophisticated city, with its museums, theaters, art-house cinemas, and bookstores, all full of interesting, fashionable people. That's where she yearned to be.

Well, she'd gotten there, and things weren't going so great, and now her dad was dead and she was back home for a week.

Life comes at you fast.

Her weeklong stay was due to the Jewish custom of *shiva*, not to be confused with the Hindu god. No, for the Jews, shiva, which means "seven" in Hebrew, refers to the traditional mourning period that begins after a loved one's burial and lasts for seven fun-filled days. During this happy time, friends and family visit the home of the bereaved to bring condolences and, more usefully, food. The ritual is called "sitting shiva." Who came up with it? Cammy had probably learned about its biblical origins in religious school, but she'd retained next to nothing from all those stultifying Sunday mornings.

She did recall, however, that more observant Jews took shiva to further extremes. They tore their clothing, sat on low stools, covered up their mirrors. At least she'd been raised Reform, in the "lightest" brand of Judaism, and didn't have to practice that type of ancient lamentation.

Still, the prospect of seven days of visitors streaming in and out of the house, offering earnest expressions of sympathy, seemed like a nightmare to Cammy, private person that she was. Not to mention seven straight days spent in close quarters with her mom, which was a whole other story. But she was here, and she had to get through this goddamn week somehow.

First, though, she had to bury her father.

★ ★ ★

Groggy and gassy—a delightful morning manifestation of her IBS-prone "Jewish stomach"—Cammy crawled out of bed and shuffled downstairs in search of coffee. The wooden steps groaned underneath her feet, just as they had whenever she'd stayed out too late as a teenager and tried to sneak back in and up to her room. Inevitably, she would find her mother's shadowy form looming in the doorway of her parents' bedroom, arms crossed in silent disapproval. Caught again. It was tough to be stealthy in a creaky, hundred-year-old house.

Entering the kitchen, she saw her mom hovering in a stupor by the coffee machine as it burbled and gurgled. That's one thing they had in common: a major coffee dependency. Cammy's dad had been even worse, drinking the stuff day and night as if it were the elixir of life. A family of java junkies.

"Hi," Cammy said.

Beth started, shaken from her trance. She had on a faded nightgown, and her hair was matted on the side where she slept. "Morning, babe. You want some coffee?"

"Yes, please."

"How 'bout some toast? I can make you some whole wheat toast."

"No thanks."

"English muffin?"

"I'm not hungry."

"Are you sure?"

"Yes, I'm sure."

"How 'bout just one slice of toast?"

"Mom, I don't want any toast."

"You need to eat something. Today's a big day—"

"I know today's a big day. We're burying Dad. That's why I'm not hungry, okay?"

Beth flinched, and Cammy instantly regretted the harshness of her tone. This was a typical interaction of theirs: nagging, bristling, then boom—a nasty jab and a pang of remorse. They never seemed to know how to talk to each other. Her dad had usually managed to defuse these tense moments with his easygoing old-school humor and a cringe-inducing Borscht Belt joke, but now that he was gone, they were on their own. How in God's name was this dynamic going to work?

The machine beeped. Beth poured hot coffee into two of the blue-floral-patterned porcelain cups they'd been using for decades. Cammy took one and murmured, "Sorry."

Her mom didn't respond. She gazed out the window above the sink at the overgrown lawn. Unlike the Schmidts next door, who mowed their grass with all-American fervor, the indoorsy

Adlers often let their landscaping go. "I just can't believe it," she said at last.

"What?"

"That we're doing this. Burying him."

"Me neither."

"Two days ago, I was with him, talking to him. How can that be? It's surreal, isn't it?"

"Yeah, Mom. It is."

This they could agree on.

★ ★ ★

Both dressed in black—grief couture—and shielded from the gray October light by sunglasses, mother and daughter climbed into Beth's white Toyota Corolla. Cammy had to move a stack of papers off the passenger seat in order to sit down.

"Where do you want me to put these?"

"Just throw them in the back."

The back of Beth's car was a cornucopia of clutter: papers, binders, receipts, takeout bags, water bottles, loose tissues, and sundry other detritus. After all, the Corolla served not just as her vehicle but also as her mobile office: She was a real estate agent. Cammy's mom spent her busy days on the go, traversing Bergen County to show clients high-priced homes nicer than her own. A master of friendly small talk and gentle yet persistent nudging, she fielded calls round the clock to keep up with the ever-competitive North Jersey housing market. (Everyone wanted to live *near* New York but not *in* New York.) As her envious peers admitted—most of them middle-aged ladies too—the woman was good at her job.

"Mom, are you ever going to clean out your car?"

"Someday."

They drove in silence to Star of David Cemetery, an "exclusively Jewish" burial ground in Saddle Brook, a sleepy town about fifteen minutes away. Cammy counted the diners they passed, an old game she used to play when she was a bored only child stuck in the back seat. Diners were Jersey's gift to the world—largely Greek-owned palaces of Americana with glowing stainless steel siding, offering up exhaustive menus and, best of all, twenty-four-hour breakfast. She couldn't begin to calculate the number of hours she and her high school friends had spent hanging out at these spots, shooting the shit while eating cheese fries smothered in gravy.

"I'm going to sue them," Beth said out of the blue.

"Who?"

"The hospital. Or the rehab place. Or both."

"Sue them for what?"

"For killing Dad."

"What do you mean?"

"He was healthy when he went in for that surgery last week. They cleared him for it, they said it was a minor procedure. Then he gets pneumonia in the hospital, and they move him to rehab. The rehab people said he was getting better, but I could tell he wasn't. He seemed weaker. He couldn't stop coughing. Then they go in to check on him, and he's stopped breathing. He's gone. They took a healthy man in his sixties, and they killed him."

Beth said all of this in staccato bursts, keeping her Ray-Banned eyes on the road. She reminded her daughter of Joan Crawford in one of those melodramatic movies from the 1940s: an angry widow bent on revenge.

As accusatory as her mom's description sounded, from what Cammy understood, the sequence of events was pretty accurate: from healthy to dead in the span of a week. A Filipina nursing assistant who liked her dad and his bad jokes had stopped into his room on Saturday night and found him unresponsive, without a pulse. She'd called Beth immediately, crying and apologizing. The doctors still had no explanation for it. Perhaps an underlying, undiscovered respiratory condition exacerbated by the pneumonia? Her father *had* been a cigar smoker decades ago. Hey, folks, let's play *Name That Cause of Death!*

"Mom, maybe you shouldn't think about lawsuits right now."

"What else should I be thinking about?"

"Grieving? Dad died two days ago."

"I can grieve and sue people at the same time."

Okay.

They reached the entrance of the cemetery, whose wrought-iron gate featured a large Star of David, the centuries-old symbol of Judaism. It tacitly announced, "Only Jewish dead people welcome." This exclusivity struck Cammy as only fair given all the establishments that had once closed their doors to members of the Hebrew persuasion: restaurants, country clubs, colleges. Take that, Gentiles; you ain't gettin' into this here cemetery.

As they drove onto the grounds, she saw manicured lawns, sturdy trees beginning their autumn transformation, and a sea of tombstones. Rows and rows of them, like the Grim Reaper's domino set. Had this many Jews really died in North Jersey? It seemed crazy, impossible.

No, it was just life.

"Where's Dad?" Cammy asked.

"Hold on." Beth pulled over and snapped open her purse, which was no less cluttered than the back of the car. She took out a folded sheet of paper.

"What's that?"

"A map of the cemetery. They faxed it to me." Yes, her mom still owned a circa-1990s fax machine that operated slightly faster than a carrier pigeon. "They circled where Dad's plot is."

Beth unfolded the paper, revealing a poorly photocopied map with microscopic text, divided into dozens of tiny numbered sections. A smudged, hand-drawn circle marked the location of the burial plot. It looked like the scrawl of a pirate seeking hidden treasure: X marks the spot! Oddly, the paths through the cemetery had names derived from both the Old Testament and the US presidency: Moses Avenue, Judah Road, and Israel Way intersected with Washington Avenue, Jefferson Road, and Lincoln Way. Was this some sort of half-baked nod to American Jewish assimilation? In any case, the map was barely legible.

Beth lifted her shades to peer at the gridded confusion. "I can't read this without my glasses," she said, shaking her head. "Can you navigate?"

"Mom, I can hardly read it either."

"Do your best."

"How do the others know where to go?"

"I took a picture of the map and texted it to them. They're all early birds. I'm sure they're there already."

Cammy glanced at the clock on the dashboard: 9:56. The ceremony was scheduled for ten. What kind of lousy people were late for the burial of their own husband and father? "We should've left ourselves more time."

"I wasn't paying attention."

"Neither was I."

"Well, they're not going to bury him without us."

This was true.

Beth resumed driving, and Cammy took charge of the hieroglyphic map. She wished she had the enormous magnifying glass her grandma Ruth had used to read her cherished *Time* magazine. Alas, despite Cammy's squinting efforts, the following few minutes quickly devolved into a black comedy of errors, a roundabout journey through the cemetery marked by wrong turns, reversals, and the requisite soundtrack of bickering. "No, Mom, make a *left* on Judah." "You said make a right." "No, I said left." "Fine, I'll turn around. Are you sure you're reading that thing right?" "Nope, not at all."

At five past ten, after completing yet another desperate loop, they spied activity up ahead: cars, people, and, sure enough, a hearse. They'd made it. As Beth pulled up and parked the Corolla, Cammy heard her mother take a deep, trepidatious breath. Here goes nothing.

On cue, a light rain began to fall.

Mercifully, the decision had been made to keep the burial small and private, so there were only a handful of attendees standing out in the drizzle. Aunt Miriam, younger sister of the deceased, a slight, redheaded bundle of neuroses whose ever-shifting collection of cats no one in the family could keep up with; Toby Goldfarb and her gangly husband, Stan, an avid amateur juggler; and, last but not least, today's master of ceremonies, the leader of Congregation Sons of Israel himself, in all his sagely splendor—Rabbi Gary Wiener.

Before Beth and Cammy could get out and join them, the driver's door of the hearse swung open, and a thin, somber man in a dark suit appeared. He slid open a large umbrella and jogged over to their car.

"Who's that guy?" Cammy asked.

"I think he's from the funeral home."

Beth rolled her window down. The thin man leaned his face in—unnecessarily close, Cammy felt—and said, "Hello. Are you the bereaved?"

"Yes. I'm the—the widow." She'd almost said "wife." It seemed unfair that the children of a dead person still get to be their children after they're gone, but their wives must become widows and their husbands widowers. Maybe Cammy could coin a new term out of solidarity: "chidow."

"Would you and your daughter like to see him?"

"What?"

"Would you like to see your husband before the burial?"

"You mean—"

"I can take you over to the hearse, and we can open the casket for a moment if you'd like."

Beth turned to her daughter, dumbfounded. Neither of them had been anticipating this option.

Open caskets, gilded coffins—none of that morbid Christian/Catholic pageantry was part of the Jewish tradition, which Cammy, a committed agnostic on her best days, appreciated about the faith. To the contrary, the Jews wanted their dead in the ground pronto—within twenty-fours, technically—and in as simple and unadorned a receptacle as possible. That made sense, didn't it? Just get the damn thing over with. Why have a procession file past a bejeweled sarcophagus to gape at the embalmed, painted, frozen face of a corpse?

So then what was this business about getting a last glimpse of her dad? A little loophole? She didn't want to do that. Or did she?

"Yes," Beth said. "I want to see him."

Cammy was startled. She thought they'd at least confer before reaching a decision. "Mom—"

"You don't have to come if you don't want to. But I want to see him."

Beth got out of the car. Cammy hesitated, then followed. Sheltering them from the misty spray with his umbrella, the thin man led them to the hearse, from which another dark-suited employee emerged. The two funereal colleagues exchanged efficient nods, and the second man darted around to open the vehicle's back door. These guys were pros. Cammy felt her mom's trembling hand grip hers.

And lo and behold, there it was: the plain pinewood box that would house Cy Adler for eternity. Humble accommodations, to be sure, but not lacking a certain modest dignity. The second man, who clearly had to do all the dirty work, lifted the top of the coffin.

CAMMY SITTING SHIVA

Cammy stared into her father's face, examining it for a final time, taking a mental picture of its topography. The salt-and-pepper beard she'd never seen him without, and now never would. The features so similar to her own: the ample Adler nose that snored mightily, the full Adler lips that parted when he guffawed at one of his own punchlines. His eyes were closed, those intense but mischievous eyes that contained traces of his old-world Polish Jewish ancestry. He was wearing his favorite beige wool sweater, a cozy layer to protect against the coolness of the earth in which he'd soon reside. The sweater must've been her mom's choice.

"I'm never gonna see him again," Beth said. "I'm never gonna see him again."

Cammy had been so absorbed in her own private contemplation, she'd failed to notice that her mother was breaking down, losing her shit, utterly decompensating right beside her. Beth kept on repeating that mournful mantra, "I'm never gonna see him again," punctuating it with convulsive sobs. Cammy glanced over at the others—her aunt, the Goldfarbs, the rabbi—who'd turned away out of respect. It was interesting how people gave each other a free pass to behave primally, to display pure animal emotion, in moments like these.

"It's okay, Mom," Cammy said, placing an awkward hand on Beth's shaking back. A pretty paltry consolation, but she couldn't think of a better one.

The thin man nodded again at the second man, who closed the lid, sealing Cy off from his weeping wife, his dazed daughter, and the cares of the world he had lived in and left behind.

★ ★ ★

The burial itself was blessedly brief.

Rabbi Wiener spoke about how funny Cy was, how he'd always had a new, often inappropriate joke to share, at which he would invariably laugh harder than whoever happened to be his lucky (or unlucky, depending on one's perspective) audience. Aunt Miriam bawled and blabbered about how he'd been the perfect brother, a saint among men, even though Cammy knew she'd driven him up the wall when he was alive. The Goldfarbs said nice, unremarkable things about his loyal friendship, his laid-back nature, his entertaining conversation. And Beth managed a few tearful words of gratitude for their three decades of marriage, for the "beautiful daughter" he'd given her and to whom he'd been such a wonderful father.

To everyone's visible puzzlement, the beautiful daughter chose to say nothing.

She didn't feel like it.

The rabbi led the group in the Kaddish, the ancient Jewish prayer for the dead: "*Yitgadal v'yitkadash sh'mei raba b'alma di-v'ra chirutei . . .*" Cammy instinctively mouthed the words, which she knew by heart from her childhood years of compulsory synagogue attendance. (After her bat mitzvah at age thirteen, she was out of there for good.) For reasons she'd learned but forgotten, the prayer was in Aramaic, not Hebrew. What did it mean? Something about praising God and his greatness, surprise, surprise. Didn't even mention death directly. Talk about beating around the bush.

Now it was time for the dreaded concluding custom: tossing shovelfuls of dirt on the coffin. Cammy supposed this act was intended to signify closure or some such lofty concept, but she found it bizarre. It almost seemed outright insulting to the deceased. You wouldn't hurl dirt on the body of a living person, would you? Not if you didn't want to get punched in the face. Then again, you wouldn't stick them underground either.

In all his solemn glory—the man simply loved being solemn—Rabbi Wiener picked up a small shovel and approached the grave, into which some stocky cemetery workers had earlier lowered the casket. "*Al mekomo yavo veshalom,*" he intoned. "May he go to his place in peace." (What place was that, by the way?)

He stuck the shovel into a mound of freshly dug earth and dropped a bit of the soil onto the coffin. Cammy winced as it hit the wood with a dull thud. He passed the tool to the Goldfarbs, who followed suit. Then Aunt Miriam, then Beth.

Finally, it was Cammy's turn. Her mom handed her the shovel. But as she took a few heavy steps toward the grave, she realized she couldn't do it. She didn't want to do it. She didn't want closure. Not now, not yet, not like this.

"Go ahead, Cammy," the rabbi prodded.

She wanted to say, "Fuck off, Wiener," but she held her tongue. Instead, she jabbed the shovel into the mound of earth in protest, so that it stood as straight and upright as her own signature stubbornness. What were they going to do, argue with her? Make a scene because she wouldn't fling dirt on her father? Nobody said a word.

Cammy half expected her dad to pop out of his resting place to break the tension with one last off-color joke—an outrageous crack, a Cy Adler special, that would scandalize them all. She waited and waited, even after the others turned to leave, even after her mom squeezed her hand and began to trudge back toward the car.

He didn't come.

◆ 2 ◆

WHAT IS IT WITH Jews and food?

This was the question Cammy asked herself upon arriving home from the burial with her mom to find the house filled with a smorgasbord of noshes and nibbles. High-piled platters covered every square inch of the kitchen counters and the long dining room table. There was a dizzying variety of fluffy bagels and flavored cream cheeses. There was lox, smoked salmon, tuna, whitefish. The triumvirate of fatty Jewish deli meats: brisket, corned beef, pastrami. Lentil soup, chickpea salad. Trays of fruits and veggies along with their accompanying dips. An entire bowl of hard-boiled eggs. Not to mention the desserts—the cookies and cakes and rugelach and the rest. Presiding over them all like a proud impresario was a commercial-size coffee urn.

"Mom, where did all this food come from?"

"People brought it over."

"What people?"

"Friends from the temple."

"How'd they get in the house?"

"I left it unlocked. It's a tradition."

"What is?"

"The, uh, the 'meal of consolation.' It has some Hebrew name—the rabbi told me, but I forget. The community feeds the family who's grieving."

Cammy had never heard of this particular tradition, but it didn't surprise her. Jews found a way to put food at the center of virtually every celebration and commemoration, whether joyful or sorrowful. Except, of course, for the holiest occasion of the year, Yom Kippur, the Day of Atonement, during which you had to fast and ask forgiveness for your sins—though even that holiday ended with a ceremonial meal, the so-called "break fast." They managed to get food in there too. And God said, "Let there be eating."

"What's with the shitload of eggs?" Cammy asked.

"Can you not curse right now, please?"

"Sorry."

"I think they symbolize life and death or something."

Oh. Lovely.

"How are we supposed to consume all of this?"

"We're not," Beth said. "People are coming over for lunch."

"Wait, they are? When?"

"Now."

"You didn't tell me that."

"I thought you knew."

"No, I thought we'd have some time to like come home and decompress after the cemetery—"

"It's the first meal, babe. It's the start of shiva." And again, "It's a tradition."

Cammy found it amusing whenever her mom tutored her in the ways of Judaism, because—guess what?—Beth wasn't really Jewish! Well, okay, now she was, but she hadn't been born into the tribe. She'd grown up as Elizabeth Summers in a barely practicing Christian family in California, moved east to New York, met Cy and married him, fallen in love with the faith, taken a yearlong conversion class, dipped herself in the *mikvah*, the ritual purification bath, and become one of the "chosen" just in time for Cammy's birth.

Anyone who didn't know Cy and Beth well would've thought it was the other way around. He liked to stay home and watch his beloved Yankees on Friday nights while she went out to services, dragging her whining daughter with her if she could. To this day, Cammy didn't understand exactly what it was that drew her mom to the religion. Judaism seemed to give Beth a sense of identity and belonging, and her devotion to it was somehow bound up with her devotion to her husband, despite his own irreverent indifference to dogma and observance. Cammy had inherited this trait of her dad's, to her mother's chagrin. The two of them would sit in the back of the synagogue and poke fun at the rabbi's sermons as an embarrassed Beth shushed them.

"Mom, would you mind if I just went upstairs and lied down for a little bit?"

"What are you talking about?"

"Honestly, I don't feel like seeing a bunch of people right now."

Beth looked at her as if she'd lost her mind. "No. You can't do that."

"Why not?"

"Because they're coming here for us. To comfort us."

"So *I* have to like perform for *them*?"

"Also, it would be disrespectful to Dad."

"How? You think Dad would care if I stayed down here for lunch or not?"

"*I* want you here. It's you and me. We're the—the bereaved." That they were. "Babe, please don't be difficult about this. Not today. Just be a mensch, okay?"

Mensch. A loaded word. It literally meant "person" in Yiddish, Cammy recalled, but what it really referred to was a good person, a decent, honorable soul who could suck it up and do the right thing. When someone asked you to be a mensch, they were appealing to your better nature. The only issue was, at this muddled moment in her life, she wasn't so sure she had one.

"All right, don't play the mensch card, Mom."

"The mensch card?" Beth sighed, eyeing the abundance of food on the counter as if it could guide her in dealing with her obstinate offspring. "You know what? I would really love to not argue with you on the day of Dad's burial."

"I don't wanna argue either. I just asked if I could go upstairs and rest."

"And I told you, you can't do that."

"But—"

Cammy didn't have a chance to offer a retort. Just then, the front door opened, and the parade of visitors began.

Rabbi Wiener, Aunt Miriam, and the Goldfarbs entered together as a group. Then came more of Beth's friends from the synagogue, most in their sixties or older, some aided by canes and walkers. Condolence calls must've been a regular pastime for this crew. Acquaintances from town poured in as well, like the lawn-mowing neighbors, the Schmidts, and other River Hillians (yes, that's what the residents of River Hill called themselves) who knew the Adlers through this or that local connection. The snooty Long Island cousins showed up. Maybe the most colorful guests to appear were the guys from Cy's weekly Tuesday-night poker game, a potbellied bunch of amateur North Jersey card sharks.

Mother and daughter stood stoically by the door and greeted them all. How many grave faces did Cammy see? How many hugs and handshakes did she receive? How many times did she hear those trademarked words, "I'm so sorry for your loss"?

Enough that she quickly went on autopilot, accepting the assembly line of sympathetic gestures with her own grateful nods and mumbled thank-yous.

She did find entertainment, however, in watching folks make a beeline for the kitchen to grab paper plates and load them up with goodies. They were eating like there was no tomorrow. The specter of death made them ravenous. What better way to cling to life than to stuff your face with tasty snacks?

Perhaps the oddest encounter Cammy had was with Neil Schwartz, one of the guys from the card game. Neil was in his fifties but looked much older. He had a round face, a messy comb-over, and a rumpled quality that extended from his condiment-stained clothes to his very being. Cammy knew from her dad that the poor schmuck had failed at a dozen different business ventures, yet he returned each week to lose even more money at poker. This was one reason why his wife had divorced him.

"I'm sorry about your father," Neil said hoarsely, wheezing a bit as he spoke. He was a close talker, and his breath smelled like tuna salad.

"Thanks, Neil. I appreciate it." She'd met him at the annual Super Bowl parties the members of the game had thrown for themselves and their reluctant families.

"I loved his jokes. He cracked us all up."

"Everyone says that."

"You know, I played cards with your dad for twenty years."

"Wow."

"And I'll be honest with ya. When he first joined the game, he wasn't very good. He used to try to bluff and pull tricks. Never worked. He lost all the time."

"Huh . . . I didn't realize that." Why was he telling her this?

"Well, you were a little kid then. But as the years went by, he started playing smarter. Got more conservative with his hands. And he won a lot. Cy ended up being quite a poker player."

"That's—that's great to hear."

"Yeah. Just goes to show." To show what? Was this account of her dad's improvement at cards supposed to be touching? Cammy waited for a further explanation that didn't come. Neil brushed some bagel crumbs off his shirt. "Anyway, I'll miss the guy." And with that, he let out a slightly alarming cough and waddled away to rejoin his fellow gamblers.

People were so weird.

At last, all the company seemed to have arrived. They spilled from the kitchen into the dining room and out to the living room. They ate and chatted and reminisced and laughed, solaced by the knowledge that they were still here among the living. Cammy felt apart from the gathering, detached and disconnected. Something about it rubbed her the wrong way. She had an acute urge to yell out, "Hey, assholes, put down your fucking food for a second! My dad is dead!" This might've caused a disturbance, though.

So she stood alone, like an invisible woman, by the fireplace her family never used, studying the framed photographs of her father that her mom had arranged on the mantelpiece. There he was in black and white as a cute little boy in the sixties, then as a bow-tied high school graduate with a crop of seventies hair and sideburns. In a picture from the eighties, he lounged in a desk chair in his advertising office, pre-beard, his hands clasped behind his head and a cigar dangling out of his mouth. The carefree New York bachelor. He looked dapper on his wedding day in '94, smiling broadly, with an arm wrapped around Beth's waist. And the last photo was of him holding pudgy toddler Cammy aloft, as if about to toss her into the sky.

Snapshots, she thought. These are what you leave after you're gone.

"Cammy, I am like *so* sorry about your dad."

She heard the singsong Valley-Girl-by-way-of-Long-Island voice behind her and knew it could belong to only one person: her cousin Arielle Freedman.

A relation on her father's side, Arielle hailed from the upper-middle-class, heavily Jewish enclave of Great Neck, on the island's North Shore, though she now had a place in the city, in douchey Murray Hill, land of the finance bros. The pejorative term "Jewish American Princess" was no longer politically correct, but Cammy secretly felt it applied to her spoiled cousin, who had long, straightened, bleached-blond hair; dressed in Kardashian chic; and spoke every "like"-filled sentence as if it ended in a question mark.

Since Arielle was just a year younger than Cammy, they'd always been paired together at family functions. "Go play with your cousin." "Go talk to your cousin." An odder, more ill-matched couple could not have been conceived.

"Thanks, Arielle," Cammy said, turning to find her meticulously made-up face.

"How are you like holding up?"

"You know. Hanging in there."

"It must've been like such a shock."

"Yeah, it was."

"I like can't even imagine." Arielle shook her head dramatically, then decided to change the subject. "So how's everything else going?"

Really? "Oh. Um. Okay."

"Are you still—Wait, like what've you been doing lately?"

"Temping. Copywriting. For different companies."

"Oh, right. That must be like . . . super flexible."

"It pays the bills. Barely."

"And weren't you like trying to write a book or something?"

"I was, but I gave up. I'm on to plays now."

"Ooh, plays. Have you seen *Hamilton*?"

"Actually, no, I haven't."

"Wait, for real? If you wanna write plays, you like *need* to see it."

"I'll get on that."

Arielle brushed some hair out of her eye with sparkly fake fingernails. "I'm still down on Wall Street. Financial services. They just promoted me to assistant director, so that's like pretty exciting."

"Congrats."

"Thanks. We should totally get a drink in the city sometime."

"Yeah, totally." They said this every time they saw each other, and, without fail, it never happened.

"You're in Queens, right? In like a basement or something?"

"Yep."

"Well, come on out of your cave and meet me in Manhattan, girl!"

Just when Cammy was considering crawling into the fireplace for cover, she caught sight of a human lifeline coming through the front door: Francesca DeMarco, her oldest and closest hometown pal. Thank God.

"Sorry," she said, darting past a nonplussed Arielle to meet her friend.

Fran had short dark hair, a lean build, and an unmistakably Italian face. She'd put on black pants and a black sweater for the occasion, having likely changed out of her regular work attire—jeans, T-shirt, apron, baseball cap—in the bathroom of the Italian deli she ran with her dad in nearby Englewood. It was the best Italian deli in Jersey, bar none, and that was saying a lot.

Cammy gave Fran the realest hug she'd given anyone all day. They'd texted yesterday, but this was the first time they'd seen each other since the death.

"Dude, how are you?" Fran asked.

"I don't know."

"How was the burial?"

"It sucked."

Fran scanned the roomful of visitors. "There's a fuckton of people here."

"Tell me about it."

"You burned out?"

"Yes."

Looking around furtively and lowering her voice, Fran asked, "You wanna smoke a J?"

"What?"

"I brought one just in case." She patted her back pocket. "I thought you might need it."

Cammy suppressed a laugh. "You brought a joint to my dad's funeral lunch?"

"Inappropriate?"

"No, I love it. But how are we gonna smoke that now?"

"We'll just go out back for a minute. Behind the shed. No one'll notice."

Cammy did deliberate for a second on the ethics of getting high in this unusual context, but no moral red flags arose. She hadn't asked for this onslaught of guests and the anxiety they were causing her. In fact, she'd actively tried to avoid them and been denied. She needed to relax, which was the very reason pot existed, paranoia notwithstanding. Dilemma resolved.

She and Fran made their way through the packed kitchen and out the sliding glass patio doors that led to the weedy backyard. They slunk around to the rear of the paint-chipped storage shed that had provided concealment for many of their illicit teenage deeds: drinking, smoking, making out with boys. More than a decade later, it still had its utility.

Fran whipped out a masterfully crafted joint and a blue BIC lighter.

"How are you so good at rolling joints?" Cammy marveled. "I'm terrible."

"It's a gift."

They rested their backs against the shed in familiar poses, lit up, puffed and passed. After a couple of hits, Cammy felt a loosening of tension, a gentle tide of relief.

"Listen," Fran said, "I know you've probably been hearing a lot of bullshit today, and I don't wanna add to that—"

"It's okay. It's not bullshit coming from you."

"All right. Good. 'Cause I just wanna say . . . your dad was the fucking greatest."

Fran meant it. She didn't have a phony bone in her body, which was one of the things Cammy liked most about her. It was also probably a big part of why Fran had gotten along so well with her father. From the moment Cammy had first brought her new friend home from elementary school, Fran and Cy had bonded over their ardent Yankees fandom (Cammy was apathetic about sports) and their love of a good laugh. They were both straight shooters, allergic to posturing and pretense. Cammy's dad had stopped into Fran's family deli every week for an Italian sub and a round of jocular banter. They'd gotten a real kick out of each other.

"He *was* the greatest," Cammy said, and she meant it too.

Fran took a deep, philosophical hit and exhaled. "So how long does this shiva thing last?"

"Seven days, technically."

"Seven days? Christ."

"I know, it's crazy. It's like a nonstop open house when all I want is privacy."

"How are you gonna deal with it?"

Cammy coughed like an amateur. "I have no idea," she rasped.

"Well, I'm here if you need me."

"Oh, I definitely will."

Passing the joint to Fran, Cammy saw that it had been reduced to a small, smoldering roach. On a related note, she'd now crossed the Rubicon: She was officially high. This presented a problem she'd lacked the foresight to consider minutes earlier—that she'd soon have to reenter the house and rejoin the lunch, stoned out of her mind.

"Oh my God, I'm high," she announced, snapping to attention.

"Wasn't that the point?"

"No, but like what are we supposed to do now?"

"Go back in and be chill," Fran said, cool as a caprese salad. "Nobody's gonna suspect anything."

"Do my eyes look bloodshot?"

Fran examined them. "I mean, not really."

"Not *really*? What about the smell? Do you think we smell?"

Fran shrugged, which wasn't very encouraging. She rubbed out the remains of the joint on the side of the shed and flicked it into a heap of leaves. All things return to the earth, Cammy reflected, the marijuana granting her a cosmic perspective.

The zonked-out friends glid across the yard, through the sliding glass doors, and back into the kitchen brimming with people and food. The instant she set foot inside, Cammy froze up, struck by total sensory overload. Everyone suddenly had the distorted faces of gargoyles. The cacophony of their voices was deafening. The pungent odor of fish and meat pervaded the room. Weed did this to her sometimes, especially when her unconscious was roiling. She really shouldn't have smoked.

"Yo, are you bugging out?" Fran whispered.

"Yes." Cammy reached into the large bowl on the counter, picked up a slippery hard-boiled egg, and plopped it into her mouth. Chew, chew, swallow.

"Did you just eat that whole egg?"

"It represents life and death."

Fran looked concerned. "Lemme take you upstairs and get you some water."

"Okay."

They'd hardly made a move when Beth appeared in front of them, frazzled from all the condolences she'd been fielding. "Oh, hi, Fran," she said. "Thank you for coming."

"Of course, Mrs. Adler. I'm so sorry." Fran was impressive; she didn't even seem high.

They hugged, and Beth turned to her daughter. "Where were you? I was looking for you. Ms. Weiss wanted to say hello."

"I—I was outside." Cammy had cotton mouth. Articulating required concentration.

"Outside? Why?"

"To get some fresh air."

"What happened to your eyes?"

"What?"

"Your eyes are all red."

Uh-oh. "They are?"

"Did you eat something?" Beth asked, referencing Cammy's vexing triad of food allergies: peanuts, tree nuts, and, most insidious of all, sesame.

"No, I just had an egg."

Her mom took a step closer, narrowed her eyes, and sniffed. "What's that smell?"

"Mom—"

"Are you kidding?" Beth had grown up in the sixties and seventies; she knew the skunky scent of grass. She'd even partaken herself as a Joni Mitchell–loving teenager in the Bay Area, but those days were long past. Now she was appalled. "At Dad's lunch? Really?"

Cammy shot a sidelong peek at Fran, who'd stepped away to let the parent-child squabble play out. She shook her head guiltily, as if to say, "Sorry, dude. You're on your own."

"What's wrong with you?" Beth said, seeming at a loss to comprehend the brazen impropriety, the sheer shamelessness of her daughter's behavior.

What Cammy did next didn't help: She started to laugh. It was the kind of giggly, irrepressible high laughter that isn't caused by anything concrete: a joke, a funny situation. It's more a response to the grand absurdity of life. She knew anyone watching would be stunned to see her chortling like a lunatic a mere few hours after her father's burial, but she couldn't control herself.

"Stop it," Beth muttered through gritted teeth.

"I'm not a mensch, Mom," Cammy said, catching her breath. She turned her palms up and laughed again. "I don't know what to tell you. I'm just not a mensch."

Rather than attempt a reply, Beth spun around and disappeared into the dining room. She clearly couldn't handle this right now.

Cammy felt a hand on her shoulder. It was Fran, who said, with characteristic pithiness, "That was bad."

✦ 3 ✦

Eventually, everyone left. Friends cleaned up and put the copious leftovers in the fridge so the bereaved didn't have to. Without any further conversation, Cammy and Beth went off to their respective bedrooms and napped for the rest of the afternoon.

That evening, they sat on the cream-colored sectional in the living room, in front of the TV. Beth had put on TCM, Turner Classic Movies, Cy's favorite channel. Hitchcock's *Vertigo* was playing, with an obsessed James Stewart driving through the Technicolor streets of San Francisco in pursuit of the elusive Kim Novak.

Cammy knew it well because her dad, a devout cinephile, had raised her on a steady diet of classic films. They'd sat together in this room on countless nights, snacking on microwave popcorn and watching "essentials," as he called them, like *Citizen Kane*, *Casablanca*, *Sunset Boulevard*, and *Singin' in the Rain*. Cinema had been one of their bonds, a shared language, their love of timeless celluloid stories inseparable from their love for each other.

Now Cammy was sifting through a mildewy cardboard box full of her father's old belongings that she'd lugged up from the damp basement. Among the miscellaneous mementos were his leather-bound Hoboken High School yearbooks; diplomas from there (Class of '74) and from the City College of New York (Class of '78); letters he'd saved, both hand- and typewritten on yellowed paper; washed-out photos of family and friends; and clippings of the smart-ass movie reviews he'd authored for *The Campus*, City College's student newspaper, which he'd always remained proud of. ("*Earthquake* Crumbles" read his headline mocking the disaster flick.)

A pale Polaroid lying at the bottom of the box caught Cammy's attention, and she scooped it up to take a closer look. The picture showed her dad, sporting his bushy seventies mop, at some kind of party, standing next to a petite, pretty young woman with delicate features and curly blond hair. He had on a dark chalk-stripe suit and a red-and-white polka-dot tie, while she wore a white smock dress with billowing bell sleeves and lace trimming. Her outfit screamed *Rumours*-era Stevie Nicks. They were locking eyes, arms intertwined.

Who was this striking woman in such an intimate pose with her father? Cammy didn't recognize her, and the only clue to her identity was scribbled in pen on the back of the photo: "C & D, 6/14/78." She held up the Polaroid to Beth. "Mom, who is this? Who's 'D'?"

Her mother had a cup of lukewarm decaf she wasn't drinking. She glanced at the picture before turning back to the television. "An old girlfriend of Dad's, I think. From college."

"Really? What was her name?

"I don't remember."

"I never heard him mention anyone with a D name."

"Why would he have? It was forty-something years ago."

"He mentioned other girlfriends he had." On occasion, Cy had related amusing anecdotes from his "B.M." dating days: Before Mom. "And why did he save this photo?"

"I don't know." Beth's tone suggested she wasn't in the mood to speculate about her late husband's prior relationships. Understandable.

Curious as she was, Cammy decided to drop her inquiry into the enigma of D—for the time being, anyway. She placed the Polaroid back in the box. Then, feeling a twinge of guilt over her earlier antics (getting high, etc.), she sought to clear the air. "Hey, so I'm, uh, I'm sorry about today . . ."

"It's fine," her mom said, too worn out to stay mad.

"The lunch, all those people—it was just . . . a lot."

Beth clinked her cup down on the glass coffee table and muted the TV. She shifted positions to face her daughter. "Well, do you want to talk?"

"Talk?"

"We haven't really had a chance to talk since it happened. About Dad. And how we're doing. Do you want to?"

Did Cammy want to have a heart-to-heart with her mother? Was she ready to try to sort out and verbalize the inchoate feelings of grief, anger, and confusion swirling inside her? "Not right now."

Beth seemed disappointed by this answer. "Okay. But at some point we should."

"Yeah."

"And . . ." Her mom paused and pursed her lips, as she often did when figuring out how to phrase something tactfully. "I'd also like to talk about you."

"Me?" This sounded like the beginning of an intervention.

"You haven't been home much lately, babe. I want to know about your life."

"My life is awesome, Mom," Cammy deadpanned.

"Like I know you and David—"

"Broke up. We broke up. It's all good. 'It wasn't meant to be,' as they say."

"That's too bad. He was so nice."

"Gee, thanks."

"And everything's okay with work?"

"Yep. Work's great. I'm temping away."

With each question Cammy glibly deflected, Beth appeared less convinced of her daughter's well-being. "You know," she said, "you can stay here longer than a week if you want."

"No, I can't, Mom."

"Why not?"

"I have a temp gig starting next week."

"Can't you do it from home? Tell them your father passed. They'll understand."

"I need to get back to the city."

"Why? What's the rush?"

"Being in Jersey makes me claustrophobic."

"What?"

"And being in my childhood room is, like, infantilizing. I don't know. I'm here for the shiva, but then I need to get back."

Seeing Beth frown, Cammy felt bad again. Her mom had held out an olive branch, had attempted to reach out and connect with her, and she'd shut it down. Why?

Beth got up, walked into the kitchen, and returned to the couch with a bottle of pills.

"What are those?"

"Ativan. They're for anxiety."

"Since when do you—"

"I called Dr. Katz last week. I told him I was worried about Dad and I couldn't sleep. He prescribed these for me. It's temporary."

"Oh."

Beth unscrewed the bottle cap, plucked out a white tablet, and swallowed it with some decaf. In almost thirty years, Cammy had never seen her mother take any medication for her mental health, and, irrationally, the sight of this freaked her out. The childish part of her brain still believed that moms were impregnable fortresses of stability and strength.

"I think I'm gonna take a walk," Cammy said, standing up.

"Now? It's late."

"I feel restless."

"It's cold out."

"I'll wear a jacket."

Cammy went to the hall closet, where she found her old maroon peacoat hanging proudly. She'd had it since high school, and it still fit. She used to feel so cool wearing this thing around, like a world-weary sailor on shore leave. Putting the coat on gave her a nostalgic tingle.

"I'll be back in a bit," she said before departing.

"Where are you going?"

"Nowhere. Just walking."

"Be careful."

"It's River Hill, Mom."

"I'll probably go to bed soon. These pills make me drowsy."

"Okay. Well. Goodnight, then."

"Goodnight, babe."

Beth picked up the remote and unmuted the TV. Cammy was unsettled by the solitary image of her mom on the couch with the pills and the decaf and Jimmy Stewart spiraling in the background. She shouldn't be leaving her alone. Not very menschy.

It felt good to get outside, though. She needed to walk off her fidgetiness.

Cammy's house sat at the bottom of a hill on a street called, appropriately, Hill Avenue. (River Hill, Hill Avenue—whoever had come up with these place names was super imaginative.) At night, all was quiet here. The autumn wind whispered, the trees rustled, television screens glowed in the windows of houses. It was a Monday, and everybody was in for the evening. If New York was the city that never slept, this was the town that hit the snooze button.

Main Street was no different. Reaching the intersection, disturbingly winded from a few blocks' uphill trek, Cammy was met with a dazzling array of sights: a liquor store (closed), a Chinese takeout restaurant (closed), a gas station (closed), and the fluorescent CVS (open), which shone like a corporate diamond on the otherwise darkened main drag.

No wonder she'd wanted to make it out of here.

Cammy had a funny memory of her middle school and early high school years, when she and her friends hadn't yet been gifted shitty first cars by their folks. Back then, sans wheels, they would meet up on weekends in the center of town with nothing to do but wander into Happy Market for a syrupy slushy, loiter in Wood Park (another creative moniker), and hope someone's generous parent would give them a ride to the Garden State Plaza mall. Despite their mundanity, those idle days had been filled with a heady mystery: You never knew whom you might run into, whom you might share a slushy with, whom you might end up liking or fighting or kissing.

Where was that mystery now?

A River Hill police car cruised by, and a cop with a doughy face glared out the window at Cammy. She probably did look suspect standing on the corner at this hour. Still, cops around here had way too much time on their hands. As he drove past, she realized she recognized the guy: It was beefy, buzz-cutted Officer Rocco, who'd come into her fifth-grade classroom to lead a D.A.R.E. unit—that is, Drug Abuse Resistance Education. With the help of Daren the Lion, a cartoon mascot, Officer Rocco had taught that marijuana was a "gateway drug" that led inexorably to hardcore narcotics. Judging by the number of local kids who'd grown up to overdose on fentanyl, his scare tactics had failed.

Lest she be stopped and interrogated—a slim though real possibility in this ridiculous town—Cammy had to figure out someplace to go. But where? What was open?

Ooh, she had an idea. Over in neighboring Englewood, home of Fran's deli, there stood the diviest of dive bars: the Golden Eagle Tavern, aka the Dirty Bird. It was just a few minutes' walk away. Notorious for drunken brawls and other such mayhem, the Dirty Bird was the spot your parents warned you to steer clear of. Cammy had only ever gone there a couple of times, as a joke. Its dinginess seemed suited to the present condition of her soul. Perfect.

Heading north on Main, past the sad-eyed Virgin Mary statue that kept vigil outside St. Paul's Catholic church, she thought of her mom and the chasm between them. Her dad's death should've been bringing them closer together, so why was there still such a palpable distance? Why couldn't they communicate? Why did they exist on opposite sides of an invisible wall?

Here was the origin of the problem, as Cammy saw it: Her mother and father had played diametrically different roles in her life. Cy had been the fun one, the friend, the partner in crime. Just about every weekend when she was young, he'd taken her on "adventures," as he called them, into the city—to movies, shows, museums, Yankees games. They'd jump in the car, and she'd ask, "Where are we going, Dad?" "We're going to follow our noses," he'd say, pointing to his sizable schnoz. Sometimes Beth came along too, but often she didn't. Cy introduced Cammy to the Beatles and *The Godfather* and the best pizza in New York (John's of Bleecker Street, hands down). They were two peas in a proverbial pod.

Beth, on the other hand, had been the practical parent. The disciplinarian. The one who made sure her daughter was dressed and ready for school in the morning, with a nutritious packed lunch. (Why couldn't she have Dunkaroos like the other kids, dammit?) Who got on Cammy's case about doing her homework and making her bed and brushing her teeth and not staying up too late. Who asked her where she was going—just like tonight!—and whom she was hanging out with and when she'd be back and if any boys were involved. "Mom, why can't you be chill like Dad?" "Because Dad gets to entertain you. I have to raise you."

This good-cop–bad-cop bifurcation likely wasn't the healthiest approach to child-rearing. And it had resulted in Cammy's current strained relationship with her mom. The fact was, outside their continual tug of war of nagging and bristling, of petty quarrels and half-hearted apologies, they didn't know each other very well. Or understand each other. Now, with Cy no longer around to act as a buffer, they were at sea, floating down the grimy Hackensack River without a paddle.

Speaking of grimy, Cammy looked up to see the Golden Eagle's neon sign flickering on the next block. A couple of the letters had burned out, so it read GOL EN E GLE, like an anagram puzzle. The place had an ugly cement exterior and one tiny, prison-style frosted window. You got the queasy feeling that if you entered this tavern, you might never come out.

She entered.

Holy shit, she said to herself as she stepped inside. If Dante had witnessed the Dirty Bird on a Monday night, he would've chucked the *Purgatorio* and written about this joint instead. It was hard to say which was grosser: the dusty, sticky wooden floor or the booths with stuffing oozing out of torn vinyl upholstery. The smell of piss emanated from the lockless bathroom in the corner. And the ancient, grizzled men—all men—hunched over their beers were straight out of a Bukowski novel. (Cammy had dated too many Bukowski fans.)

In other words, this was exactly what she was in the mood for.

She sidled up to the bar, aware of the incongruity of her presence here. *If only these haggard dudes knew I feel like them deep down,* she thought.

"What can I get for you?" the bartender asked. Unexpectedly, he had a young voice and, upon inspection, a young face. A freckled, carelessly good-looking face. The rakish face of a fuckboy.

Wait. She knew this face. It belonged to Shane O'Leary from high school.

"Whoa," he said, as surprised as she was. "Cammy? Cammy Adler?"

"Yeah. Wow. Shane. Hi."

"What the fuck are *you* doin' here?"

"I—I'm home for a little bit. Actually, my dad just died, so . . ."

"Oh. Shit. I'm sorry."

"Thanks. And you—you work here?"

"Just part-time. I fix cars during the day. I pick up night shifts here to make some extra cash."

"Oh, okay."

He glanced at the regulars and half grinned. "It's a fuckin' dump, isn't it?"

"It's got character."

"Yeah, right. What're you drinkin'?"

"What kind of bourbon do you have?" She wanted something that tasted bad.

"Jim Beam."

"Ouch."

"Only bottom shelf here, baby."

"I'll have it neat."

"Hellz yeah. How 'bout a double? On the house."

"Why?"

"'Cause your dad just died. I'll have one with you. Monday shifts blow."

He went to fetch the bottle. In high school, his nickname had been Sugar Shane. A basketball phenom, he'd been part of the popular crowd—specifically, a group of sports-loving, hard-partying bros whom Cammy and Fran had aptly dubbed the Dicks. They'd thrown their weight around at school, done keg stands in backyards, blacked out and gotten belligerent, and bullied anyone beneath them on the social food chain. All the standard stuff. Girls had liked Shane in particular because of his swagger, his height, and his shaggy-haired resemblance to prime-phase Ashton Kutcher.

Yet now he was wearing frayed jeans, a faded Eminem sweatshirt, and a backward Mets cap, serving Budweisers to the lost souls at the Dirty Bird. Pride cometh before the fall.

He set two glasses of questionable cleanness down on the bar and filled them to the brim with Jim Beam. They toasted and gulped down the acrid elixir.

"So," he said, "I bet you're like in the city doing smart shit."

"I'm in the city, yeah. I'm not doing anything very smart."

"Where'd you end up going to school? Somewhere fancy, right?"

"NYU."

"Expensive."

"I'll be paying off those loans till I die."

"I started at BCC, but I quit after a year. Wasn't for me." BCC stood for Bergen Community College, sarcastically known as Harvard on the Highway. "I figured maybe I could play ball somewhere, but turns out being good in River Hill doesn't mean you're gonna be good in college. Big fish, small pond, you know." Cammy did know.

"How're all your old buddies doing?"

Shane slugged some more bourbon. "Fuck. Well, Jimmy's in AA. Pete's on probation—"

"For what?"

"Drug stuff. He got into meth."

"Oh, that reminds me—you know who I just saw on the street? Officer Rocco."

"That guy's an asshole. He gave me a DWI a couple years ago. On July Fourth."

"Bummer."

"Let's see, who else? Pat works at the Verizon store. Tom's a security guard. And Phil's in the Army."

"Do you still see them?"

"Not much. Once in a while."

"You guys were like kings in high school."

"It's all been downhill from there." He said this not with resentment, but with a self-deprecating resignation. Cammy had to admit she kind of liked the new, humbled Shane. And he did still resemble Ashton Kutcher, albeit a small-town Jersey version who was showing the subtlest hint of a beer belly. "Want another round?"

She sure did.

Before long, Cammy was doing something she never would've dreamed of a decade ago: She was partying with Sugar Shane. They threw back shots of Jim Beam, which tasted less like vomit with each valiant swig. They swapped gossip about their old classmates and the diverse fates that had befallen them. (Matt Vanderberg was serving thirty-five years in federal prison in West Virginia for online sextortion!) They played darts, Cammy missing the board wildly and adding to the holes in the peeling wall. All the while, the mummified men at the bar didn't appear to move once. It was as if the two shit-faced millennials had the dump to themselves.

"All right, I got a question for you," Shane said. By this point, they'd slid into one of the ripped-up red vinyl booths, and he'd completely abdicated his duties as an on-the-clock employee.

"Oh no, what?"

"What'd you think of me in high school? Real talk."

Cammy snorted. "That's easy. I thought you were a dick."

"A dick?"

"As a matter of fact, Fran and I used to call all you guys the Dicks."

"Shut up."

"It's true. We'd be like, 'Oh, don't look now. Here come the Dicks.'"

Shane contemplated this. "I guess that's fair. I guess we were sorta dicks."

"*Sort of*? You were like the quintessential archetypes."

"The what?"

"Never mind. But . . ." Here she paused, because what she was about to say would tip them over the precipice into the gaping canyon of bad choices. "I also thought you were hot."

His eyes lit up with possibility. "Oh yeah?"

"Yeah. It kills me to say it, but I did."

This was the truth: Cammy was a reasonably intelligent person who, in keeping with the natural order of things, was typically attracted to other reasonably intelligent people. Nonetheless, since sometime around middle school, she'd harbored a secret, base fantasy of hatefucking a dumb Jersey bro in a backward cap. For reasons better left to Freud to decode, the cap and its reverse orientation were essential details in said fantasy. Shame had kept her from ever revealing this lurid desire to anyone, even unblushing Fran, though it had provided fodder for several satisfying masturbatory sessions through the years.

"Well, I thought you were a nerd," Shane smiled.

"Duh. Of course you did."

"Cute, though."

"You're full of it."

"Nah, I'm serious. I just couldn't ever say it."

"Say what?"

"That the dorky little Jewish girl was cute." Vaguely anti-Semitic? Don't worry about it. "My boys woulda made fun of me."

"Right. Your 'boys.'"

"But hey, fuck 'em. We're all grown up now."

They hung out and drank for another couple of hours, until closing time came at two AM and the decrepit barflies finally got up and limped out of their habitat.

"I've just gotta wipe down and take out the trash," Shane said.

"Cool."

Cammy followed him as he locked up and carried big garbage bags out to the alley next to the tavern. She was seeing double. Sugar Shane times two. Two spoonfuls of sugar. Then, in one fluid motion—a remnant of his former athletic prowess—he hurled the bags into a dumpster, swung his muscular mechanic's arm around Cammy, and stuck his tongue down her throat. It wasn't delicate, but she didn't want delicate. She wanted the backward cap and all the raw, moronic machismo it represented. They made out in this romantic setting, up against the hard cement wall, his hands on her ass over her black mourning dress.

"We could fuck in my car," Shane suggested helpfully. "I have condoms."

"I shouldn't have sex tonight. I buried my dad this morning."

"Jesus. Okay."

"We can keep making out, though."

"Where?"

"Here's fine."

"In the alley? Aren't you cold?"

"Nope. I'm nice and warm, thanks to Mr. Jim Beam."

"All right," he said with a dopey shrug. What a mensch.

You know, Cammy mused as Shane nibbled at her neck, maybe bros get a bad rap.

Day Two: Tuesday

♦ 4 ♦

CAMMY SLEPT PAST NOON the next day. When she awoke, fully clothed and horribly hungover, her first thought was to wonder whether she'd dreamed of hooking up with Shane O'Leary in an alley outside the Dirty Bird. Then she reached for her phone and saw a text from "Sugar Shane" that had come in at 3:41 AM: *awesome seeing u. thx for a fun nite. wanna do it again?* Plus an ambiguous sunglasses emoji.

Nope, not a dream. That had really happened. Wow.

You know what, though? Even if he'd written "u," "thx," and "nite," not to mention the stupid smiley face, the man had used proper punctuation. Two periods and a question mark. Good for him. That year at Bergen Community had paid off after all.

To her dismay, Cammy also saw two missed calls from her mom, one made around eleven and the other at midnight. What was she going to tell her? That she'd roamed the deserted streets of River Hill for four hours in the cold? A convincing lie would need to be crafted.

Shifting to her Gmail, she skimmed the usual bullshit temp offerings that littered her inbox until a surprising name leapt off the screen: Rebecca Strum. Subject line: "Condolences."

Dear Cammy,

River Hill being the minuscule hamlet that it is, I heard at school yesterday that your father had passed. Apparently, Ms. Weiss in the history department is friends with your mother, and she thought I'd want to know. I was sorry to hear the sad news. On the few occasions I met your dad—at those dreaded "parent-teacher conferences"—I enjoyed his company and his comedy, which came as a refreshing relief from the helicopter parenting I am, alas, so often forced to contend with in my role as a lowly public educator.

In any event, I haven't heard from you in quite a while. What are you up to these days? Are you still in the manic metropolis? Still writing? You used to send me updates on your doings every now and then, which I appreciated, but it's been a long spell since our last correspondence. I hope you haven't fallen into some kind of rut.

If you're around, as I assume you are, you're welcome to drop in and visit me at the high school. I finish teaching at three and then remain in my classroom for an hour or so, toiling over assignments that I hope may combat, however slightly, the cultural dumbing down to which my students are otherwise ceaselessly subjected. (I have seen the ruin of Western civilization, and it is called TikTok.)

Ms. Weiss informed me that guests are invited to your home in the evenings this week for shiva. I would come to pay my respects, but public displays of mourning give me the creeps; I prefer to grieve privately. I suspect you share my aversion.

Nevertheless, it would be very good to see you.

RS

Cammy finished reading the email, dropped her phone on the bed, and smiled up at the ceiling. Dr. Strum's emails always made her smile, with their eloquence and formality redolent of a bygone era. She'd been Cammy's English teacher throughout high school—three years of honors, one year of AP—and, more significantly, her most influential mentor. The sole PhD among the largely dimwitted faculty at River Hill High, Dr. Strum dressed like a librarian, in long skirts and cardigans, and seemed to have stepped out of the nineteenth century. She'd only been in her forties when she taught Cammy, but you'd never have known it. She worshipped literature, disdained popular culture, and responded to students' bad grammar and diction by pitching paperbacks against the walls. Fools were not suffered gladly in room 203.

Outside of her dad, no one had encouraged Cammy more in her love of reading and writing than Dr. Strum. This encouragement came in the form of frequent book recommendations—more like admonitions—many of which sailed right over her immature teenage head. (Hey, you try getting through *Let Us Now Praise Famous Men* in high school.) It also took the form of stern criticisms written in red pen, with impeccable cursive, in the margins of Cammy's pretentious papers: "This isn't a coherent argument." "Your thinking is lazy here." "I know you can do better, and so do you." Despite this doling out of tough love, Dr. Strum had had high hopes for her favorite pupil. During one of their many after-school Socratic dialogues, she'd once said to her, "You know, you may just rise above the morass."

This is exactly why Cammy hadn't emailed Dr. Strum lately: because she hadn't risen above the morass. In fact, she was mired in it. She had no literary achievements to show for herself. No advanced degrees. Not even a completed piece of work she was proud of. So, as much as she wanted to take her former teacher up on her invitation to come visit, another part of

Cammy felt reluctant and ashamed. Faced with Dr. Strum's penetrating visage—angular face, spectacled eyes, straight gray hair—how would she explain the disappointing last decade of her life? She couldn't even explain it to herself.

And what was with all this blast-from-the-past shit, anyway? Officer Rocco, Shane O'Leary, Dr. Strum. Who would pop out of the woodwork next? This was what sucked about being home: the constant reminders of the past, and of how far you *hadn't* come since then.

From the vantage of her twin bed, with its faded, childish night-sky-patterned sheets, Cammy looked around her room. Posters of her old heroes stared back at her: punk-rock Patti Smith with her hands defiantly on her hips; Geena Davis and Susan Sarandon as Thelma and Louise, fleeing the law in their blue Ford Thunderbird; Joan Didion, the coolest writer on the planet, brandishing a cigarette. All badass women who wouldn't be caught dead in these infantilizing environs. They'd risen above, taken big swings, made their mark. (Sure, Thelma and Louise were fictional, but still.)

How had they done it? And why couldn't she?

★ ★ ★

"Your dad was a saint," Aunt Miriam blubbered that night at the shiva. This had been her incessant refrain since the burial: Saint Cy. She had Cammy cornered in the dining room. "He was the best brother in the world. He would've done anything for me. I don't know what I'll do without him."

Cammy just nodded. Miriam was right to be worried. Not to be cruel, but she happened to be one of those fragile, helpless people who rely on others for everything and then reward their efforts with gushing gratitude that never, ever stops. The "saint" business was part of this pathology. It was true that Cy had steered his red-haired, high-strung younger sister through

CAMMY SITTING SHIVA

countless difficulties, from getting a driver's license later in life (she was afraid to drive) to divorcing André, the macho Moroccan Jew who'd conned her into marrying him while she was on a trip to Israel in her twenties. (He'd refused to give her a *get*, the Jewish divorce document that only husbands can present to their wives. How fair!)

"And your father loved you so much, honey," Miriam sniffled.

"Yeah, I know he did."

"He was so proud of you."

"For what?" Cammy muttered under her breath.

"What did you say?"

"Nothing."

She had to escape. Once Miriam got her hooks in you, she could hold you captive for hours. And the last thing Cammy needed was to spend the second night of shiva caught in the vortex of her aunt's pathos. Abruptly excusing herself, she bolted into the kitchen and ducked into the adjoining half bath, where she shut the door behind her and breathed the air of freedom.

To be precise, the air smelled like Poo-Pourri toilet spray. One of tonight's guests must've taken a dump in here, which, although not religiously forbidden, did seem like a breach of the tacit shiva oath. It doesn't exactly honor the bereaved to stink up their bathroom.

Plonking herself down on the closed toilet seat, Cammy texted Francesca: *Help. Miriam alert. What're you doing?* A reply came back almost instantly: *bowling.*

Bowling? With who?

myself

You're bowling alone on a Tuesday night?

yeah why not? fuck you

Sorry for judging.

you wanna come?

Cammy considered this. How insane would it be for her to dip out of the shiva without telling anyone—a Jewish-Irish goodbye, if you will—in order to go bowling? Would this be more or less offensive than smoking weed during yesterday's post-burial lunch or, for that matter, leaving her mom home alone last night and hooking up with a former high school jock in an alley? Truth be told, it was all pretty bad. But so what?

Actually yeah, I do. Can I?

for sure. you know where I am

Indeed, Cammy did.

Now the only challenge was to sneak off undetected. Exiting the bathroom, she edged her way along the wall of the kitchen, careful to avoid eye contact with any chatty visitors. She had to make it to the living room, then to the front door, and she'd be in the clear.

But as she passed the doorway to the dining room, Cammy saw something that caused her to halt in her tracks: her mother and Miriam huddled together in a dim nook by the china cabinet, conferring in hushed, serious tones. They looked like a couple of suburban secret agents. Beth had a small object cupped in one hand that she was showing to her sister-in-law. Was it— Yes, it was: the Polaroid from the box—the photo of Cy and D, the unidentified woman!

Though Cammy possessed neither lip-reading ability nor ultrasonic hearing, she was a pretty skilled eavesdropper, and Miriam had a high-pitched voice that carried. She distinctly overheard her aunt say with concern, "Do you think we should call her?" Then: "It's the right thing to do, isn't it?"

Call whom? D? Why? To inform her of Cy's death, maybe?

Did that mean the nameless "old girlfriend" from college was actually an important enough figure in his life to warrant such a personal call? What was the real story with this woman, and why had Beth been weirdly vague about her last night?

Cammy wanted to crash their private conversation and find out, yet she knew that doing so would keep her here and derail her getaway plan. And getting away from maudlin Miriam and the other assorted mourners was currently her primary objective.

So she filed this odd scene in her mental dossier and fled.

★ ★ ★

There had been a period in middle school when everyone started having birthday parties at the bowling alley. This came after the roller rink era but before the laser tag phase. These fads were mysterious. Nobody ever announced them—"Okay, we're done with rollerblading, now we're on to bowling!"—but all the kids picked up on the shifts as if through a collective consciousness. Pity the poor child whose clueless parents didn't get the memo and threw them the wrong kind of party. Ice skating during the laser tag craze? Loser!

Cammy recalled this preteen social farce as she stepped through the doors of Bowler City, a delightfully decaying establishment in unscenic Hackensack. The scent inside gave her an immediate Proustian rush. It was a rank combination of greasy French fries and pizza, cheap beer, and that deodorizing spray they used on the bowling sneakers. She loved it. The place was as she remembered, from the 1980s decor to the blips and bleeps emanating from the arcade room to the psychedelic wall mural depicting pins and balls floating in outer space.

The Tuesday-night crowd was sparse. Old guys with beer guts bowled alone, zenned out on the lazy rhythms of the nonsport, bottles of Coors Light within arm's reach. Were they the same gang who'd been at the Dirty Bird last night? No, but close. Among them was the youngest solo bowler in sight: Fran, who had on patched jeans and her old River Hill High School Cross-Country hoodie, gray with red lettering. She'd been quite a runner back in the day. A pitcher of beer and two glasses sat on the table behind her. Clutch.

Cammy approached her friend's lane. Fran was just about to throw. She strode to the foul line, wound up, and released a speckled, mustard-colored ball that looked like a gaseous planet. It hurtled toward the defenseless pins with startling speed, knocking all ten of them down with a crack of thunder. Fran pumped her fist in the air and shouted, "Strike, motherfucker!" as she wheeled around to find Cammy giving her an awed slow clap.

"What's up, dude? You just get here?"

"Yeah, a second ago."

"Did you see that?"

"I did. Impressive."

"That's my third strike this game."

"When'd you get so good at bowling?"

"I come here a lot."

"How often is a lot?"

"Like two or three nights a week."

"Are you serious?"

"It helps me unwind. Being at the deli all day with my dad is exhausting." Charming and obstinate in equal measure, Fran's father, Leo DeMarco, was an Italian—from Italy—who'd come to America in the seventies to make his fortune in food.

"How is your dad?" Cammy asked.

"He's all right. He's getting older. Slipping a little."

"What do you mean 'slipping'?"

"He's started forgetting stuff. Ordering the wrong supplies at the store. Not paying the bills on time. Leaving the place unlocked overnight. I have to stay on top of all that now."

"Is it just his age, or . . . ?"

"Me and my mom finally dragged him to some doctors last month. You know, he 'doesn't believe' in them." Fran sighed. "They said it might be early signs of dementia."

"*Dementia?* Oh no . . ."

"Well, he's in denial, so we're basically pretending it's not happening."

"I'm sorry. That's—that's rough." Cammy thought about the different ways you can lose people: suddenly, with no warning, as she'd lost her dad, or slowly before your very eyes, as Fran might one day lose hers. Two awful alternatives. Pick your poison.

"Eh, what can you do, right? It's a bitch." This was how Fran cushioned life's blows: with a feisty fatalism that could probably be traced back to her Calabrian peasant ancestors. "Okay, no more depressing talk. I'm supposed to be cheering you up." She pointed to the pitcher. "I got us some PBR."

"PBR? Wow."

"Don't be a snob. You like it. And isn't it a hipster thing now?"

It was. And Cammy herself did have an unironic soft spot for the bargain lager. Pabst Blue Ribbon brought back pleasant memories of her early, happy-go-lucky drinking days as a high school senior, of beer pong tournaments played in kids' basements. The splash of a ping-pong ball landing in a red cup full of PBR had rich resonance.

They sat down in plastic swivel chairs, and Fran poured their glasses.

"Thanks for inviting me out," Cammy said, taking a watery sip. "My aunt had me trapped."

"That lady's a piece of work," Fran nodded. Even she'd been subjected to some of Miriam's obsequious gushing over the years. ("Oh, Francesca, you're *such* a sweetheart. Cammy is *so* lucky to have you as a friend. I just know you're going to be in each other's lives forever.") "Your mom was cool with you leaving the shiva?"

"I didn't tell her. I just left."

"Oh, she's gonna love that."

"Whatever. If I don't wanna be part of this like coercive mourning ritual, that's my constitutional right."

"Fair enough. Not sure that's in the Constitution, though."

"It should be. 'One whose dad has just died shall be left the fuck alone if she wants to be.'"

"Hear, hear."

Cammy smiled. "Hey, so guess what happened last night?" She always relished the opportunity to tell Fran about some crazy shit she'd done, because the reverse was much more often the case.

"What happened?"

"I hooked up with Shane O'Leary."

"You *what*?"

"No joke. In the alley behind the Dirty Bird."

Fran did a legit spit take, nearly spurting PBR all over the table, and demanded a swift explanation. Cammy regaled her with a vivid account of the previous night's festivities: running into Sugar Shane, carousing with him at the bar, their romantic tryst by the dumpster.

"That's nuts," Fran said at last, which was high praise coming from someone as difficult to shock as her. "So does this mean you're over David?"

"No. We only broke up a few weeks ago. We were together almost a year." Fran hadn't ever met David—Cammy's current city life was separate from her former Jersey life, and never the twain shall meet—but Cammy had told her about him during their semiregular catch-up sessions on the phone. "That doesn't mean I can't engage in recreational hookups to dull the pain."

"Touché. But wait, I forget—why'd you cheat on David, again?"

Why *had* Cammy betrayed her faithful boyfriend by sleeping with that hunky, Brando-esque actor she'd met at one of the

Drama Collective's meetings? "Honestly, I don't know. I was drunk. It was stupid."

"And why'd you tell David you did it?"

"I don't know that either. I don't know why I do a lot of things lately. I guess I'm kind of . . . floundering?"

This remark was punctuated with a resounding boom, as if the Lord himself were confirming Cammy's critical self-assessment. Spinning around, she saw the earthly source of the sound: A bowling ball had slipped out of the hand of an old-timer a couple of lanes over, thunking onto the wood and straight into the gutter. "Goddamn shit," he swore. She empathized.

"Does David even know about your dad?" Fran asked.

"No. I haven't told him."

"You should. Maybe he'll feel sorry for you and take you back."

"Yeah, that wouldn't be manipulative at all."

"Desperate times call for desperate measures."

"So I should use my father's death to emotionally blackmail my ex into forgiving me for cheating, so he'll get back together with me?"

"Just a suggestion."

"I'm not *that* desperate. Yet."

"See?" Fran said, pleased. "You still have some dignity. Maybe you're not doing as bad as you think you are."

"How did you just steer this depressing conversation into a positive takeaway for me?"

"Magic." Fran downed the rest of her glass, belched unabashedly, and refilled it with beer. "But yeah, this is why I don't do relationships. Too much drama."

Cammy chuckled at her friend's oft-stated commitment to noncommitment. "You really never want a partner?"

"Eh. Maybe when I'm like fifty."

Fran had reached the age of thirty without having a long-term significant other, and it seemed entirely possible that she could keep the streak going for another two decades. She had an expansive, adventurous sexuality that bucked the bounds of monogamy. She liked guys. She liked girls. She liked one-night stands. She liked threesomes. Why deal with the Sturm und Drang of sustained entanglements when you could have the fun without the headaches? Cammy, who fancied herself a freethinker but was in reality quite conventional when it came to relationships, had long lived vicariously through the tales of her bestie's escapades, which never wanted for graphic detail.

Fran glanced up at the pixelated scorecard screen. She was on her seventh frame. Three proud Xs signified the strikes she'd rolled. "I'm paying for this lane, so I should probably finish the game."

"Oh yeah. Sorry."

"You wanna take my next turn?"

"What? Why?"

"For fun. Guest roll."

"But I don't have the sneakers."

"You don't need the sneakers."

"And I suck. I haven't bowled in forever."

"That's okay. I'm killing it. You can't fuck up my score that much."

Buoyed by these words of encouragement and fortified by a bellyful of Pabst, Cammy rose. She walked over to the rack to retrieve Fran's yellowish, planetary-looking ball. The thing was only twelve pounds but felt oddly heavy. She needed to start working out. Holding it, she was reminded of a song she'd sung with her preschool class at touchy-feely Apple Montessori: *"He's got the whole world in his hands, he's got the whole world in his hands . . ."* A bit religious for secular education, no? Anyway.

As she assumed her starting position and slid her fingers into the ball's snug holes—oh, the double entendres!—a strange thought entered Cammy's mind: If she could only bowl a strike, she would be able to get her mess of a life in order. She'd figure out how to grieve for her father, how to get along with her mother, how to move on from David, what to do with herself. The notion was wholly irrational, of course, but it possessed a superstitious power. Yes, everything depended on this roll.

Summoning muscle memory from those middle school birthday parties, she took a few steady steps forward, bent her knees, stretched her arm back, swung it around, and let the ball glide off her fingers. It rumbled down the center of the lane, in a surprisingly straight line, toward the pins of destiny, which stood poised, waiting. Time slowed. Her hopes were high. But then, at the very last second, as though of its own volition, the ball veered sharply to the left. She watched in dismay as it curved, barely grazing the corner pin before tumbling into the gutter and out of sight. The pin wobbled—would it fall?—but remained standing.

Cammy slunk back to her seat a failure. She hadn't hit anything: a tragicomic metaphor.

"You hooked it," Fran said, furrowing her brow in disapproval.

"Thanks, I saw."

"Why'd you hook it?"

"I didn't mean to."

"Well, you've still got one more throw."

"You take it. I'm good."

"Come on. You're just rusty. Don't give up."

"Giving up is what I do best," Cammy said with finality, images of pages from abandoned writing projects flitting through her head.

"All right." Fran got up as the ball shot out of the return machine with a pneumatic whoosh. "I can salvage this."

"Godspeed."

Cammy poured herself some more beer. Lifting the glass to her mouth, she happened to turn as a trim man in tight-fitting light blue jeans and a navy sweatshirt passed by, carrying a pizza from the refreshment area back to his lane. The man had a great ass. She was partial to guys with great asses. People talked about women's asses all the time, but men's didn't get nearly enough attention. They were a crucial feature.

On further inspection, however—and yes, she took the time to inspect—this wasn't just any well-shaped behind. Its sculpted contours, and the athletic gait of its owner, stirred something in her: an association, a recollection. Crazy as it seemed, she knew this butt.

The man rejoined his group at the far end of the room. There were four of them, all apparently under forty, the only other non–senior citizens in the place. He set the pizza down on their table and took a seat, finally granting Cammy a frontal view.

Her hand shook. She almost dropped her glass. For the handsome, chiseled face she was staring at, crowned by a sweep of lush black hair—as lush as the extraordinary ass she'd been ogling moments ago—belonged to none other than Nick Ramos, the first boy she had ever loved.

♦ 5 ♦

Nick Ramos was a dancer.

The first time Cammy saw him strut his stuff was at the eighth-grade talent show, a painful pageant of off-key singing, out-of-tune instrumentals, and, saddest of all, flubbed magic tricks. The performative bar was low, very low. Then Nick took the stage. He wore black warm-up pants, a sleeveless white T-shirt, and a pair of sleek white Nikes. An obnoxious kid somewhere in the auditorium snickered, but Nick was unfazed. The bouncy disco groove of Justin Timberlake's "Rock Your Body" kicked in over the speaker system, and he began to move.

Now, normally, Cammy would've snidely snickered herself. She was a bookish, snobbish, judgmental thirteen-year-old who scorned the pop culture prized by her peers, including Top 40 music and the tacky dancing that accompanied it. (Hence the in-your-face Patti Smith poster she'd hung in her room earlier that year.) But she couldn't bring herself to snicker at Nick. She was too transfixed by the effortless grace of his movements, which synced perfectly with the rhythm of the song, and by the bold confidence he demonstrated while engaged in an activity that the pubescent power structure deemed better suited to girls.

No such boxes could contain Nick. On that fateful April day, he put even Justin Timberlake, the man who brought sexy back, to shame, and turned the scuff-marked stage of River Hill Middle School into a Vegas arena. He also danced his way straight into Cammy's hormonally charged heart, where he would remain lodged for the next four longing-filled years.

Alas, she couldn't have picked a less attainable crush. The insurmountable problem was that Cammy and Nick really had no common ground, no loci in which their teenage paths converged. Not because he was some dumb, proto-fratty jock, like Shane and the Dicks. On the contrary, he had a reputation for niceness, albeit in the aloof way that a handsome, talented young guy destined for entertainment stardom can afford to be nice to everyone.

Rather, the issue was that their high school identities were simply too different. Cammy was Dr. Strum's protégé, the smart girl who wrote good essays and made quick-witted comments in class. And Nick was, well, Beautiful Dancer Boy.

Yes, Beautiful Dancer Boy. This was what she called him, both in her own mind and when rhapsodizing about him to Fran, the only person to whom she confessed her unrequited love. Silly as it sounded, the sobriquet couldn't have been more fitting. Whether making showstopping appearances at the yearly talent shows—any mockery from the audience had long since turned to abject wonder—or gliding through the halls as if elevated slightly off the floor, he was a golden child. Too golden for the likes of brainy, introverted Cammy, who had no choice but to pine after him from afar.

Their paths did cross, however fleetingly, each spring, when the school staged its annual musical. Nick always led the chorus of dancers, naturally, and got to display his kinetic pyrotechnics at the climax of the chosen show's biggest number. (During Cammy's tenure, the Drama Club put on splashy productions of, in chronological order, *Damn Yankees*, *Grease*, *Man of La Mancha*, and *Crazy for You*.) Cammy wasn't a performer—God no!—but she did play in the pit orchestra. Her instrument? The trombone. Why oh why had she picked the most unwieldy, least becoming horn of them all to be her burden? Because of a whim: One day in sixth grade, she'd thought the slide looked cool. The rest was humiliating history.

At rehearsals, Cammy sat sequestered with the other band nerds in a literal pit in front of the stage, peering up at the comely cast as they ran through their songs and routines. Even in this setting, surrounded by others who embraced the limelight, Nick stood out. The general consensus was that he was bound for a professional career as a hip-hop dancer or choreographer, and rightfully so. Every pivot of his muscular legs and thrust of his supple hips sent shock waves through Cammy's body and soul as she clutched her ridiculous instrument.

And that ass. Enough said.

When there was downtime in the theater, she tried to casually wander in his direction, catch his attention, and make unforced small talk that inevitably felt forced. Sure, he laughed along at her meager attempts at repartee: "Oh, isn't such and such teacher an asshole?" "Did you hear what so-and-so got detention for?" "Isn't this school just so lame?" Nick couldn't really vibe with Cammy's jaundiced view of things, though, because unlike her, he felt totally comfortable in his own skin, at one with his place in the universe. As he should have.

Once, while they were chatting on a break, the slide of her trombone, which she'd failed to lock in place, slipped off and clanged against the stage floor. Everyone turned to stare. Like a true gentleman, he picked it up and handed it to her with a sympathetic smile. She thought she might sink into the blackness of the stage from embarrassment.

And then there was the senior prom, that ultimate high school rite of passage. Ever the contrarian, Cammy considered not attending as an act of Patti Smith–style protest against conformity, etc., but Fran managed to talk her out of this, raising the unsettling prospect of a lifetime of FOMO. So she went to the prom with pimply, pedantic Carl Fisher, a fellow honors student every bit as dorky as his name would lead one to believe. It was an arrangement of convenience for both of them. Immediately upon arriving at the characterless Marriott ballroom in Teaneck that had been rented out for the occasion, Cammy proceeded to ignore her date, hang out with Fran, and gawk at her crush from a distance.

Nick looked predictably dashing in his burgundy satin tux, a harbinger of red-carpet outfits to come. His date for the evening was blond, statuesque Brianna Baker, a triple threat (actor! singer! dancer!) who starred in all the musicals and belonged in the cast of *Glee*. They weren't actually dating, which was a nice consolation, but they did spend the whole night tearing up the dance floor together, shaking and shimmying to the hits of the day: Kesha's ode to drunken revelry, "Tik Tok"; Lady Gaga's inescapable "Bad Romance"; Black Eyed Peas' "I Gotta Feeling," with its incongruous Hebrew shouts of "Mazel tov!" and "L'chaim!"

Fran had smuggled a flask of Bacardi Limon into the Marriott by hiding it in her ruffled dress, thereby passing the purse inspection carried out by beady-eyed Principal Tortelli himself (mocking nickname: Tortellini). Every half hour or so, she and Cammy took turns stealing into the ladies' bathroom to swig the citrusy rum in a stall. In their defense, they weren't the only underage attendees engaged in such prohibited conduct, as evidenced by a forgotten line of cocaine Cammy spotted next to a sink on one of her trips. She did pause for a second, wondering whether to give the good old nose candy a try, but to her sheltered seventeen-year-old self, this seemed a bridge too far.

By around eleven, the bottle of Bacardi had been drained, and Cammy was buzzed enough to do something reckless. As the hokey DJ congratulated River Hill's graduating seniors and announced the final song of the night—"a slow one for all the sweethearts out there"—she stood up from the corner table where she and Fran were sitting.

"What're you doing?" Fran asked, a hint of alarm in her voice.

"I'm going in," Cammy said purposefully. "Last dance, last chance."

"Okay, wait, hold on a second—"

But it was too late for sensible warnings now. Cammy was already striding to the center of the wooden dance floor, to the opening strains of "Angel," Shaggy and Rayvon's perennially popular, reggae-infused ballad. *"Girl, you're my angel. You're my darling angel. Closer than my peeps you are to me, baby."* (Okay, so the lyrics weren't exactly Joni Mitchell caliber, but they did the trick for a prom finale.) Spurred by rummy confidence, or rudeness, she cut right in front of a stunned Brianna Baker and asked Nick to dance.

"Oh, uh . . ." Gallant as ever, he glanced over Cammy's shoulder at Brianna, as if to say, "Would it be okay if I humored this poor mortal by dancing with her?" Like a benevolent goddess, Brianna must've taken pity on her, for the next thing Nick said was, "Sure."

It was happening!

A current of electricity passed through Cammy as she rested her hands on Nick's broad shoulders. And when he placed his on her waist, the charge increased exponentially. They were in the classic awkward slow-dance formation, but for all the breathless exhilaration she felt, they might as well have been fucking buck naked on the floor. A lock of his gelled hair had come loose and fallen across his forehead. She wanted nothing more than to tenderly smooth it back, the way Barbra Streisand does with Robert Redford in *The Way We Were*, a weepy seventies fave of her mom's.

Instead she said the most mundane thing imaginable: "So have you had a fun night?"

"Yeah. It was a good time. You?"

Cammy shrugged. "It was okay. I'm not really into the whole prom thing."

"Why not?"

Rather than launch into a lengthy antiestablishment diatribe, which would likely ruin the mood, such as it was, she merely said, "I guess I'm a curmudgeon."

Nick smiled, and Shaggy's angels sang. "You're eighteen, and you're a curmudgeon?"

"Still seventeen. I don't turn eighteen till August."

"That's even crazier."

"I mean, I probably would've had more fun if I could dance like you and Brianna. You guys were killing it out here."

"Brianna's an awesome dancer."

"You're better," Cammy said before she could stop herself.

"I don't know about *that*." His modesty sounded authentic. Did this guy have any flaws?

"Come on. You're a star. Everyone thinks so."

"A star in River Hill, maybe."

"You'd be a star anywhere." Hearing these moony words leave her mouth—a mouth much more inclined toward elitist snark—she realized how flagrantly she was fawning. She needed to tone it down, say something neutral. "So . . . you're gonna study dance at school?"

"Yep. University of Arizona."

Arizona! What? Why was he going all the way to *Arizona*? In the back of her mind, Cammy had been comforted by the assumption (based on nothing) that Nick would probably head to some conservatory in the Northeast, within spitting distance of New York. Then she could hit him up on Facebook and try to kindle a college romance; by that point, she'd be cooler and more deserving of his attention. Scheme foiled. "Why Arizona?" she asked, faux nonchalant.

"They've got a great dance program. And I like warm weather."

"Is that in Phoenix?"

"No, Tucson. Near the border. I have family there, so that's another reason."

"Cool. Very cool."

"And you're going to NYU, right?"

"Yeah." Although she was now contemplating a preemptive transfer to U of A. No, that would be stalking.

"For English?"

"That's the plan."

"I wish I could write like you. I always loved your stories in the lit mag."

Wait, what was this? He'd read the high school's literary magazine, the *River Hill Review*? (Dr. Strum was responsible for its aspirational academic name.) She'd thought no one in the student body even opened the wretched thing, with its navel-gazing poetry and purple prose. And more than that, he'd actually read her bleak tales of suburban ennui?

"Wow. Thanks for reading those. I didn't think anyone did."

"I mean, they were kind of depressing, but really well written."

"Depressing's what I was going for."

As a kid whose soaring dance performances inspired people, lifted them up, Nick seemed puzzled that someone would set out to do the very opposite. "Oh. Okay. Then good job."

Cammy could sense that the song was winding down. Shaggy was intoning his last throaty reggae verse: "*Now, life is one big party when you're still young. And who's gonna have your back when it's all done?*" Who indeed? Shifting from foot to foot, intoxicated by the boyish fragrance of Nick's cologne and perspiration, basking in the glow of his clear bronze complexion, she knew that time was running out. In a couple of weeks, school would be over, and in a few months, he'd be off in the Arizona desert, wowing the young women in the dance department. She had to act now or forever hold her peace.

Lifting her hands from his shoulders and clasping them behind his neck, Cammy inched her body closer to Nick's, so that his hands slid from her waist to the small of her back. She liked how they felt there. "Hey," she began tentatively, "so I don't wanna like . . . make things weird." Well, thanks to that preface, they were officially weird. Her Bacardi-induced inhibition was fading fast. Come on, keep going. "But, um . . . I—I like you, Nick."

There, she'd said it: the four monosyllabic but meaning-laden words she'd been holding inside her since the eighth-grade talent show, when he'd first swung and swayed into her consciousness. She would've preferred to say "love" instead of "like," but that would've been utter madness. The ensuing seconds passed like eons. And how did her object of affection at last respond?

"I like you too, Cammy." He said it courteously, innocuously, playing dumb.

Heedless of the fact that the music had stopped and the dance floor was emptying out, she pressed on. This was her Molly-Ringwald-at-the-end-of-a-John-Hughes-movie moment. She hadn't watched *Sixteen Candles*, *The Breakfast Club*, and *Pretty in Pink* over and over again on TBS for nothing. "No, I mean I *like* you, Nick. I *like* like you. And I know it must seem totally out of the blue, but it's really not, 'cause I've felt this way for a while. I just haven't had the chance—or the courage, I guess?—to tell you. And high school's over now, and we're going away to different places, and I just need you to know that I think you're amazing—"

"Cammy, there you are! We're all waiting for you out in the limo!"

A whining, nasal voice interrupted her Ringwaldian monologue. It was the last voice in the world she wanted to hear at this particular instant. It was the voice of her neglected, nebbishy date, Carl Fisher. She turned to see his round, flushed, scolding face behind her. "Carl, I'll be right there—"

"Everyone's waiting," he repeated. "We're trying to go to Ben's."

As was the custom, Cammy had traveled to the prom in a hired limo with nine other people, including Carl and Fran; the whole group had gone Dutch to pay for it (or, more accurately, their folks had). Their post-event destination was the McMansion of Ben Miller, a jerky kid whose primary social asset was his Wall Street parents' laissez-faire attitude vis-à-vis teenage alcohol and drug use, which went on unencumbered in his lavish finished basement. Apparently, Cammy's limo mates were anxious to get there and start drinking, and she was holding them up by lingering here. If only they understood why!

"All right, I'm coming," she said, hoping Carl would leave and give her another minute with her man. But he just stood there. He wasn't going anywhere. Perhaps this was revenge for how she'd snubbed him the entire night. She turned back to Nick, whose glistening face betrayed no reaction to her amorous outpouring. "I'm so sorry. I have to go."

"That's okay. I do too." Imperious Brianna Baker was at his side now, tugging at the sleeve of his jacket. "I think prom's done," he added, stating the obvious.

"Yeah. This is so abrupt, though. I'm sorry for like... springing all that on you at the last minute." Searching her head for a way to save this, Cammy remembered that she'd gotten Nick's number a couple of months before, during a break from rehearsals for *Crazy for You*. "Can I call you, maybe? To talk some more?"

"Sure. You can call me."

"Okay. I will. Thanks for the dance. Bye, Nick."

"Bye, Cammy."

She hesitated, and then, to the surprise of Carl, Brianna, and even herself, she took a brisk step forward and planted a soft, yearning kiss on Nick's lower cheek, dangerously close to his full, pillowy lips. It may have been the most daring thing she'd ever done.

And that was that.

Cammy never did call him. In fact, they never spoke again. After risking mortification to express her love, why didn't she follow through? The simple answer was that without the aid of liquid courage and the adrenaline rush of prom, she lost her nerve.

The last two weeks of high school flew by in a whirl of activities intended to celebrate the senior class: a trip down to Six Flags Great Adventure, with its gravity-defying roller coasters; a free-for-all field day in Wood Park; an inexplicable daylong ping-pong tournament. This was followed by the pomp and circumstance of graduation, where Cammy accepted the English department's award from Dr. Strum, yellow tassel dangling comically from her blue cap. Amid all this hubbub, she picked up her phone each evening and stared at Nick's name in her contacts list, but she couldn't bring herself to dial.

Cammy drifted through the summer before college in a hopeful haze. Hopeful because of the promise of NYU and the intellectual and artistic life it offered. (She didn't know yet that the university was an overrated corporate cash cow.) Hazy because she got high with Fran just about every night, after days spent half-assing it as a counselor at a local educational day camp for spoiled rich kids. Losing her virginity in the back of a car to

Dustin, a lanky, wisecracking co-counselor, helped keep thoughts of Nick at bay. She resigned herself to regarding him as "the one who got away"—not that she'd ever had him to begin with.

"Why don't you just call him?" Fran asked one balmy day in late August, as they sat on a bench at an overlook off the Palisades Interstate Parkway, smoking a joint. Across the Hudson, the setting sun lit the city skyline in a brilliant orange blaze.

"I don't think he wants me to call him."

"But you'll never know if you don't."

"I already poured my heart out to him at prom. It's been two months. If he wanted to talk to me again, he would have."

"Maybe he's just shy."

"Nick Ramos is the opposite of shy. He's not into me. That's it." Cammy said this with the stoic fatalism of a Humphrey Bogart antihero (her dad was a big Bogart fan), puffing on the J. "And why would he be? He's Beautiful Dancer Boy, and I'm . . ."

"Hot Writer Girl."

"I'm not hot."

"I think you're hot. You're smart-hot."

"What's smart-hot?"

"It's like its own thing. It's not just physical. Like your smartness somehow becomes hotness."

"You're my best friend. You have to say that."

"Fine, don't believe me." Fran pitched the finished joint over the railing in front of them, beyond which a steep cliff led down to the riverbank. "I still think you coulda fucked him."

"That wasn't the objective," Cammy said, rolling her eyes at her friend's unromantic nature.

"It wasn't?"

"Okay, it was part of it. But the real objective was . . . a passionate love affair."

"Oh. Yeah, I guess it's too late for that."

Cammy stood up and stretched her arms. "Well, you know what Tennyson says."

"Who?"

"Alfred, Lord Tennyson."

"Who the hell is that?"

"One of Dr. Strum's favorite poets."

"Figures."

"'Tis better to have loved and lost than never to have loved at all.'"

Fran pondered this maxim. "Bullshit."

★ ★ ★

Oh, and as for the rest of prom night: Cammy went to Ben Miller's house along with her limo crew, several of whom gave her the stink eye for having kept them waiting. Once there, she drowned her heartsick sorrows in plastic Solo cups filled with Natural Light, aka Natty Light, a cheap brew far worse than PBR. At around two AM, thoroughly blitzed, she found herself facing off against her pestering date, Carl, in an epic beer pong match. With the game on the line, despite her blurred vision, she miraculously sunk the winning shot.

"That's what you get, Carl!" she yelled loud enough for everybody in Ben's opulent basement to hear. "That's what you get for ruining my Molly Ringwald moment!"

Carl, of course, didn't get the reference.

♦ 6 ♦

"Nick," Cammy said, having crossed the length of the bowling alley to speak to him for the first time in eleven years.

He saw her and stood up from the table where he was sharing a pepperoni pizza with his three companions. "Cammy! Wow. What a—Hi."

"Hello." She felt like Ingrid Bergman in *Casablanca*, wandering into Bogart's nightclub (Rick's, which rhymed with Nick's!) to the melancholy music of "As Time Goes By." Except she and Nick had never been lovers, and a world war hadn't separated them, but whatever.

They exchanged a brief half hug. She recognized his fresh scent. He still looked good.

"It's been forever," he said, seeming sincerely pleased to see her.

"Yeah, it has."

"How are you? What're you up to?"

"I'm okay. My dad just died." Jesus, Cammy, how about a filter?

"Oh my God, I'm so sorry."

"Thanks. That's why I'm home. I mean, I *should* be at the house sitting shiva with my mom right now"—Did Nick know what shiva was? Probably—"but instead I'm here bowling."

He looked unsure how to respond to this. "Uh-huh."

"Fran's over there." She pointed across the room to her pal, who waved overenthusiastically.

"Fran! Such a character. You guys are still friends?"

"Ride or die."

"That's awesome."

"And how 'bout you? What're you . . ."

Nick gestured to the three friendly-looking people at the table behind him. "These are my co-workers." He indicated a woman with a purple-streaked pixie cut and a kind face. "Iris is leaving, so we're having a little going-away party for her. She likes bowling."

"Oh. Fun. But, uh, co-workers? What do you do?"

"Oh, I work at this community center for underserved kids. The Clubhouse. It's right by here in Hackensack. We have after-school programs, tutoring, mentorship. I teach hip-hop dance."

Cammy heard her herself saying, "That's so cool," though what she was really thinking was, *what*? According to the great expectations of everyone in River Hill, Nick was supposed to be a full-fledged star by now, dancing, choreographing, appearing next to some pop singer on the Super Bowl halftime show. So what in the world was he still doing here in humdrum Bergen County, working at a center for kids? Not that that wasn't admirable and altruistic and everything, but it didn't match up at all with his projected ascent to the stratosphere. Unfortunately, there was no unobnoxious way to ask about this. (E.g., "Hey, why haven't you lived up to your potential?")

"And you're in the city?" he asked.

"Yep."

"Writing?"

"Sort of?"

Mercifully, Nick didn't press her on this nonanswer. "How long are you home for?"

"Just this week. Shiva lasts a week. One loooong week."

"Well, I'm sure you're mostly spending time with your family and stuff—"

"As little as possible, actually."

He didn't press her on this perversity either. "Then if you have some free time—"

"I have nothing but free time."

"—you should stop by the Clubhouse, check it out."

"I should?"

"Yeah. It's a really cool place." He smiled, prompting a familiar flutter in her heart. "And it would be fun to catch up."

"Yes . . . it would."

"Nick, you want another slice?!" one of his colleagues called.

"Ah, I'm being summoned," he chuckled. "But it's great seeing you, Cammy."

"You too, Nick."

"And again, I'm so sorry about your dad."

Walking back to her lane, Cammy did her best to process the improbable events of the preceding few minutes: After over a decade, she'd run into her long-lost high school crush, whose personal trajectory appeared to have altered drastically, though she had no idea why. Strangely, despite having ended up in drab Hackensack rather than onstage in the spotlight, Nick came off as content, at peace. And stranger still, he wanted to see her again, to "catch up"; he'd even invited her to his workplace. Unless he was just being polite or feeling pity because of her father's death. But Cammy had a pretty foolproof bullshit detector, and his interest and his invitation had struck her as genuine.

Huh.

Fran was waiting for her, eager and wide-eyed. "You better tell me what just happened right now," she said, "or I'm gonna bounce this bowling ball off your head."

* * *

The Madonna Cemetery in Fort Lee is perched at the highest point in all of Bergen County, offering a panoramic view of the marshy Meadowlands down below. (You can't tell how polluted they are from so far up.) In existence for a hundred fifty years, the small Catholic burial ground on the hill is a tranquil, secluded place well suited to quiet contemplation. It's also, as Cammy and Fran had discovered as wayward youths, a perfect spot for getting hammered late at night and ruminating on life's big questions.

Which is exactly what they were doing at this moment. Some things never change.

They'd left the bowling alley and decided on the cemetery as their next destination. Cammy didn't want to go home yet, and Fran was, as usual, up for anything. Besides, they now had the whole Nick situation to unpack. On their way, they swung by the Discount Liquor Outlet in Palisades Park, where they'd once used low-quality fake IDs to make purchases from cynical clerks who turned a blind eye. What they bought there tonight made PBR look like world-class champagne: two hulking forty-ounce bottles of Olde English 800 malt liquor.

This choice was a throwback, strictly for old times' sake. Yellow like piss and just as nauseating, with a trace of sickly sweetness to add insult to injury, Olde E, as they called it, was another remnant of their shared past. ("Hey, let's grab a couple forties before we head to the party.") Neither of them had had it in years. Cammy wondered if she were regressing—if the weed and the bowling alley and the cemetery and the malt liquor were all an elaborate coping mechanism to help her avoid her grief—but she already knew the answer.

She had several missed calls from her mom and a series of increasingly vexed texts: *Where are you? Where's my car? What are you doing? Call me right now.* Yes, not only had she absconded from the shiva without so much as a word to her mother; she'd also taken her Corolla to get to Bowler City. Oh, well. She'd deal with that mess later.

Now she was too busy listening to Fran, who, out of nowhere, was making an impassioned case that Cammy should move back home to Jersey. They were seated on the grass in the October chill, between the ivy-covered gravestones of deceased Catholics, sacrilegiously drinking their forties. The smoggy night sky hovered overhead.

"Move back home? Why would I do that?"

"'Cause you said you're floundering in the city."

"I'm not floundering badly enough to come back to *Jersey.*"

"What's wrong with Jersey? *I* live here."

"I know, but—"

"You talk about it like it's the shittiest place on earth."

Cammy didn't correct this perception. "I promised myself I'd make it in New York."

"Well, no offense, but it sounds like that's not really panning out for you."

"Wow, thank you."

"No, I mean, you don't like the work you're doing. You always complain about that basement you live in. You and David broke up—"

"Fine, yes, my life currently sucks. Agreed. But . . . what would I even do here?"

"Hang out with me."

"Okay."

"Seriously, though, you could get out of the rat race. Get some clarity. I bet that would be good for your writing."

"What would I do for *money*?"

"Don't worry, I've thought of that too."

"Oh, so you're just planning out my new life for me?"

Ignoring Cammy's skepticism, Fran set her giant bottle down and leaned forward, brimming with excitement. Her elbow was resting on the tombstone of one Ann Binetti. "All right," she said, as if about to confide a secret. "I think my dad's gonna be stepping back from the deli soon. He's stubborn as hell, but he knows it's time. And he's leaving the place to me, of course. The thing is: I don't wanna keep it just a deli."

"What do you wanna do with it?"

"Turn it into a restaurant!" Fran extended her arm to emphasize the point, inadvertently bumping the bottle, which spilled a few malty drops of Olde E on poor Ann's grave.

"A restaurant?"

"Yeah! Like vintage Italian, but also hip and modern. Deep down, it's what I've always wanted, but I've been scared to say it out loud. Especially 'cause my dad would've thought I was nuts." She imitated the Italian accent of gruff Leo DeMarco: "'We got a good business already! Why we change it?'"

"I think that sounds incredible," Cammy said, and she really thought it did. "But what does it have to do with me?"

"You can help out. You can work with me."

"Me? What're you talking about? I don't know anything about food or restaurants or—"

"I know you don't. I'll be in charge of the food, obviously. But I'll need someone to handle like marketing and advertising and PR and whatever. Writing the menu, even. I've been running an old-school deli—I don't have the first clue about any of that crap. Isn't that the kind of stuff you do in the city?"

"Well, yeah . . ." Cammy admitted, reflecting on the innumerable hours she'd spent attending marketing "strategy sessions" and writing snappy, sales-y copy for all manner of clients. Though she may not have loved the work, she did have a knack for it.

"Give it some thought. It could be so much fun, the two of us working together." Fran flashed a grin. "And you know I'd be a super chill boss."

It was plain from Fran's appealing delivery of this little pitch that she hadn't just come up with it on the spot. She'd been waiting for a chance to sit Cammy down and sell her on the idea of returning to Jersey and changing her life. It reminded Cammy of her mom's mini intervention last night on the couch: "You know, you can stay here longer than a week if you want." Were they conspiring to get her to come back here? Sure, the present state of her life was nothing to brag about, but did it seem in such desperate disarray that she needed to move home and start over from scratch?

"Honestly," Fran went on, "part of this is me being selfish. I miss you, Cammy. I wish you were around more. I wanna spend time with you."

"No, I—I miss you too."

Such displays of open sentiment were rare between the two of them, and they lapsed into a self-conscious silence. Fran picked up her bottle to take another sip. "Look, I know you hate like New Age cosmic shit—"

"I do," Cammy confirmed.

"So do I, most of the time. But maybe this is the stars aligning. Think about it: Like, your dad passing is this terrible tragedy, but it's brought you back here. And *I'm* here, offering you an opportunity. And now *Nick* is magically in the picture, inviting you to his Treehouse—"

"Clubhouse. And I'm pretty sure that was a platonic invitation."

"No, I think he saw adult Cammy and found her sexy and intriguing, and he wants to make up for lost time."

"You're ridiculous."

"I am often ridiculous," Fran acknowledged. "But right now, I think I'm right. I think maybe this is where you belong."

Where you belong. The phrase made Cammy feel woozy. (Or was it the Olde E?) Ordinarily, she would've dismissed any talk of "stars aligning" as superstitious babble. She wasn't someone who took astrology or any of its mystical offshoots seriously. Yet as she sat on the frosty grass at the cemetery on the hill, under the actual stars themselves, which were still perceivable through the Garden State smog, Fran's words gave her pause.

What was so awful about the idea of moving home, anyway? Why did she have this simplistic binary in her brain that equated New Jersey with failure and New York with success? She'd been banging her head against the city's manifold brick walls since college, and she wasn't happy. Why keep banging? Wasn't that the very definition of insanity—to do the same thing over and over again and expect a different result? How liberating it would be to say "goodbye to all that," as Joan Didion had in her famous essay about leaving the Big Apple (also at age twenty-nine, Cammy recalled!). To return to the welcoming bosom of Bergen County, to work with Fran, to write with a clear head, to (re)kindle with Nick . . .

Could this have been her dad's parting gift to her? A chance to take stock of her life and start fresh?

Before she could voice any of this, Cammy was startled by the crunch of tires on gravel. A car was pulling into the cemetery's parking lot. She and Fran traded apprehensive looks. Was someone coming to pay their respects to a dead relative at ten o'clock on a Tuesday night? Unlikely. Or was it a serial killer, a necrophile, here to perform some unholy rite? *You've been listening to too many true-crime podcasts*, she chided herself.

The reality was even worse: As the vehicle came into view, it became apparent that it was—oh God—a police cruiser. Cammy and Fran stood up stupidly, like proverbial deer in headlights, though Fran at least had the presence of mind to hide the two bottles of malt liquor behind Ann Binetti's gravestone. (Thanks, Ann. You're a trooper.) Spotting them, the anonymous officer at the wheel switched on the car's brights and whooped its shrill siren once, just for good measure, which made Cammy jump.

This was not good.

"What do we do?" Cammy whispered.

"Be cool," Fran said, sounding not cool at all.

The cop parked and got out of the cruiser, leaving the high beams on. He sauntered toward them in no particular hurry, a squat silhouette backlit by the blinding white light. When he got close enough for Cammy to discern his features—doughy face, buzz cut—she was shocked to find that she knew him. This was not just any lawman but Officer Rocco of the River Hill Police Department, who'd driven by her on Main Street last night, who'd instructed her not to use drugs in fifth grade, whom Shane O'Leary had called an asshole for giving him a DWI on a recent July Fourth. Fran clearly recognized him too.

As they sing down at Disney World, *"It's a small world after all . . ."*

"What's going on here?" Officer Rocco said with the blasé brusqueness of a man in possession of low-level power. (Incidentally, Rocco was his last name, his first being Joe, Cammy recalled. Joe Rocco: a moniker as blunt as the end of a baton.)

"We were just, uh, hangin' out, Officer," Fran said, as though it were the most normal thing in the world.

"In a cemetery? At this hour?"

"My dad died a few days ago," Cammy volunteered without thinking.

Officer Rocco looked uncertain what to do with this information. "Sorry for your loss," he mumbled. "He's buried here?"

"Um . . . no. He was Jewish. He's in the Jewish cemetery in Saddle Brook."

Now he was really confused. "So why did you just tell me that?"

"I'm not sure."

"Stop talking," Fran hissed out of the side of her mouth. Cammy realized that the non sequitur about her father had probably made her appear drunk, which, to be fair, she kind of was.

"Have you two been drinking?"

"No, Officer, we haven't," Fran replied with remarkable conviction.

"You sure about that? 'Cause I think I smell alcohol."

"Well," Cammy clarified in a helpful tone, "we were at the bowling alley in Hackensack before this, and we *did* have a couple beers there, but that's it."

"So you both drove your cars here under the influence?"

"No, no, no—we just had a couple PBRs!" (A pitcher.) "Low ABV. Under five, right?"

"Right," Fran nodded responsibly. "Four-point-eight, I believe."

Officer Rocco narrowed his suspicious eyes. Cammy could see him sizing up the situation, endeavoring to understand what the hell two thirty-year-old women were doing loitering in the dark at the Madonna Cemetery. This was an unusual case for the guy.

"You do realize this is private property, don't you? The cemetery's closed. You're trespassing."

"And we're so sorry about that, we really are," Cammy rambled as Fran gave her a death stare. "The thing is, we used to hang out here back in the day, when we were in high school. Not 'cause we're creeps or anything; we're not into dead people. There's just a great view, right? Best view in Bergen County. Which doesn't make it okay to trespass, but—Anyway, we came here tonight to relive the old days, and we'll leave immediately. So sorry to bother you with this. I'm sure you've got real crime to fight out there."

Cammy had no clue where this nonsensical spiel had come from, but for a triumphant second, it seemed to have worked; Officer Rocco was poised to let them go with merely a stern warning. That is, until the clinking of glass prompted him to glance over at the two near-empty bottles of Olde E that had just toppled onto the grass next to Ann Binetti's grave.

"Not drinking, huh?" he sneered.

Great.

★ ★ ★

Long story short, Officer Rocco determined that the two cemetery crashers weren't fit to drive and ordered them to accompany him to the River Hill police station, where relatives would have to come pick them up. Their cars—or, to be exact, Fran's car and Cammy's mom's car—would be towed there as well. "But you're River Hill police, and we're in Fort Lee," Cammy attempted to argue à la Alan Dershowitz. "Do you have jurisdiction here?" As it turned out, the cemetery technically straddled both towns. Dammit.

En route to the station, squeezed in the back of the cruiser like a criminal, Cammy tried to appeal to Officer Rocco's good nature. She reminded him that she and Fran had once been students in his elementary school D.A.R.E. course, where he'd taught them to "just say no." This stratagem also fizzled. Her annoyed accomplice pinched her leg to shut her up.

The worst part, the lowest of the low, was having to call her mother from the station to ask for a ride home. Beth was horrified, too disgusted to speak. When Cammy began explaining the details of what had happened, of how she'd ended up in the custody of the law, her mom simply hung up the phone.

And when Beth did show up to collect her delinquent child, she arrived with—guess who?—the king of sanctimony himself, Rabbi Wiener. He'd driven her over in his silver Tesla, which Cammy had noticed at the burial yesterday morning but forgotten about. The rabbi drove a Tesla now! She didn't understand anything anymore.

Wearing an expression of profound exhaustion that made Cammy swell with guilt, Beth signed some papers at the front desk that allowed her to retrieve her daughter and her Corolla. (Fran had already left with her grumbling dad.) Outside, in the vapory light of the police station parking lot, the rabbi was waiting for them.

"I'd like you to come see me at the synagogue, Cammy," he said solemnly. Again, the man loved solemnity. "I'd like to talk to you."

"About what?"

"How you're acting out. How you're manifesting your grief for your father."

"I didn't mean to get like semi-arrested, okay? This was a freak thing."

"But you're being destructive. You're not honoring the shiva."

"Sorry, but why is this your business?"

"It's hurting your mother. It's getting in the way of *her* grief. You left tonight, and she didn't even know where you were. She was worried."

"Shouldn't that be between me and her?"

"She asked me to speak to you. She said she hasn't been able to get through to you since your father passed."

Cammy looked at her weary mom and felt a perplexing mix of sympathy and resentment. Then she returned to the rabbi. "Well, thanks for the offer, Rabbi *Wiener*, but no thanks. I'll pass on the chat. I'll grieve how I want to grieve, and I'd appreciate if you'd stay out of it."

Beth covered her mouth in disbelief.

On the ride home, they said nothing to each other. What was there to say? Cammy knew she was behaving badly—"acting out," in the rabbi's trite words—but she blamed it on the crazed crucible of death and grief and pain she was caught up in. Her mother was collateral damage. They couldn't find a way to connect; they didn't share a common language in which they could grieve together. And the pressure cooker of the shiva, with its daily parade of mourners and consolers, was only making things worse. It was all a colossal clusterfuck.

When she got back, Cammy trudged up to her room and closed the door. Plopping down on her bed, she flipped open her MacBook. As if guided by an unseen force, she created a new Word document and started writing something. The beginning of a play.

She stayed up for hours writing.

Day Three: Wednesday

♦ 7 ♦

It was light outside and the birds were chirping by the time Cammy shut her laptop and passed out. When she opened her eyes a few hours later, the first thing she did was to reread the twenty pages of playscript she'd written in her feverish all-night fugue state. They were, shockingly, about a young, mixed-up guy who comes home to Jersey to sit shiva with his mom after his dad's untimely death. The protagonist, whose gender she'd switched to get a little distance from the material (as if that were remotely possible), was named—wait for it—Cameron.

Fine, so the autobiography wasn't even thinly veiled! So what? This was real, this was immediate, this was what she was going through. "Write what you know"—wasn't that the old dictum? Not "write what you know, but only after a reasonable period of time and with sufficient objectivity." Fuck that tame shit.

Hell, in the opening stage directions of *Long Day's Journey Into Night*, which Cammy had written a paper on in college, Eugene O'Neill had famously described his own dysfunctional family's living room down to the most minute detail. He hadn't disguised the parallels at all. Then again, he *had* waited thirty years to tackle his personal demons in that play, and he'd ordered that it not be published until a quarter century after his death.

Bad example.

Anyway, here was the important thing: Her pages were good. She really thought so, which was a rarity. Though Cammy had many faults and frailties, far too many to count, an inflated sense of her own talent wasn't one of them. Quite the opposite: She usually thought her work sucked, hence all the crap she'd given up on or thrown out over the years.

But these pages were different. They had the unmistakable bite of truth to them. She'd written a funny-sad initial scene between the son and the mother (Bev instead of Beth!) that deftly captured her and her mom's own fraught dynamic, their inability to communicate in the wake of the death. It was still a first draft, of course, with rough edges to be smoothed out, but it had potential. The dialogue crackled with painful humor. The scene was alive.

All at once Cammy saw a new escape hatch materialize in her mind's eye—a way out of the Life Slump in which she'd been languishing. What if she could take her grief and inner turmoil and transform them into art? Okay, okay, let's not get too grandiose here. More simply and modestly: What if she could write a good play? Wouldn't that be a healthy, productive way to channel her angsty energies? Healthier, at least, than weed and liquor and hookups next to dumpsters?

Maybe she could actually finish this one. Maybe it would amount to something. Maybe what her writing had been missing all this time was the force of raw experience—and now, with her dad's death, the worst thing that had ever happened to her, she had that secret ingredient at her disposal.

All right, slow down, Cammy. You've only written twenty measly pages. You have a long way to go.

Still, she couldn't deny the fizzy feeling in her gut: After a lengthy creative dry spell, and when she'd least expected it, inspiration had struck.

She remembered today was Wednesday. The Drama Collective would be having its weekly gathering tonight in the city. She could take a bus in, attend the meeting, share her pages with the group, hear them read aloud by actors, be encouraged by her fellow members' glowing feedback. (It was sure to be glowing.) Christ, after three days in prosaic, pedestrian Jersey, the over-the-top theatricality of the theater kids wouldn't even be annoying; it would be a relief. And it would be nice to see zany Gretchen, whose thirtieth-birthday party Cammy had fled when she'd gotten the news about her father.

But wait. How could she go to the meeting? Tonight was the third night of shiva. Yet another interminable evening of friends and family milling around, offering condolences, crowding her, giving her no room to breathe. It never ended! And it wasn't as if, one day after skipping out and winding up in the hands of the police, she could ask her mom for special permission to leave again. No, she was on thin ice now, her current credibility score resting somewhere below zero.

Ugh.

Cammy wanted to scream in frustration, but she didn't. Instead, she got up and went downstairs for coffee. She was surprised to find her mom fully dressed and made up in the kitchen, wearing a black power pantsuit from her real estate wardrobe. Beth looked crisp, ready for action. This was a marked change from yesterday, most of which her mom had spent wandering around the house in a nightgown, adrift in grief. She'd changed into clothes only at the last minute, just before six, when the shiva guests were set to arrive.

"Are you going somewhere?" Cammy asked. She'd considered leading with a half-hearted apology for last night's shenanigans, but really, why bother?

"I'm going to CarePlus," Beth said, businesslike.

"What's CarePlus?"

"The rehab place. Where Dad died."

"Oh." Cammy felt bad for not knowing the actual name of the facility where her father had spent his final few days. "Why are you going there?"

"To get their records on Dad. For the lawsuit." Oh yes—Cammy had almost forgotten about her mom's plan to sue the medical authorities for "killing" her husband. She couldn't sue the guiltiest party, though: God.

"You're doing that *today*?"

"Why not?"

"I don't know. It's so soon. Are you sure you're in the right headspace to like . . . revisit the scene?"

"What do you care?" Beth shot back sharply. And here came the deluge: "First, you get high after the burial. Then, last night, you leave the shiva without telling me. You take my car. You're out running around, drinking, getting in trouble with the police—"

"Mom, that wasn't supposed to happen—"

"You clearly don't give a damn about my feelings. You clearly don't want to be here with me. So why do you care *what* I do?"

"It's not that simple, Mom." Cammy groped in vain for words to explain the tumult inside her head, to account for all her impulsive behavior. "I'm just—I'm having a hard time—"

"*You're* having a hard time? I just lost my husband of thirty years."

"And I just lost my dad!" Was it a contest? "And I'm trying to deal with that. And being home. And seeing everyone. And it's a lot, okay? So I'm sorry if I'm, like . . . not exhibiting perfect mourning decorum."

"I'm not asking for that," Beth said, her pitch rising. "I'm asking for the bare minimum. For you to act like an adult. For you to be here for your father's shiva."

"But I don't like the shiva! All these people coming over, night after night. Having to put on a show for them. Aunt Miriam sobbing in my face for an hour. It's oppressive. It's the *opposite* of what I need right now."

"What *do* you need?"

"Space!" Cammy heard herself shout. "A little fucking space!"

"Well, suck it up! Be a mensch!"

"Oh, now we're back to the mensch thing?"

Beth rested her hand on the kitchen counter, as though it could provide some moral support. She steadied her voice. "If you're having a hard time, why don't you go see the rabbi?"

"Again, no thank you."

"You were very rude to him last night."

"Was I? My bad."

"What do you have against him?"

"He's pompous. He's full of himself. Dad thought so too. That's why we used to crack jokes about him in temple, remember?"

Her mom winced at the memory. "He's a good man, and he cares about us. He wants to help us get through this."

"So *you* talk to him, then. I'm good."

Beth threw up her hands. She was done. She reached for the cup of coffee she'd been drinking before this skirmish with her daughter. It was probably cold now. She finished it off anyway and began to leave the room.

"Wait," Cammy said, prompting her mom to stop. "I—I wanna go with you."

"What?" Beth looked bewildered.

"I wanna go to the rehab place. I wanna see it."

"Why?"

"'Cause . . . it's the last place Dad was alive. Can I come? I promise I won't do anything crazy. I'll just be there."

Cammy knew how bizarre it was for her to be making this request mere moments after their fight. But suddenly it felt important that she get to experience the site of her dad's death firsthand, to stand within its walls. Perhaps Beth understood this, or perhaps she just didn't have the stomach for another conflict; whatever the reason, she replied with a terse, "Fine."

So Cammy put on jeans and a sweater, poured some coffee into a thermos for sustenance, and headed out with her mom to where her father had drawn his last living breath.

★ ★ ★

Another silent car ride. They'd expended their energy on the clash in the kitchen, and it was best to let things settle. On Beth's preferred radio station, 106.7 Lite FM, Belinda Carlisle was singing "Heaven Is a Place on Earth." Was it really?

They rode past Overpeck County Park, a sprawling recreational area situated along the Hackensack River. Naturally, since this was Jersey, it had once been a landfill. But there was no evidence of that contaminated past on this sunny fall day. Folks were out and about, running the track, walking their dogs, pushing baby strollers. Arcadia in Bergen County.

When Cammy was a kid, her dad had taught her to play tennis on the Overpeck courts. Cy was a self-taught player himself, with eccentric strokes and a scrappy counterpuncher strategy that essentially amounted to this: Keep returning the ball, even if your returns are ugly, until your opponent makes a mistake. Sometimes he played pickup matches with strangers in the park—people who had proper technique and high opinions of their skills—and beat them through sheer inglorious persistence. Which drove them nuts. Oh, and rather than drink water between sets, he'd refresh himself with a cold can of Beck's beer right there on the court.

All this to say: As with so many other things in her life, Cammy had learned tennis the Cy Adler way. And she'd loved every minute of it.

They drove into Teaneck, a town with a large Orthodox Jewish population. Out the window, Cammy glimpsed a young Orthodox woman around her own age, modestly dressed, head covered with a hat, walking with four cute little children. Four kids! Can you imagine? That could easily be me, she thought, if I'd been born into different circumstances. Still, she guessed that the woman felt rooted, secure, free from the self-doubt and self-loathing that were Cammy's daily bread. But to live like that, ruled by religion, repressed by the patriarchy? No, thank you.

She stole a quick glance at her mom. Beth was gripping the steering wheel tightly, psyching herself up to return to the rehab facility. Why was she so set on this lawsuit idea? Probably because it gave her someone specific to blame for her husband's premature death. A tangible target for her anger at losing him before she was supposed to. Otherwise, the whole thing was too senseless.

Cammy thought of what her mom had said before in the kitchen: "I just lost my husband of thirty years." Yes, it was weirdly easy to forget that Cy hadn't only been *her* dad; he'd also been her mother's partner, lover, best friend. Over three decades they'd made a home together, raised a kid together, talked, argued, taken trips, celebrated holidays, watched TV, played Scrabble, fretted about finances, gone out to dinner, shared inside jokes—all the quotidian details that form the mosaic of a marriage, a life. And now, abruptly, without warning, it was over.

Of course she wanted to sue somebody.

They pulled up to CarePlus, a nondescript beige building that resembled a Holiday Inn Express more than a medical establishment. The sign on the front lawn read "CarePlus—TRUST IN OUR CARE." Well, her dad had done that, and look how he'd ended up.

Beth parked the Corolla in a "Visitor Parking" spot, although, technically, they weren't visiting anyone. Alas, there were no spaces set aside for "Vengeance Parking." She switched off the ignition and sat behind the wheel, staring straight ahead. Cammy wasn't sure what to do. She didn't want to open the door and get out until her mom did. This was Beth's show. Finally, her mother said, "Okay," to no one in particular and exited the car. Cammy followed.

They strode across the parking lot toward the building's entrance, to the metronomic soundtrack of their own footfalls on asphalt. Beth had the air of a woman on a grim mission. In her real estate pantsuit, powdered and coiffed, she really did cut a formidable figure. Little wonder that she sold so many houses. You'd almost be afraid *not* to buy one from her.

There was nothing overtly grim about the lobby of CarePlus, however. The beige Holiday Inn aesthetic was in full force inside as well, complete with carpeted floor, cozy couches, and pastel wallpaper bathed in warm sconce lighting. Who would ever suspect this wasn't a three-star hotel, but rather a place where people came to recover from debilitating illnesses and operations—or, when that didn't work out, to die?

"Good morning," said the throaty-voiced receptionist at the front desk. She was one of those middle-aged, fake-tanned Jersey ladies who'd likely once smoked Virginia Slims (or still did) and whose fashion and cosmetic sense was permanently arrested in the late 1980s. "Can I help you?"

"I called earlier," Beth said, skipping the niceties, not even pretending to be friendly. "I'm here for my husband's records."

The lady's expression changed. "Oh. Of course. I'm sorry." Her garishly mascaraed eyes darted from Beth to Cammy and back again. "And his name is—was . . . ?"

"Adler. Cy Adler." To twist the knife, Beth added, "He died here Saturday night."

"I'm so sorry. One moment, please."

As the shamefaced receptionist got up to go to a filing cabinet, Cammy realized she was actually enjoying seeing her mom be so standoffish. Good for her; get it all out. But she wasn't at all prepared for what happened next.

Hearing a ping, Cammy turned and saw a woman in blue scrubs emerge from an elevator down the hall. Tall and thin, her brown hair up in a bun, she was coming toward the lobby with the brisk, efficient steps of a busy nurse.

"Oh my God," Beth whispered. "That's *her*."

"Who?"

"Helen. She was the nurse in charge of Dad."

"I thought you said the nurse was Filipina."

"No, that was the assistant, Flor. Flor's the one who found him. She was nice. But Helen"—her eyes flared—"*she's* the one who's responsible."

"Mom," Cammy said, touching Beth's arm lightly to keep her from charging at the hated nurse and pouncing. Her mother broke free. She was going to pounce.

Nurse Helen was close enough to the front desk now to see and recognize Beth. She slowed her approach, as if considering whether to change course and make a run for it. How to describe the fearful look in her eyes? It was the look of a low-level gangster who's betrayed his brutal boss and then crosses paths with him on the street. Nowhere to hide.

Cammy stepped back to watch the inevitable showdown. The receptionist cowered in her bunker behind the filing cabinet.

"Do you remember me?" Beth spat, sounding like that wrathful Mafia don.

"Y-yes, hello, Mrs. Adler," the nurse stammered.

"I just want you to know I'm here to get my husband's records because I'm planning to sue you and this whole place."

"I—I'm so sorry about what happened—"

"'*What happened*'?" Beth was breathing fire. "You mean how my husband died? How he had a routine surgery, got pneumonia, and came here to get better? And in less than a week, he was dead?"

"I know—"

"Do you?"

"It was a terrible shock—"

"Was it? 'Cause I was coming here every day to visit him, and I'm not a doctor or a nurse, but *I* could tell he wasn't doing well. He was weak, he couldn't stop coughing. I'd never seen him so frail. And *you*, you kept telling me, 'Oh, no, Mrs. Adler, he's doing fine. It's just the pneumonia. He needs a week or so to recover.' And then that last night, the last night I ever saw him, he threw up. My husband *never* threw up. And I said to you, 'Are you *sure* he's okay? Because something doesn't seem right.' And you reassured me again: 'Yes, he's all right. We're taking good care of him.' And later that night, he was gone. A sixty-eight-year-old man in great health. He should've had another twenty years at least." Beth stopped to catch her breath. Then, in a voice quavering with rage, she dropped the bomb: "You killed him."

The receptionist let out a muted gasp from her hiding place by the filing cabinet. Shell-shocked, Nurse Helen said, barely audibly, "Mrs. Adler . . . please . . ."

Beth wasn't finished. "Now I don't have a husband. Now my daughter doesn't have a father. All because of you and your neglect and incompetence and this, this pathetic fucking shithole!" Cammy was taken aback; she didn't think she'd ever heard her mother curse in a public setting like this. "But don't worry—I'm getting a lawyer, so get ready to be sued."

The nurse could no longer withstand the barrage. She promptly burst into tears and dashed into a staff bathroom located off the lobby. Cammy almost felt sorry for the woman. Her mom's accusations had been insanely harsh. Yet they no doubt contained some truth; it wasn't hard to imagine gross negligence taking place in this antiseptic Holiday Inn with the absurd name of CarePlus. No sympathy for you, Helen. Not today.

Meanwhile, the flustered receptionist had crept out of her foxhole to photocopy Cy's records. Beth and Cammy stood there at the desk, listening to the whirring of the Xerox machine. The receptionist kept her permed head down, desperate to avoid any leftover vitriol from the avenging widow. She collected the copied pages, slid them into a manila folder, and held it out with a shaky hand. "Here you go."

Beth didn't bother to say, "Thank you." She grabbed the folder, spun around, and stalked out of the beige building, Cammy trailing behind her.

Mission accomplished.

* * *

After, they went to eat at Wendy's. There was one near Beth's real estate office in Fort Lee. For some reason, the dramatic scene at the rehab place had produced in both mother and daughter an urgent craving for a greasy meal. Like their dependence on coffee, this was another thing they had in common: Wendy's was their favorite fast-food joint.

At the drive-through, Beth ordered a cheeseburger, fries, and a Diet Coke from the crackly, disembodied voice on the speaker. Cammy opted for her old standbys: a "classic" chicken sandwich (the fried one, not the grilled), fries, and a vanilla Frosty. Fran had always given her shit for liking vanilla. "Who the fuck gets a *vanilla* Frosty? Literally *everyone* gets chocolate." One more area in which Cammy was perverse.

They sat in the Wendy's parking lot at eleven thirty on this Wednesday morning, the medical records balanced on the center console between them, Lite FM on low, wolfing down the salt and fat and sugar. It was just what they needed.

Slurping her frozen dairy dessert, Cammy decided now was as good a time as any to broach the thorny issue of tonight. She wanted to go to that Drama Collective meeting in the city. She wanted to bring her exciting new pages. But the goddamn shiva stood in the way.

"Mom."

"What?" Beth said, biting into a fry.

"I wrote something last night. I started a play."

"Oh, you mean after I bailed you out of jail?"

"Can we not have another fight, please?" Cammy waited a second, then continued. "What I wrote—it's super personal. It's about . . . all of this. Dad and everything. And I actually found it, like, really cathartic, and I'm proud of it." Now for the delicate part: the big ask. "The thing is, there's this theater group in the city that I joined, and they meet every Wednesday night to work on stuff, and I think it would be really good for me—for my mental health, I mean—if I could go to the meeting tonight and share these pages—"

"So you want to skip the shiva again," Beth interrupted, cutting to the chase.

"Well . . . yeah. But hey, at least I'm asking this time." A weak joke. "You can tell people I'm sick or something." She tossed in an extra bargaining chip: "I'll stay tomorrow night, I promise."

Cammy thought her mom might very well explode again and lay into her as she'd laid into Nurse Helen at CarePlus. She didn't, though; maybe she'd done all the exploding she could for one day. "Whatever," her mother said in a tone of tired resignation, a tone that made Cammy feel even shittier than an explosion would have. "Do what you want." And Beth solaced herself with another salty French fry.

♦ 8 ♦

BACK HOME, LIKE SUPERMAN turning into Clark Kent, Beth stripped off her power pantsuit, put on her faded nightgown, and became the adrift widow again. She popped an Ativan and went up to her room to lie down. She'd been a hellbent badass this morning, and now she had to rest up in preparation for the shiva guests tonight.

Cammy stayed downstairs in the living room and threw on daytime TV. Judge Judy was yelling at some people. Nice.

The musty cardboard box containing her dad's stuff was still on the floor by the sectional. She reached inside and took out the Polaroid she'd discovered the other night—the one of her father arm in arm with the petite, blond-haired mystery woman, labeled "C & D, 6/14/78."

D. Who was she? A college girlfriend of her dad's, her mother had said dismissively, unable to come up with the woman's name. Yet the very next evening at the shiva, Cammy had spied Beth furtively showing the photograph to Aunt Miriam. "Do you think we should call her?" she'd overheard anxious Miriam ask. There was clearly more to the story.

Cammy had other reasons to wonder: First, she was certain that her father—to whom she'd been so close, who'd harbored no secrets from her—had never made even a passing reference to this person. And second, he hadn't held on to pictures of any other former flames. Why this one? Had she been his first love? Broken his heart? What was her special significance?

Cammy carefully examined the figure in the photo: the Stevie Nicks–esque smock dress with the bell sleeves, the slightly ethereal quality of D's pretty face, her inscrutable expression as she gazed into young Cy's eyes—a mix of happiness and a darker shading that was more difficult to pin down.

But as much as she stared, Cammy couldn't crack the code of the woman's identity, her history, her connection to her dad. D remained a puzzle, a surprising lacuna in her knowledge of her father's past, which she'd thought was virtually complete. Strange.

She slipped the Polaroid into her jeans pocket for later investigation, then felt a wave of exhaustion hit her. She'd slept only a couple of hours last night thanks to her marathon writing session. Within a few minutes, lulled by Judge Judy's berating bray and the carb overload from Wendy's, Cammy was fast asleep on the couch, dreaming fitfully of D.

★ ★ ★

She woke up at a quarter to three feeling refreshed and, oddly, a little jazzed. Jazzed because tonight, in the midst of this weeklong forced mourning march, she was going to escape the clutches of Jersey and be back in the city. Even for just an evening, she'd be free from home and its attendant miseries. In the company of the Drama Collective, she'd be around young, artsy New York types again! (And yes, they often got on her nerves as well, but the grass is always greener . . .)

Needless to say, Cammy knew that a daughter's absence from her father's shiva two nights in a row—or at all—would be frowned upon by pretty much any decent, upstanding person. But she also knew that her aversion to the suffocating ritual had nothing to do with her love for her dad, which was as strong as ever.

On top of that, she knew that if he were watching from wherever he was (heaven? oblivion?), he'd support her decision. He'd smile and say something like, "Don't sit around moping on my account. Go to New York. Be with your friends. Show off your work." And with a sly wink, he'd add: "Don't worry about Mom. She'll get over it."

Thanks, Dad.

The Drama Collective gathered at seven in Midtown, so she could take a bumpy, fumy NJ Transit bus into the city at six and get there on time. Which left her with a few hours to kill this afternoon. How should she spend them?

Well, there was the Nick option. Last night at the bowling alley, he'd invited her to stop by the Clubhouse, the center where he taught disadvantaged kids how to dance. Should she ask to borrow her mom's car (Beth would be thrilled) and drive over to see the adult version of her teenage love? Was it possible, as Fran had insisted, that he wanted to rekindle their youthful romance, which had actually been a romance only on Cammy's end?

No, too soon. If she went to see Nick today, she'd seem overeager, just as she had when she'd spilled her guts to him at prom all those years ago. What was the old saying? "If you learn nothing from history, you're doomed to repeat it." Something like that. Play it cool, Cammy. Wait a day or two.

There was also another invitation that had been nagging at her since yesterday morning: the one from her former English teacher and mentor, Dr. Strum. She picked up her phone, opened her email, and reread what Dr. Strum had written:

> If you're around, as I assume you are, you're welcome to drop in and visit me at the high school. I finish teaching at three and then remain in my classroom for an hour or

so, toiling over assignments that I hope may combat, however slightly, the cultural dumbing down to which my students are otherwise ceaselessly subjected. (I have seen the ruin of Western civilization, and it is called TikTok.)

Oh, Dr. Strum, you endearingly grumpy elitist. It would be so good to see her. They hadn't met in person in years. The downside, of course, was that Cammy would have to sit face-to-face with her cherished teacher—who'd possessed such great belief in her potential—and acknowledge that she hadn't done jack shit with her life thus far. A demoralizing prospect.

On the other hand, maybe Dr. Strum could give her some wise, stiff-upper-lip advice—replete with relevant literary quotations—that would help her put her life back on track. The same brand of tough love she'd once applied to Cammy's half-baked AP English essays: "I know you can do better, and so do you." What was a mentor for if you couldn't turn to them in your hour of need?

In the final analysis, the pros outweighed the cons. Amid this week of reckonings with the past, it was time for Cammy to pay her guide and guru a long-overdue visit.

★ ★ ★

She'd done the walk to the high school hundreds of times, clunky knapsack bumping against her back, and here she was a decade later, sans backpack, doing it again. The autumn nip in the air, the cars whooshing by on Grand Avenue, the familiar houses along the road—all of it conjured up a million misty memories.

It was after three now, and school had let out, so Cammy passed clusters of kids moving in the opposite direction, on their way home. The carefree ones goofed around, teasing and laughing, while the loners trudged in solitary silence. They all looked so young and small to her, more like middle schoolers than high schoolers. When she was their age, she'd thought, delusionally, that she was grown up. But they were *children*.

She turned off Grand and walked down the long paved path that led to the main entrance. (The seniors with cars got to park behind the school and go in the back door—the "cool" way. Cammy recalled the immense satisfaction of achieving this milestone in her janky Ford Focus.) A couple of kids shot her wary glances, as if to say, "What are *you* doing here, lady?" On the not-so-hallowed ground of her alma mater, she felt old and out of place.

This feeling only increased when she reached the glass double doors and found that she couldn't open them. They were locked. Okay. Awkwardly, she tried tapping on the glass in the hope that someone would hear and let her in. No luck. Peering inside, Cammy saw not a soul—just the gleaming display of athletic trophies that still stood in its same prominent position. The school's sports-centric priorities were safely intact.

Well, this was fun. You make a pilgrimage to visit your favorite teacher, and you can't even get in the fucking place.

Just then, she caught sight of a figure around the corner, by the side of the building. A stooped older man with a few wisps of hair left, wearing the uniform of a janitor: light-blue shirt, dark-blue pants. He was lighting up a cigarette with an arthritic hand. Wait, could it be—It was Rudy! He'd been a janitor back in Cammy's day, and even then the guy had seemed ancient. How had he not retired by now? And how was he still getting away with smoking those cigarettes on school property?

"Rudy!" she called, inordinately excited, bounding up to him as though he were an old friend.

He took a startled step back, having zero clue who she was. His bulldog cheeks and bulbous nose were bright red with rosacea. "Yeah?"

"Sorry, sorry, you probably don't remember me. My name is Cammy Adler. I graduated from here like ten years ago. Eleven, actually."

"All right . . ."

"We used to talk in the cafeteria sometimes. You told me about how you were in Vietnam?"

Rudy squinted and shook his head. "Sorry, kid. I been workin' here forty-three years. I seen a lotta kids come and go. And my memory ain't what it used to be."

"That's okay. It's still good to see you. I would've thought you'd retired."

"I could," he shrugged, "but then what the hell would I do?"

"Yeah, I feel you." Cammy got the distinct impression that Rudy was one of those isolates with no spouse and no family; all he had were his janitorial job, his war stories, and the sweet relief of these secret cigarette breaks.

"Whatcha doin' back?"

"Well, I wanted to see Dr. Strum, my old English teacher—we're still in touch—but the doors are locked. I can't get in."

"Oh yeah, they keep 'em locked all the time now. No one's allowed in the building 'cept 'authorized personnel.' Everyone's got swipe cards. Even the kids."

"Huh? Why?"

"Safety, I guess. Ya know, with all the schools gettin' shot up these days. It's like 'Nam out there." Rudy took a doleful drag. "Tell you what. I ain't supposed to, but I'll swipe you in." He added with a wrinkled smile, "Long as you don't tell anyone 'bout my ciggy."

"It's a deal."

The janitor stubbed out his cigarette on the yellow-brick wall and, to avoid leaving evidence, stuck the butt in his back pocket. Then he let her into the building and went on his way. Fare thee well, good sir.

Cammy stood in the deserted hall of her high school, taking it all in: fluorescent lighting, tiled vinyl floor, rows of red lockers, River Hill Rhinos banners and motivational posters ("Go for it!") on the walls, the smell of cleaning solution in the air from after-school mopping. Everything was as she recollected but, like the kids out on the street, *smaller*; she felt like Gulliver in Lilliput. Distantly, she heard the brassy cacophony of a band practice in the music room. It was football season, the time of year when all the band members had to put on hideous marching uniforms, sit on cold bleachers in the frosty weather, and play peppy songs during the endless games. Shudder.

She took a left and headed toward room 203, Dr. Strum's domain, which lay at the far end of the hallway, not too close to any other classrooms. Dr. Strum preferred this secluded location. "I like to keep away from the clamor," she used to say. Most of the clock-watching teachers here hightailed it home as soon as the final bell rang, but not her. She remained planted at her desk, often well past four, crafting assignments or counseling students or, in idle moments, doing what she loved most in the world: reading.

Cammy was delighted to find that a photocopied Emily Dickinson poem was still affixed to Dr. Strum's door. It was her credo:

There is no Frigate like a Book
To take us Lands away
Nor any Coursers like a Page
Of prancing Poetry—
This Traverse may the poorest take
Without oppress of Toll—
How frugal is the Chariot
That bears the Human Soul—

Emily, Emily, with your idiosyncratic capitalization and your expressive dashes! The simple, beautiful words made Cammy want to weep. They reminded her of the joy of discovering books as a kid, of marveling at their transporting power. She thought of reading Roald Dahl novels with her dad and then, later, becoming Dr. Strum's avid pupil, soaking up her literary knowledge like a sponge. Could she ever recapture what she'd felt then—that stirring sense of passion?

Rather than cry, she knocked.

"Come in," said the professorial voice on the other side of the door.

Cammy entered. Years ago, Dr. Strum had spent her own money to furnish her classroom with wall-to-wall bookshelves, creating the effect of a sanctum of literature. She sat at her desk, which was strewn with books, stacks of what appeared to be student papers, and her famous yellow legal pads. ("I do my best thinking in legal pads.") There was also the obligatory cup of Yorkshire Tea, a brand she bought from an obscure store that specialized in English goods.

The woman was something else.

When she saw her old protégé, Dr. Strum stood up, smiled, and held out her hand. Mushy hugs weren't her style. She was wearing a long brown skirt and a forest-green cardigan. "Hello, Cammy," she said. "I was hoping you'd come."

"Hi, Dr. Strum." Even as an adult, Cammy couldn't bring herself to drop the formality and call her teacher "Rebecca"; it was unthinkable. They shook hands. "Thanks for your email. It was really nice to hear from you."

"Well, again, I was very sorry to hear about your father."

"Thank you."

"He was a charming man. I know you two were close."

"We were."

"How are you holding up?"

"Oh, I don't know. It's been a rough week. The shiva and everything..."

"Yes, communal grieving can be a bit much, can't it?"

"To say the least."

"Mm. Have a seat, won't you?" Dr. Strum motioned to a worn wooden chair next to her desk, which was reserved for those devoted students—disciples, really—who came to see her after school.

As they both sat down, Cammy observed that her mentor had aged remarkably well. In her fifties now, she was fit and trim beneath her bookish attire, likely due in large part to her longtime weekend hobby: bicycling through the nature preserves of Bergen County. Her face had retained its angular precision, and her round glasses and gray hair were the same as ever.

"I'm teaching *Walden*," Dr. Strum said, nodding to the piles of ungraded essays.

Cammy chuckled, recalling her own struggles with the dense transcendentalist tome. "I remember *Walden*."

"The students can't understand why Thoreau would go off and live alone in a cabin in the woods for two years. They think he must've lost his mind. I tell them, he explains it right in the text." She recited fluently from memory: "'I went to the woods because I wished to live deliberately, to front only the essential facts of life, and see if I could not learn what it had to teach, and not, when I came to die, discover that I had not lived.' And they say, 'But he didn't even have a phone!'"

"Kids these days," Cammy said with a laugh.

"They're not dumb, but the culture is doing its damnedest to *make* them dumb. To turn them into mindless, phone-addled consumers. Their antennae are shrinking. Their attention spans are dwindling. They don't have the patience required to read— and I mean really *read*—a challenging book. They're used to thirty-second snippets. So you can imagine what it's like trying to lead them through the thicket of *Walden*."

"Not easy?"

"No. Far from it. Yet I row on against the tide."

Downbeat as it was, Cammy felt curiously comforted by her teacher's sociocultural critique. She'd missed listening to her hot takes.

"You know," Dr. Strum mused, touching the rim of her teacup, "I think your AP English class might've been the last truly inspired group I had here. And you—you were at the very top of it. You devoured every book I threw your way."

"I did. I even made it through *Middlemarch*."

"And your writing got sharper and sharper."

"Thanks to your harsh comments. I still have PTSD from that red ink in the margins."

"I had high standards for you, so I pushed you. I wanted you to think more clearly, to write more precisely. That's my job, such as it is." She studied her onetime star student with searching eyes. Then she asked meaningfully, "So how *are* you, Cammy?"

The question caught her off guard. "How am I?"

"I used to hear from you more often. You'd drop me a line, let me know what you were up to, what you were working on. Now I hardly hear from you at all."

"Well . . . I guess there hasn't been much to report."

"Why not?"

This was exactly what Cammy had been afraid of: having to reveal to Dr. Strum the lamentable state of her life. She quipped evasively, "Let me put it this way: If I could run off to a cabin in the woods, like Thoreau, I would."

"So you're not doing well? You're unhappy?"

"I . . . I don't know. Honestly, I've felt pretty aimless the last few years. I'm doing these mindless temp gigs in the city, writing marketing drivel."

"What about your own stuff? Weren't you working on a novel?"

"I was a while ago, but I got sick of it. See, that's the problem: I've tried to write things. I've taken all these pricey classes in the city. But I haven't been able to finish anything, or at least anything I didn't end up despising." Now that the floodgates were open, Cammy couldn't stop the torrent: "And I go around with this heavy feeling in the pit of my stomach, this feeling I can't shake, that I'm not living up to my potential. That I'm letting *you* down, as silly as that sounds. And my dad always believed in me too, but now *he's* gone, and he never got to see me make something of myself. Oh, and I torpedoed my last relationship, and my mom and I aren't getting along, and—Yeah. I even hate hearing myself whine like this, 'cause I know I sound like a privileged crybaby. Bottom line: I'm a mess."

She'd done it. She'd fessed up. She'd word-vomited her soul-sickness all over Dr. Strum's desk.

Her teacher didn't say anything at first. She opened a desk drawer, plucked a tissue from a box, and handed it to Cammy—which is when Cammy realized her eyes were wet. Oh God, she literally *was* a privileged crybaby.

Dr. Strum cleared her throat. "Are you all right?"

"Yeah. I'm sorry—"

"No need to apologize. We're all entitled to a little meltdown every now and then."

"*You've* had meltdowns, Dr. Strum?"

"Certainly, in my younger days." Cammy attempted to imagine this composed, erudite woman losing her shit, but it was impossible. "Now, may I offer a few thoughts?"

"Yes. Please."

"First of all," she said, no-nonsense, "you're not letting me or your father or anyone else down, so please disabuse yourself of that foolish notion."

"But—but didn't you have high hopes for me?"

"I did, and I still do. Which leads to my second point: How old are you now, Cammy?"

"Twenty-nine. Going on thirty." She thought of Gretchen's gleeful cry at her birthday party in Brooklyn: *I'm thirty—I'm almost dead!*

"Exactly. You're young. But you talk as if your life is over, as if it's all passed you by."

"It feels like it's *passing* me by."

"Rubbish. You're finding your way. There's no shame in that. What good does it do to flagellate yourself?" It was an excellent question. Dr. Strum took a sip of her authentic English brew and sighed. "You see, as much as we would like it to, life usually doesn't proceed in accord with our initial hopes and expectations. Do you think, for instance, that I set out to teach *high school*?"

Funnily enough, Cammy had never considered this. "No?"

"Correct. I wanted to be a professor, a scholar. I earned my PhD at Buffalo. I wrote what I thought was a rather brilliant dissertation tracing the influence of Sterne's *Tristram Shandy* on Melville and *Moby Dick*." Cammy nodded dumbly; she'd read neither. "But upon graduation, I found myself unable to secure a tenure-track position within the rarefied groves of academe."

"Why?"

"Well, some of the ideas in my dissertation were—how shall I put it?—a tad unorthodox. And it probably didn't help that I came off in job interviews as a young, opinionated woman who marched to the beat of her own drum. Plain bad luck played a role as well, I'm sure." She paused. "So, to my great chagrin, I fell into teaching high school. I told myself it was only a temporary sojourn, of course. Now here we are, thirty years later."

"And do you regret it?"

"Not for a second." Dr. Strum looked around at her classroom, at her bookshelves, at the literary sanctuary she'd created in this otherwise run-of-the-mill school. Above the old-fashioned chalkboard, a long horizontal poster displayed the alphabet—the building blocks of expression. "At the risk of sounding grandiose, I believe I've had a greater influence here—made more of an 'impact,' if you will—than I ever could have at a university. I've been able to reach students at their most formative stage. Teach them how to read, how to think."

"You taught me those things."

"I hope I did. So no, no regrets." Rolling her eyes, she added, "Even if I *have* had to put up with a few thickheaded principals and some cretinous colleagues." Cammy snickered at this. Dr. Strum tapped on her desk before delivering her moral: "My point, Cammy, trite though it may be, is that life often takes us on circuitous paths. You may feel you're in a rut—"

"I do. A deep one."

"Fine. But while you're 'rutted,' as it were, life may be steering you in a direction you're not even aware of. You never know how you may end up being useful."

"Useful," Cammy repeated. How could she be *useful*? By teaching high school, like her mentor? No, she'd be awful at that. Then how? Where was *her* circuitous path headed?

"Out of curiosity, are you working on anything now?" Dr. Strum asked.

"Writing-wise, you mean?"

"Yes, writing-wise."

"I—I am, actually. A play. I only just started it, but—"

"Mm. A play. Interesting. I'll be giving my students *The Glass Menagerie* in the spring."

"I love *The Glass Menagerie*."

"As do I. Tennessee Williams's best work, in my estimation. What's your play about?"

Cammy blushed. "It's about . . . a guy who comes home to sit shiva for his father and deal with his mother. And figure out his life."

Her teacher smiled slyly. "Wouldn't happen to be autobiographical, would it?"

"How'd you guess?"

"Well, then, here's my final exhortation to you," Dr. Strum said, sitting up and adopting the stern tone she used to spur her students to excel. "This play you're writing—finish it. No matter what. Even if you want to give up, don't. All right?"

"All right," Cammy said.

♦ 9 ♦

AT SIX THAT EVENING, with Dr. Strum's encouraging words echoing in her head, Cammy boarded the rickety NJ Transit bus to New York City.

The trip from River Hill to the Port Authority Bus Terminal in Midtown took only half an hour with no traffic, but, spiritually speaking, it might as well have been a light-year. Because when you got off the turnpike and rode through the Lincoln Tunnel, you were crossing a threshold. You were leaving the petty provincialism of Jersey behind, with its cookie-cutter houses and landscaped lawns, and traveling straight into the beating heart of the cosmopolitan city. (Which, technically, was Times Square, a Boschian tourist nightmare, but you get the idea.)

Sitting on a stained fabric seat on the lurching bus, holding her laptop in its gray sleeve, Cammy felt relieved. She'd gotten her way: She was en route to the Drama Collective meeting to share her promising new pages, and she was missing the shiva tonight. "Whatever," her mother had said defeatedly in the Wendy's parking lot this morning. "Do what you want." Don't mind if I do, Mom.

Back at the house, the first guests would be trickling in now, bringing their sympathy and their snacks, eager to wallow in the sickly atmosphere of grief. Aunt Miriam would doubtless be blubbering about something or other. Tonight, though, Cammy was liberated from it all, Manhattan-bound. Free at last!

As the bus barreled into the mouth of the tunnel, she thought of one of her favorite memories of her dad. Twenty-three years ago, on a Wednesday just like this one, he'd shown up unannounced in her first-grade classroom and told kindly Mrs. Weinstein that he needed to remove his daughter from school for the day, for "family reasons." Six at the time, Cammy had had absolutely no idea what was going on. She'd grabbed her *Beauty and the Beast* lunchbox and followed her father out to the car, asking, "Where are we going, Dad?"

"On an adventure," he'd smiled.

"But where?"

"You'll see. It's a surprise."

They drove into the city, to the catchy sounds of Cy's favorite oldies station, WCBS-FM 101.1. (Even then, she preferred her dad's music—classic rock and roll, doo-wop—to her mom's bland Lite FM pablum. She was already choosing sides.) Cammy felt the renegade thrill of being out of school in the middle of a Wednesday, riding with her father, headed to who knows what fantabulous destination. (She really liked the word "fantabulous.") They were two adventurers on the road.

Her dad left the car in an underground garage, took her hand, and led her out into the bustling, sunlit streets of the Theater District. Cammy was still green enough to be bowled over, and not put off, by the sensory extravaganza: the melting-pot crowds rushing every which way, the towering billboards with their digital dazzle, the costumed cartoon characters and the hucksters hawking double-decker bus tours, the salty scent of hot dogs and pretzels mingled with the sweet aroma of honey-roasted nuts. How could this place exist? she wondered. How could it be real? It was a kaleidoscope, a dream.

Before she knew it, they were standing in front of a large building with a glittering marquee. People were lined up outside, holding tickets in their hands, abuzz with anticipation. Since Cammy had strong reading skills for her age ("exceptional," according to Mrs. Weinstein), she could easily make out the words on the marquee. At the bottom, simple white lettering read "Martin Beck Theatre." Okay, so this was a theater. She'd been to theaters before—small ones in Jersey that put on plays for kids about princes and princesses. She'd even gotten to meet a princess once after a performance. The princess had been chewing gum.

Above the name of the theater, set against a black background, was a lively logo featuring two tumbling dice and three colorful words: *Guys and Dolls*. What did they mean? Was this a show about guys who played with dolls? That sounded kind of strange.

"Dad," she said, yanking at her father's sleeve, "what's *Guys and Dolls*?"

He looked down at her with a twinkle in his eye. "It's your first Broadway musical."

Yes, folks, this was Cy Adler parenting at its finest: taking the day off from work and pulling his daughter out of first grade (without telling Beth) to bring her to her first Broadway show. Not only that, but he'd secured them front-row center seats! There wasn't even a special occasion, only a dad's love for his little girl and his desire to expose her to something wonderful.

And it *was* wonderful. Even if Cammy couldn't follow the ins and outs of the plot, even if the comic world of fast-talking New York gangsters and gamblers and showgirls was new to her, even if she didn't get all the jokes and gags, she was still utterly astonished by the experience. From her vantage point mere feet from the stage, she gazed up in awe at the lavish sets, at the men in brightly hued pinstripe suits and the women in sparkly sequined dresses as they sang and danced to the lush music of the orchestra.

Her dad glanced at her a few times during the first act to gauge her reaction and found her wide-eyed, open-mouthed. When the lights came up at intermission, Cammy announced to the entire front row that *Guys and Dolls* was the greatest thing she'd ever seen. She continued to rave about it later, over heaping pastrami sandwiches at the Carnegie Deli, and for several weeks thereafter, to anyone who'd listen.

In retrospect, though, the show itself didn't matter nearly as much as the fact that her father had given it to her as a gift, a token of his affection, a way of broadening her young horizons. He gave her so many such gifts. And she would carry that particular Wednesday's adventure in a reserved compartment of her heart forever.

★ ★ ★

Cammy alighted from the bus at the Port Authority, that dingy purgatory populated by both weary commuters and the unhoused, forgotten people of New York. She'd been passing through this terminal for years, and it had never gotten any less dank and dreary. Descending the escalator, she saw a pair of machine-gun-toting National Guardsmen standing by the Starbucks on the ground floor. It appeared as though they were there to protect the coffee franchise.

She exited out into the twilit chaos of Eighth Avenue, with its gridlocked traffic, honking horns, and sketchy characters hollering and hustling on the sidewalk. She was heading a few blocks south, to the run-down black box theater on Thirty-Sixth Street—situated directly above a porno video store—where the Drama Collective held its weekly meetings. Gretchen and her co-leaders rented the space for cheap, in return for dealing with the occasional drunk porn customer who wandered upstairs by mistake, horny and confused.

Every Wednesday evening, between ten and twenty aspiring actors, directors, and writers showed up there to hone their craft and gossip about "the business" and seek validation from each other. They were young and hungry, on the fringes, yearning for that elusive big break. Some, like Cammy, were newer to theater; others had been pounding the pavement for a while. The writers brought their in-progress pages. The actors performed them. The directors watched and critiqued. Everyone drank boxed wine. And after three or so hours, the meeting ended, and they stumbled around the corner to a dive bar on Ninth for more drinking and gossip.

No, it wasn't quite the legendary Actors Studio, but it was better than nothing.

Cammy passed the porn shop, in whose window a blue neon sign advertised "$1 PEEP SHOWS." Ew. She stopped in front of the graffitied metal door that led up to the theater. Before pressing the buzzer, she realized something remarkable: Nobody in the Drama Collective knew about her dad's death.

She'd gotten the terrible call from Rabbi Wiener outside the Williamsburg beer hall on Saturday night, hopped in a Lyft to Jersey without saying goodbye to birthday-girl Gretchen or her guests, and hadn't seen or spoken to any of them since.

What did this mean? That for the next few hours, she wouldn't have to play the pitiful role of the Girl With the Dead Dad, which she'd been constrained by all week long. She could just be Cammy again, undefined by her loss. It also meant that the group would be objective about her pages and not handle them with kid gloves because they felt sorry for her. This was good.

She was buzzed in and climbed the narrow flight of stairs, inhaling the usual mysterious weed smell. Who snuck in here to smoke? The porn dudes? Reaching the second floor, Cammy moved through the threadbare lobby—this was the kind of dump where old eccentrics self-produced their own abysmal plays—and into the theater itself. Here, within the plain, square, black-walled space, she found the members of the Collective seated on folding chairs arranged in a circle, sipping wine out of their plastic cups and chatting away. The sight of them made her surprisingly happy. Starving artists do have a certain charm.

Gretchen's saucer-size eyes lit up when she saw her. "Yay! Cammy's here!" The others turned, smiled, nodded, said hi. Gretchen pounded the palm of her hand on the empty seat next to hers. "Go get some wine and come sit next to me!" Cammy did as ordered. As soon as she sat down, Gretchen leaned over, frizzy hair bobbing, and mock-scolded, "What happened to you Saturday night? You disappeared!"

"Yeah, I know. I'm sorry."

"It was my birthday! You hurt my feelings! Just kidding, I was too drunk to be hurt. Everything okay, though?"

Cammy calibrated her lie. "I just wasn't feeling well. I went home and crashed."

"Oh no. You feeling better now?"

"Yep. All good. It was probably that German beer. It's . . . heavy, you know?"

"Totally. Totally. *Super* heavy."

★ ★ ★

The meeting progressed in typical fashion. A few nervous writers shared their work. (Nervous except for Hunter, a pompous asshole who, despite being from New England, fancied himself the next Sam Shepard and wrote heavy-handed dramas set in the American West.) The intrepid actors did their best cold readings of the material. And after each presentation, Gretchen or another of the directors led long-winded feedback sessions, asking anodyne questions like, "What are our first impressions?" "What did we like?" "What did we want more of?" One of the group's rules was that all comments should be constructive, and never explicitly negative, so when a scene was really bad, it was fun to watch people jump through euphemistic hoops.

Cammy sat quietly, following along on her laptop, offering an innocuous, intelligent-sounding remark here and there. (They read on screens instead of printing pages, out of consideration for the world's trees.) She was waiting for her moment. Then it arrived.

At around nine thirty, Gretchen surveyed the room. "Does anyone else have anything? Or should we head over to the Holland early?" The Holland was the dive on Ninth. It still had a functioning jukebox.

"Um, I do," Cammy said. Heads swiveled in her direction.

"Oh, nice! What do you have?"

"A scene from a play I just started. It doesn't have a title yet."

"Ooh, exciting," Gretchen trilled. "New stuff from Cammy. Let's hear it!"

Cringing at this enthusiastic intro, Cammy emailed her pages to the group via the theater's faulty Wi-Fi network. She asked Max, a solid actor with a shock of brown curls and a neurotic Jesse Eisenberg vibe, to read the role of Cameron, her gender-swapped alter ego. And for the part of Bev, she enlisted Jillian, a Melissa McCarthy look-alike who was only in her thirties but had a mature quality that made her a go-to for middle-aged characters.

Now came Gretchen's customary query: "Is there anything you'd like us to know before we hear the scene?"

"Nope." Cammy hated artistic disclaimers; she believed work should speak for itself.

"All right!" Gretchen nodded at Max and Jillian. "Go ahead, guys. Take it away."

And take it away they did. The two actors proceeded to perform Cammy's scene with a skill and verisimilitude that even she wasn't prepared for. You would've thought they'd been rehearsing it for a week instead of reading it for the very first time. Slipping easily into the prickly parent-child dynamic that Cammy had based on her and her mother's own sparring, they brought the dialogue to vivid life.

Wow, Cammy thought, preening herself as she listened to Max and Jillian voice her words. I knew this was good when I wrote it, but I didn't know it was *this* good. And it's just an initial draft!

When the fifteen-minute scene was over, she fully expected to be showered with praise. (E.g., "Cammy, what an *amazing* beginning. You're really becoming a playwright.") Unfortunately, however, this was not what happened.

"Okay," Gretchen said after the obligatory applause. "Thank you, Cammy, for sharing that. So . . . what did we think?" Silence. Blank stares. Were they too awed to speak? "Anybody?"

As was often the case, Hunter, the Sam Shepard copycat, volunteered his opinion first. "I'm sorry—I thought Jillian and Max did a great job, but . . . to be honest, the scene kind of confused me."

Uh-oh. Not an auspicious sign.

"That's fine," Gretchen assured him, sounding like a preschool teacher. "What confused you, Hunter?"

"Well, so in the play, the dad has just died, right? And the son's come home to be with his mom? For the, the Jewish thing—"

"Shiva," Cammy interjected. *The Jewish thing.* She had a sudden impulse to punch Hunter in his preppy poser face.

"Right. Shiva. Sorry. So like . . . why are they fighting, then? Shouldn't they be comforting each other?"

"They have a complicated relationship," Cammy said, attempting not to lose her patience. "That's the point of the scene."

Hunter scratched his patchy ginger beard. "Huh. Yeah, I don't know. Maybe it's me, but it just didn't seem relatable."

Relatable? What wasn't relatable? The wild notion that grieving people might not get along perfectly? That parents and children sometimes have conflicts? That life can be complex and messy? Cammy wanted to say, "You know what, Hunter? I don't find *you* relatable, and your Western plays suck ass. You're from New Hampshire, you fucking phony." But she managed to hold her tongue.

The next to pipe up was pigtailed Daphne, a hippieish director who draped her rangy frame in flowing, flowery dresses and who could always be counted on to throw in her two cents. "Cammy, first of all, kudos for starting something new. That's awesome." Thanks a lot. "But the thing for me was, I found the son character sort of . . . unlikable."

Cammy raised an eyebrow. "Unlikable?"

"Yeah, like why is he being so mean to his mom? Why doesn't he want to be at the shiva?"

"Because he's overwhelmed, and he doesn't know what to do with all his emotions. He's not trying to be *mean*."

"He comes off that way, though," Daphne said. She was sitting on her chair in some version of the lotus position. "I couldn't really sympathize with him. It made it hard for me to get into the scene."

The others murmured in agreement, and the pile-on continued. To their credit, the group didn't even hide behind their usual euphemisms. The plain fact of the matter was that they hadn't liked Cammy's pages one bit. They were perplexed by her ugly portrait of grief, of a mother and son arguing after having just buried their husband and father. They found the whole thing icky and unpleasant. They didn't get it at all.

Amid the onslaught of negative feedback, it occurred to Cammy that one of the perils of writing something so blatantly autobiographical was that when people criticized your protagonist, it felt as if they were criticizing *you*. When they said the son seemed like a selfish brat who was treating his mom like shit, they were in essence saying that about her. (Although they still had no idea about the real-life basis for the scene.) She felt stupid—for sharing the pages in the first place and exposing herself this way, for predicting a rapturous reception, and, most of all, for caring so much what these nobodies thought.

Yes, she was calling them nobodies, because she was pissed.

After twenty excruciating minutes, Gretchen had to step in as moderator and put a stop to the orgy of judgment. She interrupted Ezra, a proudly Jewish actor with horn-rimmed specs and a hipster mustache who had gone off on a sanctimonious tangent about the importance of the shiva ritual. "All right, guys. I think that's enough notes for now. Cammy has plenty to mull over." There was an understatement. "Before we call it a night, uh, Cammy, do you have anything else *you* wanna say?"

Under normal circumstances, she would've simply said, "No." Cammy had attended enough writing seminars over the years to know that when your work didn't go over well, you had to tough it out, absorb the blows, and exit with your head held high. (Then you could pick up a pint of Ben & Jerry's on the way home and shed a tear or two into your Cherry Garcia.) But these weren't normal circumstances. She had a special dispensation: the all-powerful Grief Pass.

"Actually, there *is* something I'd like to say," she declared, sliding her laptop into its sleeve and rising to her feet. "My dad died Saturday night, during Gretchen's birthday party." Boom. In an instant, the air had left the room. There were scattered gasps, dropped jaws. "Yeah. So these pages are very personal for me. And I appreciate all the 'constructive' feedback, but to be frank, I don't care if you think the scene is 'relatable,' or if you find the son 'likable,' or whatever. 'Cause it's raw and it's real, and I stand by it. So you can all go fuck yourselves. Have fun at the bar!"

With that, Cammy stalked out of the shabby theater, just as her mom had this morning at CarePlus. Look at that: They'd both been badasses today. Behind her, she heard a shaken Gretchen call her name, but she just kept going. Shooting through the lobby and down the stairs, she registered that this would very likely be her last Drama Collective meeting. Once you've told the members of an organization to fuck themselves, it's hard to come back.

She burst onto the street and wove around a few leering lowlifes loitering outside the porn store. When she hit Eighth Avenue, her adrenaline slowed, and she reckoned with the fairness of her actions: She'd hidden her dad's death from the group, shared her pages under false pretenses—and then, when she didn't get the reaction she wanted, she'd sprung the heavy news on everyone and cursed them out. No, probably not so fair. But definitely rash and spiteful.

Back in the gloom of the Port Authority, on line for the bus to River Hill, Cammy found herself perversely smiling. For better or worse (and yes, most would say worse), she was developing quite an impressive knack for alienating people.

Day Four: Thursday

♦ 10 ♦

Cammy dreamed that she and Nick were starring in a production of *Guys and Dolls* on Broadway. He had the role of the suave gambler Sky Masterson, while she was playing Sergeant Sarah Brown, the pious Times Square missionary. They'd reached the scene in which Sky takes Sarah on a long-distance date to a Havana nightclub, where she inadvertently drinks rum and lets her hair down. After they kiss, Sarah sings the tipsy ode "If I Were a Bell": *"Ask me how do I feel, ask me now that we're cozy and clinging. Well, sir, all I can say is, if I were a bell I'd be ringing."*

Incidentally, Cammy couldn't sing to save her life, but this was a dream, so she possessed a beautiful soprano voice.

In the middle of her big number, she peered down past the footlights and glimpsed an uncanny sight: her six-year-old self and her father seated in the front row, staring up at her. She faltered, lost her place. Try as she might, Cammy couldn't recall the next line of the song. Standing on the vast stage before a packed house, perspiring in her itchy red missionary costume, she was completely helpless. Nick, dapper in his high roller's pinstripe suit, looked on with a mixture of horror and pity. The orchestra vamped for a while but eventually fell silent.

Cammy heard her younger self whisper, "Dad, why can't the lady sing?"

Then she woke up, sticky with actual sweat.

What the hell was the meaning of *this* dream, Dr. Freud? That she and Nick belonged together after all? That she hadn't lived up to her childhood aspirations? That her father was watching her from the next world? Or did it just mean that she had too many Broadway musicals embedded in her consciousness?

Who knew? Her head felt fuzzy, probably thanks to the boxed wine she'd drank last night, and she couldn't think clearly enough to carry out an analysis.

Shambling downstairs, Cammy braced herself for an interrogation from her mother, who'd been asleep when she'd gotten back. ("So how did your meeting go?" she might ask. "Was it worth missing the shiva for?") But Beth was nowhere to be found.

"Mom?" Cammy called, passing from the living room into the kitchen. She glanced out the window above the sink; the Corolla wasn't in the driveway.

Affixed to the coffeepot—which, thankfully, had a decent amount of hot coffee left—was a yellow Post-it note that offered an explanation. "Meeting with Craig Rosen today," read Beth's slanted cursive. "Be home later. See you then." Signed, unnecessarily, "Mom."

Craig Rosen was a family friend from the synagogue who also happened to be a ferocious lawyer based out of Fort Lee. Fiftyish and fit, with a gray crew cut, he looked like a Jewish commando. When he wasn't training for Ironman competitions, he did his job with military-style aggression, litigating all over Bergen County and winning seven-figure settlements for his clients. He lived in a mansion in tony Alpine and had thrown his daughter's bat mitzvah party on a huge yacht on the Hudson. The guy was no joke.

So this was the wolf in designer clothing whom Beth was turning to for her lawsuit against CarePlus. As if suing the living daylights out of the rehab place would heal the wound of her husband's death. Cammy didn't get it, but whatever. More power to you, Mom. Take them to court. All the money in the world won't bring Dad back.

Still, she was glad her mother wasn't home. She'd been spared the dreaded interrogation. For the first time all week, she had the house to herself.

Cammy poured coffee into a chipped mug that had been her father's favorite, went back upstairs, and wrote for an hour. Despite how much the Drama Collective had disliked it, she wasn't going to abandon her grief play. On the contrary, she'd let their scorn fuel her work. "This play you're writing—finish it," Dr. Strum had admonished yesterday. "No matter what. Even if you want to give up, don't." Yes, ma'am. Fuck the haters.

At noon, once she'd reached a suitable stopping point, she closed her laptop and considered her next course of action. Guided by her surreal *Guys and Dolls* dream, Cammy felt an urge to see Nick again, to visit him at his Clubhouse, to find out if, possibly, there was something there. Yes, reconnecting with your high school crush sounded like the plot of a shitty rom-com. And yet . . . why not? What did she have to lose?

What if her destiny lay with Beautiful Dancer Boy?

★ ★ ★

Not having a car in the suburbs is a real bummer. You tramp around like a vagabond, waiting for inefficient local buses that make a million stops and take forever to get anywhere. Your fellow passengers are usually old ladies with grocery bags who can't drive because of cataracts. It's a depressing mode of travel, but Cammy, reluctant to fritter any more of her limited funds on Lyfts, had no better means of getting to Nick's community center in Hackensack.

On her way to the bus stop, though, she decided on a detour. She was hungry, and Fran's deli, DeMarco's, was within walking distance. She could drop by, get a pre-Nick pep talk from her best friend, and scarf down a high-calorie Italian sandwich, all at once. Bada bing.

Heading there, Cammy passed Congregation Sons of Israel, the small Reform synagogue to which her family belonged. Amusingly, the modest brick building sported a tall steeple—a holdover from its previous life as a Lutheran church—topped with a Jewish star. She'd spent untold tedious hours in this place, suffering through services and Sunday school, until at last she'd been bat mitzvahed and emancipated. All that God talk had never done it for her. Even as a kid, she'd wondered, why so much supplication? If God is so great, why does he need to be constantly buttered up? Seems a bit insecure.

One time, in a Sunday class, Cammy had made the mistake of voicing this observation to her teacher, Orna, an imposing Israeli woman who'd served in the country's armed forces. "How dare you!" Orna had bellowed, flinging a chalky eraser across the room. "We praise God because he gives us life, the world, everything! Not because he 'needs' it. He doesn't 'need' anything from us. He's God. *We're* the ones who need *him*."

Um, do we really, though?

Cammy thought this but didn't say it, as she feared that Orna might pick up the eraser and hurl it at her tender twelve-year-old head.

Now, to her dismay, she saw another, less frightening yet more irritating authority figure emerge from the synagogue's front doors: Rabbi Wiener.

Oh no. How could she hide?

Too late. She'd been spotted.

"Cammy!" The rabbi trotted up to her, his multicolored knit yarmulke bouncing atop his bald head. For his professional duties, he wore a suit, but since today was Thursday, an off day, he had on corduroys and an argyle sweater-vest over a collared shirt. "What a pleasant surprise. It's good to see you."

"Yep . . ."

"I was just in my office, working on my sermon for tomorrow."

"Cool."

"It's about redemption."

"Big topic."

"Yes, it is," he said, stroking his grayish goatee like the sage he imagined himself to be. "How 'bout you? Out for a stroll?"

A *stroll*? What was she, ninety? "No, I'm going to get lunch."

"Oh. Where?"

"DeMarco's."

"The Italian place? They make terrific sandwiches."

"Yeah. My friend Fran runs it with her dad."

"Really? I didn't know that. The next time I go in, I'll have to tell them I'm your rabbi."

"You don't need to do that."

Standing on Main Street, chitchatting with the Wiener Man—what could be more fun? Cammy weighed what would happen if she just took off and ran. Would he chase her? Probably not; he had a belly and wasn't in the best shape.

Before she could give this plan a shot, he spoke again, in a paternal tone that made her bristle. "You know, my invitation from the other night still stands." The other night, when they'd encountered each other in the police station parking lot after her regrettable quasi-arrest.

"What invitation?" she said, though she knew exactly what he meant.

"For you to come see me, so we can have a talk. About your grief. And your . . . behavior. And your relationship with your mother—"

"I thought I already declined that invitation."

"You did, but I'm offering it again."

"Well, I'm declining again. Sorry, Rabbi, I've gotta go. Shalom. Namaste. Whatever." She made a move to brush past him, but Wiener didn't budge.

"I get the feeling you have something against me, Cammy," he said good-naturedly.

"Against you?"

"Yes. Am I correct in that perception?"

"I mean . . . do you want me to be honest?"

"Please."

Cammy's gaze fell on the synagogue, which stood like a silent, forbidding witness to the sacrilege she was about to spew. "I guess it's not so much *you* I have something against as it is, um, what you represent?"

"And what do I represent to you?"

"Organized religion. Which I'm not the biggest fan of. No offense."

"Judaism doesn't hold any meaning for you?"

"Oh, I definitely *feel* Jewish, in an I-live-in-New-York-and-like-bagels-and-*Seinfeld* kinda way. But as for the actual religion? Nope. There's just too much bullshit for me to get on board. Fairy tales, platitudes, hypocrisy. Again, no offense."

"I see," the rabbi said, curiously unfazed. He'd apparently faced down a few heretics in his day.

"And what really pisses me off," Cammy went on, now relishing this rare chance to speak truth to power, "is that religion tells you how you're supposed to grieve: Say these prayers! Do seven days of shiva! Go through the motions!"

"Many people find great comfort in those rituals."

"Maybe so, but I don't find them comforting at all. My dad's dead, and I just wanna be left *alone*. I don't wanna have to do a song and dance for a bunch of strangers every night—"

"They're not strangers. They're your community."

"What community? I don't even live here anymore. And they might as well be strangers. They show up at the house, say 'Sorry for your loss,' devour the snacks, and go on their merry way."

Rabbi Wiener adjusted his yarmulke, which had begun to slip down the back of his smooth dome. He seemed to be considering how best to respond to the incorrigible apostate before him. "Can I ask you something, Cammy?"

"Do I have a choice?"

"Do you think . . . your father would be proud of how you're handling all this?"

The question made her skin prickle with outrage. "Excuse me?"

"Would he be proud of your actions this week? Of your absence from the shiva? Of how you're behaving toward your mother?"

"My mom and I clash, okay? That's how we are. It's how we've always been."

"You don't think she might need your support right now?"

"I don't think it's for you to say. Oh, and by the way, my dad didn't buy into any religious crap either. We used to sit in the back at temple and make jokes during your sermons."

"I'm aware."

"Wait—you mean you noticed?"

"How could I not?" the rabbi said matter-of-factly. "I'd be up at the podium, talking about the week's Torah portion, and I'd hear snickers from the last row. Your father had a distinctive laugh. It was very distracting."

Cammy chortled in spite of herself, imagining Wiener's vexation at her and her dad's impious high jinks. She wished she could hear his distinctive laugh again. She didn't want to forget its life-giving sound.

The rabbi formed a benevolent smile and came out with a whopper of a non sequitur: "You know, Cammy, I still remember your bat mitzvah."

"My bat mitzvah? Why are you bringing *that* up?"

"Because you did such a wonderful job that day. And you gave one of the best speeches I've heard any young person make."

It was true that Cammy had killed it at her bat mitzvah. Under the exacting tutelage of Orna, the Israeli drill sergeant, she'd mastered all the prayers and memorized each swirling note of the Torah portion she was required to chant. (By the luck of the draw, she'd gotten stuck with a lovely chapter in Leviticus about the rules for animal sacrifice.) As her "bat mitzvah project"—the yearlong community service every student was expected to perform—she'd volunteered one day a week at a local soup kitchen. This experience had been the subject of her speech. Its boldly original theme: "giving back."

And the reward for all her diligent study and preparation? A lame party in a hotel ballroom in Tenafly, presided over by a spiky-haired DJ who looked as if he'd stepped out of the cast of *Jersey Shore*. Such is life.

"When I watched you give that speech about the soup kitchen," the rabbi continued, "I thought to myself, 'Wow. This is a girl with a big heart.' And I still believe that."

"Gee, thanks."

"I mean it. I know how much you loved your father, Cammy. I look at you, and I see him." She felt her eyes growing watery. Crying in front of Wiener Man would be unforgivable. "I know you're hurting. But that's not an excuse to act out and hurt others. Like your mother."

"Okay—"

"There's an ancient Jewish saying: 'Hurt people hurt people.'"

"Um, I'm pretty sure that's not a Jewish saying."

"Regardless. Tell me—how can I help you grieve? How can I help you and your mom come together? How can I make this process easier for you?"

A gust of wind blew colored leaves around Cammy's feet on the sidewalk. She shivered. The churlish part of her resented the rabbi for his hackneyed aphorisms and sentimental appeals. At the same time, the vulnerable part wanted to give in and accept his offer of help, to let herself be consoled by a "spiritual leader," like a normal person.

As usual lately, the churlish part won out.

"I don't think you *can* help me, Rabbi," she said. "But I know another saying: 'Hungry people get lunch.' And that's what I'm gonna do now. Good talk, though. Good talk." Then she nodded and slipped past him, leaving the bemused clergyman alone on the street in front of his steepled house of worship.

★ ★ ★

The deli was hopping.

Folks all over Bergen County flocked to DeMarco's for its authentic Italian meats, cheeses, and bread. The ambience, or lack thereof, was an added attraction: Stepping into the place was like entering a time warp to the 1970s. Fran's no-nonsense dad, Leo, didn't bother with pleasant decor and other such frills. You came to DeMarco's for the fatty, flavorful food, and that's what you got. And if you didn't bring cash with you, you were out of luck. Leo didn't mess with credit card machines and declared only a fraction of his income to the IRS.

Cammy arrived in the thick of the lunch rush. Clad in apron and baseball cap, Fran stood behind a display case full of mouth-watering salami and prosciutto and mortadella, preparing sandwiches with lightning speed. Her bearlike father was chatting up regulars at the register.

Had Fran not told Cammy that Leo was "slipping a little," "forgetting stuff," showing early signs of cognitive decline, she never would've suspected it. With his sturdy frame, silver mane, and big forearms bursting out of rolled-up sleeves, he still appeared vigorous, like a king holding court. If you looked closely, though, you could make out a barely perceptible mistiness in his expression, as if a thin, gauzy veil had been cast over him. This was the sole hint that something was off.

Yet sure enough, when he saw his daughter's best friend, Leo recognized her instantly. He beckoned her over and kissed both of her cheeks. "Cammy, how are you?" he said in his rich Southern Italian accent. "I'm sorry about your father."

"Thanks, Mr. DeMarco." Kindly, he'd made no mention of the other night, when he'd had to pick Fran up from the police station after her and Cammy's run-in with the law.

"How's your mom?"

"She's, you know . . . sad. How've you been?"

"Eh, I can't complain." He gestured to the swarm of hungry patrons. "Business is good. But I'm getting tired. I ain't as sharp no more." With a tap of his temple, the strong man grudgingly acknowledged his frailty. "My wife wants me to quit, move to Naples."

"Oh, back to Italy?"

"No," he chuckled wistfully. "Florida."

"Ah."

"It's nice down there, I guess. I could be a . . . how-you-say? Beach bum. Give this place to Francesca."

On cue, Fran, who'd now sighted Cammy as well, yelled over the din of customers, "Yo! What're you doin' here?"

"Just came to bother you!"

"You want a sandwich?"

"Yes, please!"

"Okay, hold on!"

Cammy turned back to Leo. "Well, I hope you get to take it easy. You've worked hard for a long time."

"I have, I have. Life is funny, no? You work and work, and then your mind . . ." He puffed his stubbled cheeks and expelled air, like a deflating balloon. A poignant visual metaphor. "Listen, you and your mother take care, huh?"

"We'll try. You do the same, Mr. DeMarco."

Meanwhile Fran had gone into overdrive, churning out Italian heroes like a one-woman assembly line until every impatient soul in the store was served and satisfied. Then she whipped one up for Cammy, came around the counter, and joined her at an old, scratched Formica table.

"You're like a machine back there," Cammy said. "How do you do it?"

"I don't know. I go into some kinda trance. My hands move faster than my brain. Everything disappears except those fuckin' sandwiches I'm making."

"I think they call that a 'flow state.'"

"I call it a pain in the ass," Fran said, ever pragmatic. "Hey, is my dad giving me the evil eye? He doesn't like when I abandon my post."

Cammy glanced over her friend's shoulder at the register, where Leo was schmoozing with a pretty, middle-aged woman in business attire. A charmer to the end. "Nope, he's occupied."

"Good. By the way, was your mom super pissed the other night?"

"I'd say so. She showed up at the police station with the rabbi. He wanted to talk to me about how I've been 'acting out.'"

"Oh God."

"And she and I had a big fight yesterday morning."

"That sucks."

"Yeah. Then last night, I skipped the shiva again—"

"*Again?*"

"Yes, but I got her permission this time. Sort of. And I went into the city and ended up telling off all these pretentious theater kids I've been hanging out with."

Fran shook her head. "You're having a helluva week."

"That I am." Now that she'd caught her pal up on her most recent misadventures, Cammy took a bite of her hero. It was so good that she wondered if heaven might not simply be an eternity of fresh prosciutto and mozzarella. "Jesus, this is delicious," she said with her mouth full.

"What can I say? I've got skills." Fran leaned over the table and grinned confidentially. "So . . . can't you picture it?"

"Picture what?"

"This place as a *restaurant*. I mean, totally renovated, obviously. I'd change the name from 'DeMarco's' to 'Francesca's.' Classic Italian food with a young vibe. I'd be cooking up masterpieces in the kitchen. You'd be in the back office, doing your marketing stuff and whatever. We'd be unstoppable." She paused for dramatic effect. "Have you thought any more about it?"

In truth, Cammy hadn't, not since Fran had first broached the idea over bottles of Olde English in the cemetery Tuesday night. But she could see in her friend's eyes how eager she was to turn her vision into a reality, just as soon as Leo relocated to Naples (Florida) and handed the business to her. And Fran wanted Cammy to be a part of it—to move back home and join forces with her, to oversee advertising and PR and all the things Fran had no idea about. "I think maybe this is where you belong," she'd said on the graveyard grass. What if she were right?

"It's okay," Fran said, reading the noncommittal look on Cammy's face. "No rush. But promise me you *will* think about it."

"I will."

"I know you have some weird prejudice against coming back to Jersey. Like it would mean you've failed at life or something—"

"I never said that."

"You don't have to. I know it's how you feel. But I think this could be really great for you. For us."

Two best friends running a restaurant together in the place where they grew up: Maybe it *could* be great. Or stifling and unsatisfying. Cammy didn't know. She still couldn't let go of her self-image as someone bound to "make it" in the city . . . whatever the fuck that meant. "I'll think about it," she repeated.

"Okay. Cool. That's all I'm asking."

"Francesca!" Leo's gravelly voice boomed from across the deli. "Whatchu doin'? We got customers!" A few famished construction workers had wandered in.

Fran rolled her eyes in her dad's direction. "He wears me out." She rose from the table. "At least I'm getting away this weekend, though."

"Getting away where?"

"I didn't tell you? I'm going to A.C. tomorrow." A.C., of course, stood for Atlantic City, the Jersey Shore destination that had once been a luxury resort town but now could best be described as a wannabe Vegas with a boardwalk. It was Fran's favorite spot, and she liked to take weekend trips there to gamble at the casinos, visit the male strip club, and soak up the tawdry seaside setting. This was her version of "decompressing." "Wanna come with?"

"I wish I could, but I've still got more shiva-sitting to do."

"Wait, when does it end?"

"Sunday morning. Which feels years away right now."

"I'm sorry, dude."

"Thanks."

"Francesca!" Leo roared again.

"I'm coming, Dad! Shit!" It was funny how Fran and her father barked at each other all day every day. They had their own quarrelsome love language. Fran held up her fist, and Cammy pounded it. "I'll talk to you later. What're you up to now?"

"Well, I'm gonna finish my sandwich"—coy smile—"and then I thought I'd head over to the Clubhouse."

Fran perked up. "You mean the place where Nick Ramos works?"

"Yes . . ."

"Oh, damn! I called it! You're gonna rekindle with Beautiful Dancer Boy!"

"There's nothing to rekindle!"

"Fine, *kindle*, then."

"Look, he invited me, so I'm just gonna go—"

"I'm telling you, he wants you. I could smell it at the bowling alley."

"Yeah, right."

"Just do me a favor," Fran teased, swinging behind the counter to serve the construction crew. "When you're living your high school fantasy and making out for the first time, think of me saying, 'Told you so.'"

◆ 11 ◆

Cammy got off the bus in Hackensack, having braved its indignities, and found herself staring up at the hundred-foot-tall art deco tower of the old Sears Roebuck department store, which had closed just a few years ago. She remembered her dad telling her that, in a strange and stunning promotional coup, Salvador Dalí himself had unveiled one of his surrealist paintings there in the sixties. Dalí in Hackensack! This was something she did appreciate about Jersey: the lively lore, the sense of history. Everywhere you turned, there was a surprising story.

Nearby stood a newer building that was bright, glassy, and inviting, with big windows and a garden and a playground on the side. The sign above its entrance read, in colorful lettering styled after children's alphabet blocks, "THE CLUBHOUSE."

As pleasant as the place looked, Cammy still couldn't wrap her head around the fact that Nick had ended up *here*. The dancing sensation of River Hill High, fated for the glitz and glamour of an entertainment career, working with kids at some local center? It just didn't compute. What had happened? Maybe she could delicately—or, knowing herself, not so delicately—find out.

She walked up to the front doors and pressed a buzzer.

"Hello," a woman's voice said over the speaker. "Are you here for pickup?"

"Pickup?"

"Yes. Are you here to pick up your child?"

"Sorry—no. I'm, uh, I'm an old friend of Nick Ramos? I'm just here to say hi." She added quickly, "He invited me."

"Oh." The woman sounded a bit confused. "Well, Nick's teaching a dance class right now, but I can buzz you in and you can wait for him in the lobby."

"That would be great, thank you."

"No problem."

There was a loud beep, the doors clicked open, and Cammy stepped into the spacious lobby of the Clubhouse, which was as warm and welcoming as its exterior. There were comfy chairs and kid-friendly beanbags, and the walls were covered with children's artwork and framed photos of students engaged in various dynamic activities. When Nick had first mentioned the center, she'd pictured something drab and institutional, but the atmosphere here was actually pretty delightful. So much for her preconceived notions.

She heard music emanating from down a hallway—the unmistakable bumping bass of a hip-hop track. It had to be coming from Nick's class. Like a woman hypnotized, Cammy turned and began to follow the vibrations. Yes, she'd been told to wait in the lobby, but how could she pass up the chance to see Beautiful Dancer Boy in action after so many years?

The sound led her to a room endearingly labeled "Groove Studio." Its door was open a crack, and she tiptoed up to peer inside. What she saw transformed Cammy into a lovesick teenager all over again.

Dressed in black warm-up pants and a sleeveless white T-shirt—the same outfit he'd worn at the eighth-grade talent show where he'd first captured her heart—Nick was leading a group of elementary schoolers in an energetic hip-hop dance routine. The kids were popping and locking and dropping to the beat. As they moved, Nick drifted around the studio to offer a helping hand where needed and enthusiastic words of encouragement ("There you go, Shawn! You got this, Alyssa!").

He'd been dreamy back in high school, cavorting onstage, but somehow the sight of him now, doing this, was even dreamier. And nothing about his demeanor suggested someone who'd "settled" or failed to fulfill his ambitions. No, Nick looked like a man who was exactly where he was supposed to be. The kids were having a blast, and so was he.

Cammy watched, captivated, until he stopped the music, blew a whistle, and exclaimed, "Okay, nice work today, guys! It's healthy snack time! Go see Miss Carmen in the cafeteria!"

After exchanging high fives with "Mr. Nick," as they called him, the children rushed toward the door, flung it open, and streamed into the hall, chattering and laughing. Before she could sneak back off to the lobby, Nick laid eyes on her. "Cammy," he said, surprised.

"Hi, Nick," she blushed.

"You came."

"Of course I did."

"How long were you standing there?"

"Oh, only a minute or two. I wasn't trying to like spy on you or anything." He smiled at this. "I just heard the music, and—That was amazing, by the way."

"What was?"

"You and those kids. The dancing. So cool." Here she was, fawning again, just as she'd done on the dance floor at prom a decade ago. ("You're a star," she'd gushed back then. "Everyone thinks so.") Why couldn't she be around this guy for five minutes without fawning? Old crushes die hard.

"Yeah, we have a good time," Nick said with easy, natural modesty. He came closer, and butterflies flitted around her stomach. There was a thin film of sweat on his face that made him shine. A few strands of gray in his luxuriant dark hair were the only sign that he was nearing thirty. "All the movement is great for the kids, and the hip-hop makes it fun."

"They're crazy about you, I can tell."

"They look up to me. But honestly, they probably inspire me more than I inspire them." Nick could say Hallmark-y things like this without sounding the least bit corny. "So should I give you the tour?"

"Sure. I'd love that."

He led her around the cheery building, through its muraled halls and past the gymnasium, the cafeteria, the computer lab, the auditorium, the art studio, the music room. Each space was cleaner and more well designed than the last. There was also a separate "meditation corner" with soft mats on the floor, where kids could come to "chill out when they're feeling stressed," as Nick charmingly put it. Even a perennial skeptic like Cammy had to be impressed. The Clubhouse was the real deal.

They wound up seated across from each other in Nick's tidy, sunlit office by the lobby. A blue stability ball rested in the corner. Shelves on the wall housed a collection of motivational books, and a large poster read "HELP ONE CHILD, HEAL THE WORLD." Aware that she was alone in a room with her teen heartthrob for the very first time, Cammy felt a secret, silly thrill. Then she noticed the engraved nameplate on his desk: "Nick Ramos, Director."

"Wait," she said. "You run this whole place?"

"I guess I do," he said humbly.

"Oh—I thought you just like worked here and taught dance—"

"No, I helped found it, actually, a few years back."

"Wow. I didn't realize. That's incredible."

"It's not so incredible."

"Yeah, it is. I mean, I've spent my twenties working meaningless temp jobs and failing at being a writer. But you've like . . . *built* something."

Nick received this with a look of amused compassion. "You've still got plenty of time, Cammy."

"Do I?"

"I think so."

Perhaps she did. Yet Cammy couldn't help but feel like a piece of shit when she compared her own colossal lack of achievement with this sparkling community center she now sat in—whose existence Nick was directly responsible for. She also felt like a piece of shit for still wondering why he hadn't made it big in showbiz. But the question remained.

Nick apparently detected the curiosity in her face. "You look like you wanna ask me something."

"Um. Well—"

"Yeah?"

How could she phrase this tactfully? "Why aren't you a star?" she said. Nope, that wasn't tactful at all.

Nick's eyes widened, as though he couldn't quite believe her bluntness. "What?"

"Sorry, that sounded—I just mean, this place is wonderful and all, it really is—"

"Uh-huh?"

"But back in high school, you know, you were such an amazing dancer. And you went off to college for it. Everyone thought you were gonna end up on Broadway or on TV or choreographing for pop stars or whatever. You had this like . . . golden halo around you—"

"Golden halo?"

"Yeah, like you were destined for glory. So . . ."

"So why am I here in Hackensack instead of on *So You Think You Can Dance?*"

"Basically. I know it sounds rude, but I had to ask."

Nick turned to the window and stared out at the garden, where one of his colleagues was showing some kids how to plant seeds. His voice softened. "So you never heard?"

"Heard what?"

"It was all over Facebook when it happened."

"I deleted my Facebook in college."

"And no one ever told you?"

"Fran's like the only person I still speak to from high school. And she was *never* on Facebook."

"Oh. I just assumed you knew."

"Knew *what*?"

He took a breath. "I was in a car accident. A pretty bad one."

"A car accident? When?"

"Senior year of college."

"What happened?"

With the measured tone of one who'd related his story many times before—although maybe not in a while—Nick proceeded to tell her.

"I was home from Arizona for winter break. Just a few months from graduating. I had everything figured out—I was gonna move to L.A., get into the pro dance scene. Best-laid plans, right?" Right. "It was late Christmas Eve night, and we were driving back from a big family holiday party. Me, my parents, my grandma, and my little sister, Clara, in a minivan on the Garden State Parkway." A notoriously dangerous highway. "There was this massive semi next to us, and it suddenly swerved into our lane. Turned out the driver was dozing. It hit us, and we flipped over onto the median."

"Oh my God."

"We all got hurt. My grandma, she, uh . . ." He paused and looked away. "She almost died. But through some miracle, she made it. I had a bunch of broken bones. I had to have surgeries, wear a neck brace, use a wheelchair. I spent a month at a rehab facility, just working up to walking on my own."

"Nick . . ."

"My parents sued the trucking company, and they got a settlement. But that didn't make things any better. It was traumatic, you know. My sister still gets freaked out being in a car."

"Of course."

"For me, though, the worst part was . . . I couldn't dance anymore. Not like I used to, anyway. Not with the same agility." The acrobatic agility that had dazzled anyone who'd ever seen him perform, that would've propelled him straight to the heights. "I'd lost my gift. I wasn't gonna be a pro. And that'd been my path since I was a kid. My whole identity, really. So *now* who was I?"

Cammy sat frozen in disbelief as Nick calmly recounted this tragic tale. The cosmic irony of it all was too cruel to comprehend. What kind of diabolical deity would let such a thing happen to Beautiful Dancer Boy?

He explained how he fell into a deep depression after the accident. (She could hardly imagine this confident, vital man laid low by despair.) He moved back home to Jersey to recuperate, missing his final semester of school, and the University of Arizona granted him his dance degree out of charity. He whiled away a couple of years working odd jobs, taking too many pain pills, and generally feeling sorry for himself.

Therapy didn't help much, but a priest, of all people, did: Father Bryan over at St. Paul's in River Hill, his family's church, invited Nick to begin meeting with him once a week. Slowly but surely, the priest roused him from his malaise and urged him to consider how he might still be of use to the world, if not as a performer.

"So I started thinking," Nick said now, his voice strong again, "if I couldn't be a dancer myself, maybe I could teach *other* kids how to dance. Give them the same passion I had. I can still move well enough for that. And then I thought, why stop there? Why not address their other needs, too? I mean, people look at Bergen County as this affluent place, but there's also a lower-income population here. And these kids need somewhere safe and positive to go after school. So I heard about this abandoned warehouse, I applied for a bunch of grants from the county and foundations... and here we are: the Clubhouse."

The arc of Nick's narrative left Cammy speechless. Not only was it legitimately uplifting (and "uplifting" was a word that typically made her nauseous), but it also represented the exact antithesis of her own self-absorption and self-pity. She wanted to burst into applause. Instead she said at last, "God, Nick. I can't believe you went through all that."

"Well, it had a happy ending, right? I think I'm making more of a difference here than I would shaking my booty on TV."

"Yeah. What a story, though. You should do a TED Talk or something."

"Sorry if I sounded like I was giving a fundraising speech at the end there. I slip into that sometimes out of habit."

"No, not at all. You couldn't seem fake if you tried." Stop fawning, Cammy!

"It's funny how life turns out." Nick's beguiling gaze met hers. "Like us running into each other again."

"I know, and all it took was my dad dying for it to happen." Christ, what was wrong with her? Could she have said anything more mood-killing? "Sorry, I have trouble filtering myself."

"That's okay. I respect it. How are you doing? That must be a huge loss."

"It is. He was my favorite person in the world. I'm kind of a basket case."

"You have a right to be."

"Thanks. No one else seems to think so."

Nick rested his cheek in his hand. He belonged on the cover of *GQ*. "Do you remember the last time we saw each other? In high school, I mean."

"Ugh, how could I forget?" Cammy said, her own cheeks reddening. "I confessed my puppy love to you at prom. One of the single most embarrassing moments of my life."

"It wasn't embarrassing. It was sweet."

"Then why didn't you ever call me that summer?" Ooh, shots fired.

"I wanted to."

"Sure—"

"No, I did. But I was just . . . too full of myself and my bright future. So I dropped the ball. And I regretted it."

"Okay, *now* you're bullshitting me."

"I'm not." There was that patented Nick Ramos sincerity. "And then you came up to me at the bowling alley the other night. And I thought, 'Well, here's a chance to finally hang out with Cammy. Better a decade late than never.' That's why I invited you here."

Cammy pinched her leg under the desk to make sure she wasn't daydreaming. It hurt, which meant this was real: The object of her teenage obsession, the first boy she'd ever fallen for, who'd once seemed so far out of reach, who'd since gone through hell and back and was even more attractive for it—this boy was now a grown man expressing interest in *her*. "So . . . you're single?" she asked, just to check.

"Yes," he laughed. "I'm single. I was with someone for a while, but we broke up last year."

"I was with someone too, but I fucked it up."

"You're too hard on yourself."

Cammy shrugged. Then, throwing caution to the winds—because why not?—she smiled and said, "Do you know what I used to call you in high school? When I talked about you to Fran?"

"What?"

"Beautiful Dancer Boy."

"You're kidding."

"Nope. That's who you were to me."

"And who am I now?"

"Um, Beautiful Dancer Man?"

"But I'm not really a dancer anymore."

"To me you are." And like a true rom-com heroine, Cammy got up, gingerly shut the office door (so as not to traumatize any children), came around the desk to where Nick was sitting, and kissed him flush on his full lips. In the back of her mind, she heard Fran saying, "Told you so."

The kiss was perfect. Not a sloppy, drunken, late-night smooch, like those she'd shared with Sugar Shane, but the long-awaited culmination of years of youthful yearning. And it was also more than that, because they weren't teenagers any longer; they were adults who'd experienced adult misfortunes. He'd survived a horrible accident, and she was attempting to survive the death of her father. These painful facts added depth and meaning to the kiss.

The next thing she knew, Nick was standing, Cammy was half-seated on his desk, and they were locked in a full-on make-out session. She ran a searching hand through his abundant hair—that was the word for it, abundant—then down to the small of his back, resting it on the exalted ass, whose taut firmness surpassed even her awesome expectations. Nick was caressing the side of her neck with just the ideal amount of light pressure, which drove her absolutely crazy. When his thumb grazed her earlobe, her whole body quivered. She couldn't get enough of him.

Cammy felt desire welling up within her—desire that was somehow amplified by her grief. Sex and death, intermingled always. She wanted Nick badly, immediately. Pulling away, she said, "Do you wanna come over?"

"Come over where?"

"To my house."

"When?"

"Now."

"*Now?*"

"Yeah, can you get away?"

"I mean—maybe for a little. But aren't you staying with your mom?"

"She went out today. Hold on." Cammy grabbed her phone and called the old landline at the house to see if her mother were there. No answer. She was probably still at the attorney's office, plotting her lawsuit. "She's not home. The coast is clear."

Nick hesitated. "Cammy—"

"What?"

"This is exciting, but . . . I don't wanna take things too fast."

"I do," she said, kissing him again. "Come on."

♦ 12 ♦

They drove over to the house in Nick's Kia electric car. (Of course he had an electric car.) Cammy took his hand and led him upstairs to her room. She guided him onto the small twin bed with its night-sky sheets and straddled him, as Joan Didion, Patti Smith, and Thelma and Louise watched with approval from their posters on the wall.

"I'm sorry if this is weird," she said.

"What?"

"That we're in my childhood room right now. Being here makes me feel stunted."

"I get it. I felt the same way when I had to move home from college."

"It's like I'm right back where I started."

"You're not, though," Nick said. "You're here for a reason." Death, namely. "Sad things bring us home."

"I guess that's true." Cammy interlaced her fingers with his. "And there is a kind of poetic logic to us being on this bed."

"Why?"

"'Cause this is the place where I used to moon over you."

Nick chuckled. "'Moon.' That's a funny word."

"It's what I did. For a significant portion of high school."

"Over me? That's wild." The adorable modesty again! "Well . . . now I'm really here."

"I'm glad you're really here."

As Cammy yanked off her sweater, she remembered she was wearing a functional, unsexy beige bra. Oh, well; that would be off soon too, hopefully. But when she went to remove Nick's T-shirt, he stopped her.

"What's wrong?"

"Nothing. It's just . . ." He sighed. "There are scars. From the accident."

"I don't care."

"You don't? Some people get freaked out."

"Fuck those people."

Cammy lifted Nick's shirt gently over his head, revealing a toned torso, complete with six-pack abs, marked by several pinkish scars where stitches once had been. It turned out the chiseled Adonis had a body as vulnerable as any mere mortal's. She tenderly kissed each scar and felt him growing hard. For some reason, the look and feel of an erection bulging through nylon warm-up pants really did it for her. Human sexuality is a mysterious thing.

Thanks to the comical lack of space on the bed, she had to contort herself awkwardly to slide his pants down. (This would make a good Marx Brothers routine, she mused.) She liked that he was letting her take the lead. A long, jagged scar ran down his right leg, which must've been the one that had borne the brunt of the crash.

Cammy stood up to unbutton her jeans, bending to avoid smacking her head on the ceiling. Below her Nick lay in his snug black briefs, beautiful as ever—even more so with his new, human flaws. She wished she could teleport back in time to tell her seventeen-year-old self that her far-fetched fantasies would one day come true.

Tossing the jeans aside, she lowered her body onto his and slipped her hand into his briefs. Which prompted him to ask, responsibly, "Do you have a condom?"

"Oh shit. Do I? Wait, no, I think I do." She rolled to the side of the bed and reached to open the bottom drawer of her night table, where, in high school, she'd kept forbidden items she didn't want her mom to discover. Happily, buried under a mound of receipts and other camouflage was a trusty old pack of Trojans she hadn't touched in years. "Voilà!"

She was about to unwrap one when she heard the worst sound imaginable: the front door opening downstairs. "Oh my God. Oh my God."

"What?"

"I think my mom's home."

Nick sprung up like a jack-in-the-box. "Are you serious?"

"Yes, I'm serious! Get dressed!"

They leapt off the bed in a blur of panicked motion, throwing on pants and shirts as quickly as they could manage. Cammy heard herself mutter, "This is like a bad movie," which it totally was; horny teens in a stupid sex comedy might've found themselves in just such a predicament. But she and Nick were grown-ups, so the situation was all the more mortifying.

"Cammy?" Beth called from below. "Are you home?"

"Yeah, Mom!" She shoved the condoms back in the drawer. "I'm up here!" Now she could hear her mother's heels clacking up the stairs. She whispered to Nick, "Can you hide in my closet or something?"

"I'm not hiding in a closet," he said with dignity.

"I am *so* sorry about this."

"You didn't know she was coming home?"

"I thought she'd be back later. I don't know, I was caught up in the moment. Oh God, this is a nightmare—"

The door opened then, and Beth entered to find her daughter standing in her room with the lights off and the curtains drawn, next to a man in warm-up pants whom she didn't know. She nearly jumped in shock.

"Hi, Mom," Cammy said, switching on a lamp. Her ruse was to act normal. "This is, uh, my friend Nick."

"Who? What's going on?"

"Nick Ramos, from high school. Don't you remember—he was the one who danced at all the talent shows?"

"Hello, Mrs. Adler," Nick murmured, as respectfully as possible under the circumstances. "I'm sorry for your loss."

Beth regained her composure and appeared to be putting two and two together. "So this explains the Kia parked out front. What's your *friend* doing here?"

"Oh, we were just . . . catching up. We ran into each other the other night, so—You know, Nick actually runs this great community center in Hackensack, the Clubhouse?"

Her mom was too sharp to be distracted by this digression. "You were catching up in the dark?"

"I forgot to turn on the light."

"Mm-hmm."

"I should probably be getting back," Nick said, inching toward the door to make a hasty exit. "Call me, Cammy, okay?"

"Yeah. Okay. Bye, Nick."

"Take care, Mrs. Adler." This elicited no response. Taking the hint, he slunk past her, down the stairs, and out of the house.

Mother and daughter regarded one another in stony silence. Whatever the female version of blue balls was, Cammy had it big-time. She'd been so close to consummating with Beautiful Dancer Boy, only to have the encounter end in the most utterly humiliating manner. Just her luck. How could she face him again after this? Well, she'd worry about that later. Right now she had her mom to reckon with.

"So I go out for *one* afternoon," Beth said, "and you bring someone here to sleep with?"

"That's not what it was," Cammy lied through her teeth. "He's an old friend. I haven't seen him since high school. We were . . . reconnecting."

"Is that why there's a condom on the floor?" Indeed, one stray Trojan that Cammy had overlooked was lying near the night table. Dammit. "You really don't have any respect, do you? For me, for the shiva—"

"Mom, I'm not getting into another fight with you about the shiva." She sank down onto the bed. "And I'm sorry for trying to *enjoy* myself and release some *stress*, okay? I wasn't expecting you to walk in on us. Also, Nick happens to be a genuinely good guy, so—"

"I don't care . . . I don't care . . ." Out of nowhere, Beth began to cry.

Caught off guard, Cammy felt a stab of conscience. A middle-aged widow weeping in a pantsuit is enough to stir anyone's sympathy. "Mom, you don't have to get that upset about it. So I brought a guy home. It's not the end of the world—"

"Craig said there's no case."

"What?"

"Craig Rosen. The lawyer." That she wasn't crying about the Nick thing was some relief. "I met with him, I brought all the paperwork from the rehab place, I told him what happened with Dad. And he said they probably screwed up, but there's not enough evidence for a lawsuit." Beth pulled a crumpled tissue out of her purse and dabbed at her mascara-streaked eyes. "You know what that means? There'll never be any justice for Dad. He died when he shouldn't have, and no one'll ever be held accountable."

Cammy knew how much angry energy her mother had invested in this lawsuit idea, and how much of a blow it must've been to have litigious Craig Rosen shoot her down. Now her husband's needless death, less than a week after a routine surgery, would forever go unpunished. "Mom," she said softly, "just let it go."

"Let it go?"

"The lawsuit wasn't really gonna fix anything anyway. You'd still have the guilt."

"What guilt?"

"You know, that—that—"

"That what?"

"That Dad died on your watch." By the time Cammy registered the terrible words she'd spoken, it was too late.

Beth looked as if her knees might buckle. Her face was a mask of anguish. "What did you say?"

"Nothing. I didn't mean to—"

"Is that what you think? That I *let* Dad die? That I could've somehow prevented it? I did the best I could when I saw he wasn't doing well, but that idiot nurse"—Nurse Helen, whom she'd reamed out yesterday—"wouldn't listen to me."

"I know, Mom—"

"But you still blame me, don't you?"

Did Cammy blame her mother for her dad's passing? She hadn't confronted the ugly question until now. On a rational level, of course not: The fault likely lay with the inattentive staff at CarePlus, who'd ignored Cy's rapid decline from pneumonia and allowed him to wither away in a matter of days. But on a deeper level, some part of her maybe did feel, however illogically, that her mom should have done a better job of protecting him.

"You weren't even there," Beth said, as though she'd read her daughter's mind.

"What?"

"You didn't even come visit him after the surgery. So you don't have a right to say anything."

"Mom, I was in the city—"

"Right. The city. Living your busy city life."

"I *do* have a busy city life. And you told me Dad was just recovering and he was gonna be home in a few days! I didn't know he was gonna die!"

"Well, he did die, and you're going to have to live with that."

"Live with what?"

"That you didn't see him one last time when you had the chance."

"Wow. Wow." Cammy shot up and paced the length of her cramped room, kicking the telltale condom under the bed. "You're guilt-tripping me for *this* now? That is so fucked up!"

"No, you know what's fucked up? How you're acting this week."

"Mom, don't start with this again—"

"Every day it's something else. Smoking weed, getting drunk, getting arrested—"

"All right—"

"Today it's bringing a boy home for sex!"

"Well, you did a swell job interrupting that, so thank you."

"You know this house is supposed to be a sacred place during shiva?"

"And that precludes intercourse?"

Beth shook her head in disgust. She reached back into her purse, dug out her bottle of Ativan, and took a pill without any water to wash it down. "You know, the rabbi called me a couple hours ago. He said he ran into you on Main Street."

"What, am I being *surveilled* now?"

"He said he tried to talk to you again, but you blew him off."

"Yes, Mom, I did."

"Why?"

"'Cause I don't want his help."

"You need *someone's* help, because you're out of control."

"No," Cammy cried, "I just need everyone to get off my case so I can grieve in my own way!"

"What about me?" Beth pleaded. "How am *I* supposed to grieve when you're behaving like this? I can't take it anymore."

"Neither can I! So I'll leave!"

Cammy was too frazzled at this point to even grasp what she and her mom were really fighting about. All she knew was that they couldn't get along, they couldn't cope with their loss together, and she had to get out of here before things grew even worse. She snatched her backpack off the floor and started refilling it with the clothes and toiletries she'd retrieved from her apartment on Sunday.

"Where are you going?"

"I don't know. Out. Maybe I'll spend the night at Fran's."

"You promised you'd stay for the shiva tonight."

"Oops."

"People will be here in an hour."

"You can send them my regards."

Beth took a heavy step forward and spoke in an icy voice that her daughter barely recognized. "If you leave again now, don't bother coming back."

Cammy stopped her frantic packing and looked up. "What?"

"I'd rather you not come back."

"You mean *ever*? Are you disowning me?"

"I mean for the rest of the shiva. You're making this impossible for me."

What an ultimatum: to be exiled from the official mourning ritual for your own father. But wasn't this what she'd craved all along? "Space" to grieve on her own terms? So why, now that it had been offered, did she feel so ambivalent? Be careful what you wish for.

Still, Cammy obstinately decided to call her mom's bluff. "Fine. It's probably for the best."

As Beth turned to leave the room, she must've noticed the Polaroid sitting on the night table—the unearthed photo of young Cy and the blond mystery woman ("C & D, 6/14/78")—because she said with suspicion, "What's that doing up here?"

"I was looking at it."

"Why?"

"'Cause I don't think you told me the whole truth about who that woman is."

"What are you talking about?"

"A college girlfriend? That's all?"

"Yes."

"What made Dad save this picture all these years?"

"I have no idea," her mother said stiffly, like a coached witness on the stand.

"Oh, really? Then why were you showing it to Aunt Miriam the other night? I saw you two having some kind of secret conference in the dining room. Looked pretty intense." Checkmate. "You're a bad liar, Mom."

"So are you." And Beth was gone, off to wash her tear-stained face and reapply her makeup before the evening's guests arrived with their condolences.

Cammy slid her weathered MacBook into the laptop compartment of her backpack and tossed in the perplexing Polaroid, too. She didn't know what her next move would be. The only objective was to escape from the house and the shiva and the escalating psychodrama with her mother.

Which is precisely what she did.

Outside, the air was cool and crisp. A lovely, leafy late afternoon. It was five o'clock, the liminal hour when briefcase-toting commuters began to return from the city to reunite with their happy families. At least that was the Norman Rockwell ideal. How many other households on Hill Avenue were trapped in their own psychodramas behind closed doors? Probably plenty.

Having been banished from her home, Cammy wondered whether she shouldn't just head back to her "busy city life," as her mom had contemptuously called it. She had a temp gig in Midtown starting Monday, four days from now. But who was in the city waiting for her? Nobody. No boyfriend. No more Drama Collective. The loneliness of the coming weekend would be crushing. (Yet didn't she *want* to be left alone? Oh, the self-contradiction!)

When it came down to it, the only real friend she had in the world at this moment was Fran. And Fran resided right here in River Hill, in an apartment complex across town. Yes, loyal, straight-talking, nonjudgmental Fran was the person she needed to turn to.

Cammy would send her an SOS soon.

First, though, there was one piece of unsettled business to deal with: the photograph of her father and D that had ignited her curiosity and that was currently burning a hole in her JanSport. Cammy felt sure that her mom was hiding something about the woman in the picture—but what, and why? And now that her dad's lips were sealed for good, who could help her get to the bottom of it?

With a wince, she realized who: her father's sole sibling, the often insufferable Aunt Miriam.

♦ 13 ♦

It's not nice to call people cat ladies, but if one were being honest, Aunt Miriam did fit the mold. Since her drawn-out divorce from André, the Moroccan Jewish con artist, in the nineties, she'd turned her back on the male species and transferred her affections to felines. She adopted them as pets, volunteered on their behalf, sent daily images and videos of them to everyone in her contact list. Cats became her world. After André, who could blame her?

Miriam couldn't have been more different from her older brother, physically and otherwise. Cy had dark hair; hers was ginger red. He was easygoing and quick to laugh; she was tightly wound and prone to tears. He knew how to navigate life; she needed help with just about everything. It was hard to believe they'd come from the same set of parents, to the point that Cy had occasionally joked (in his sister's absence) that Miriam may have been the product of an illicit affair between their mother, Ruth, and a redheaded friend of the family named Mr. Kornfeld.

As annoying as Cammy found her aunt, she knew she was the one person who might be able to shed some light on the identity of D, the Polaroid apparition. So she gritted her teeth and speed-walked twenty minutes to Palisades Park, another small borough that bordered River Hill, hoping to catch her before she left for the shiva. Miriam lived there with her kitties on the first floor of a brick two-family house and worked in the main office of the town's elementary school. It was important that she have a job close to home, as highway driving terrified her.

Cammy rang the doorbell, and her aunt answered in a puffy, salmon-colored housecoat. (Was that what the anachronistic garment was called?) Miriam was sixty-one, seven years younger than her late brother, but a lifetime of worry had aged her prematurely, giving her skin a prune-like texture. She blinked behind her thick glasses, thrown by Cammy's surprise appearance, then said in a whining voice, "Well, hi, sweetie."

"Hi, Aunt Miriam. Sorry for just showing up like this."

"No, no, that's okay. Is everything all right?"

No, it wasn't, but her aunt didn't need to know that. "Yeah. I was actually, uh, running some errands in Pal Park"—a feeble fib—"and I thought I'd drop by. There's something I wanna ask you about, if you have a sec."

"Sure. Of course. I always have time for my favorite niece."

"I'm your only niece."

"Come in, come in. It's cold out." Miriam ushered Cammy into her apartment, which was less a dwelling place for a human being than a play palace for cats. Toys were strewn all over the floor—fluffy balls, stuffed mice, scratch pads—and the place smelled like a giant litter box. The TV was tuned to Animal Planet; what else? "I didn't see you at the shiva last night."

"I had a meeting in the city I couldn't get out of," Cammy fibbed again.

"How awful that they wouldn't let you miss it for your father's shiva."

"I know. Heartless."

"Here, have a seat." Miriam motioned to a hideous green sofa covered in cat hair. "Can I get you anything? Do you want some cottage cheese and fruit?" She always offered this particular snack, and Cammy always turned it down; cottage cheese grossed her out.

"No, thank you."

"How about some seltzer?" Her standard follow-up.

"Nope. I'm good."

"Well, you let me know if you get hungry. I have plenty of fresh fruit in the fridge." Miriam joined Cammy on the hairy sofa and called to her two current cats: "Honey! Princess!" No sign of either. "They're hiding, silly babies. Honey has diabetes now, but I give her insulin shots, and she's doing much better."

"I'm glad to hear that."

Her aunt lowered the volume on the TV, where elephants were frolicking at a zoo. "So. What did you wanna ask me about?"

Cammy unzipped her backpack and produced the Polaroid. "This." When Miriam saw the faded picture of her brother with the blond woman—he in his striped seventies suit, she in the white Stevie Nicks dress, arms linked—her face blanched. "I found it in a box of my dad's things. At the bottom." Cammy flipped the photo around. "On the back, it says 'C and D, 6/14/78.' I asked my mom who D was, and she said a college girlfriend of my dad's, but she acted weird about it. Then I saw you guys looking at this and whispering at the shiva the other night . . ."

Miriam put a hand to her mouth. "You did?"

"Yeah. You weren't very stealthy. So I thought you might be able to explain."

Her aunt's eyes moistened. She could cry at the drop of a hat. "Oh my."

"Oh my?"

"For the life of me, I still don't know why Cy kept that picture."

"Who is it? Who's the woman?"

"That's—Debra." Finally, a name to put to the delicate, enigmatic visage.

"Debra? So *was* she my dad's girlfriend, or—"

"Yes. Well, at first."

"What do you mean 'at first'?"

"At first she was his girlfriend." Miriam paused and reached for a box of Kleenex that was decorated with dancing cats. "And then she was—Oh, I shouldn't be telling you this."

"Yes, you should. And then she was *what*?"

"His . . . his wife."

"Sorry?"

"Debra was your father's first wife." She couldn't hold back any longer; here came the waterworks. "That picture is from their wedding reception . . ."

Cammy heard the words, but they sounded like stock lines from a bad soap opera. Her father's first wife? He hadn't had a first wife. He'd had *one* wife: Beth, her mother. What the fuck was this nonsense? "Aunt Miriam—"

"I know, sweetie. I know it must be a shock to you."

"A *shock*? Um, no, it's the craziest thing I've ever heard. You're saying—You're telling me my dad was . . . married before?"

"Yes."

"For how long?"

"Eight years."

"*Eight years*? Did he have other kids? Do I have siblings?"

"No. No kids."

"Okay, this is ridiculous."

"It's true."

"Fine, let's say it *is* true," Cammy said, humoring her aunt, playing along with her stupid joke. "Does my mom know about this alleged 'marriage'? Does *she* know she was my dad's second wife?"

"She knows."

"Then—then why don't *I* know? Why wouldn't they tell me this?"

Miriam blew her nose loudly. "I think because it was a very bad chapter in your father's life, and he wanted to put it behind him. Your mother respected that. So did I. But now he's gone"—sniffle—"and you found this picture, and you're asking me about it, so I'm telling you. I'm sorry, sweetie . . ."

As the diabetic Honey, an orange tabby, crept into the room from the kitchen, it dawned on Cammy that this was no mere flight of fancy from her eccentric aunt. Characteristic blubbering aside, Miriam clearly was speaking the truth: Her dad had had a first marriage she'd never known about, and he and her mom had deliberately kept her in the dark.

Which meant—

Cammy was so flabbergasted, she could hardly consider all the implications.

How could her father—her best bud, her partner in crime, her number-one guy—have hidden such a huge chunk of his history from her? Did this mean they weren't really as close as she'd believed? And what about her mother's willing complicity in the omission? Was the plan for everyone to just take this information to their graves, leaving Cammy forever ignorant of Cy's real life story?

"But I don't get it," she said to her aunt. "What's even the big deal about a first marriage? Why keep it a secret? How bad could it have been that my dad needed to, like, Never Speak of It Again?"

"Oh, it was bad," Miriam said in a tone reserved for discussing wars and other such calamities. "It was hell. It almost destroyed him."

"Destroyed?"

"That's right."

What on earth could have nearly destroyed vibrant, optimistic, laughter-loving Cy Adler? "Can you be any more specific?"

"You don't wanna hear about this, sweetie."

"Actually, I do."

"It's sad, and so far in the past . . ."

"It's my dad. It's his life. I have to know. Tell me. Please." Cammy tossed in a bit of manipulation for good measure: "As a favor to your favorite niece."

The ultimate soft touch, Miriam acquiesced. Armed with her cat-themed Kleenex box, she launched into a mournful account of her brother's doomed first marriage. Honey, timid no longer, leapt onto Cammy's lap to listen too.

"They met at City College in the seventies. In a literature class, I think. Two smart Jewish kids from families without a lot of money. Your father was commuting from Hoboken. Studying English." As his daughter one day would. "Debra—her last name was Baron—"

"How do you spell that?"

"Why?"

"Just curious." For future googling.

"B-A-R-O-N. She was commuting from Brooklyn. Crown Heights. A sociology major. She was bright and pretty. Your father was confident and charming. They fell in love, or they thought they did. That's how it worked back then. City College was kind of a mating ground for smart Jewish kids. Then, senior year . . . Debra got pregnant."

"Oh."

So, Miriam explained, a few weeks after graduation, the couple were married at Hoboken City Hall. June fourteenth, 1978. The Polaroid was snapped during their modest reception at an Italian restaurant in town. No wonder Debra's expression had a trace of ambivalence; she and her new husband were twenty-one and expecting a baby. A shotgun wedding hadn't been part of either of their plans. They were in over their heads.

Soon after they moved in together, to a shoebox of a studio up in Hamilton Heights, by the City College campus, Debra miscarried.

"At first they were just very sad," Miriam said. "We all were. And then they started fighting. And they never stopped."

"Fighting about what?" Cammy asked.

"Everything," her aunt said. Money was one issue. Cy was an overworked, underpaid junior account executive at a Waspy Madison Avenue ad agency, Debra a burned-out social worker in the Bronx, and they were perennially strapped for cash. They clashed with their in-laws as well, turning family gatherings into anxiety-ridden ordeals. Above all, they fought because they weren't really compatible—they'd gotten married prematurely in response to a pregnancy that quickly ceased to be—but they were both too stubborn, and too bound by middle-class Jewish social and familial expectations, to admit defeat and let each other go.

This conjugal "hell," as Aunt Miriam described it, stretched on for eight agonizing years, to the baffled horror of outside observers. Debra came to despise Cy's irreverent disposition; she called him unserious, a lightweight. He said she was cold, humorless, remote. There were heated arguments in public places, accusations of affairs, nights spent apart, with Cy holed up in a cheap Manhattan hotel. There was, somehow, another pregnancy too, though this one Debra chose to terminate, informing her distraught husband only after the fact.

The final straw occurred at a Passover Seder, where the assembled Adlers and Barons watched in dread as Cy and Debra consumed several glasses of Manischewitz wine and engaged in a knock-down, drag-out screaming match across the ceremonial table. She brandished a butter knife. It was like a Strindberg play in Brooklyn. A downstairs neighbor of Debra's parents heard the racket and called the NYPD, who showed up to check on the situation.

At last, the point of no return had been reached.

"It was a horrible scene," Miriam said, shuddering at the memory.

"Then what happened?" Cammy said, dazed by all she'd just learned. Honey was nipping at her fingers to comfort her.

"They got a divorce, like they should have in the first place."

"Where did my dad go?"

"He moved back in with Grandma Ruth in Hoboken."

"When was this?"

"Oh . . . '86, I guess. Your father must've been twenty-nine." Cammy's age now. "He was broken. I couldn't bear to see him like that."

"Broken how?"

"He blamed himself for the whole thing. He was sick with guilt about the marriage. He thought he'd made a mess of his life." Like his daughter today. "It took him a few years to put himself back together and start over."

"And what about Debra?"

Miriam shook her head. "I don't know what happened to her. I heard she moved away, but that was a long time ago." She picked up the Polaroid and studied her former sister-in-law's face. "Poor Debra. She looked so lovely that day. But she wasn't a happy person. And I don't think she liked me very much."

This last remark made Cammy chuckle involuntarily. "Sorry. Thank you for telling me all that. I'm . . . I'm pretty stunned."

"Of course you are, sweetie."

"I mean, how could my dad have kept this from me? I thought I knew everything about him."

"He wasn't *keeping* it from you. He didn't want to dwell on the past. It was painful for him. He wanted a clean slate. He met your mother, they had you, and he never looked back." Setting the Kleenex down, Miriam smiled. "You know what he used to say to me?"

"What?"

"He'd say, 'Sis, I'm the luckiest guy in the world. I got to have a second act.'" Miriam pinched her niece's cheek, the quintessential gesture of an aunt. "*You* were his second act."

Petting Honey, who'd now become her emotional support animal, Cammy tried to make sense of the contradictory feelings coursing through her.

On the one hand, she was, yes, stunned by the revelation of her dad's disastrous marriage to Debra, and hurt that her parents had concealed it from her. She'd always assumed her father had simply been an inveterate New York bachelor who'd married late when he met the right woman. But no, that wasn't the truth at all. How had he spent those wilderness years after the divorce, before he "put himself back together"? What else didn't she know about him?

On the other hand, the story of Cy's early misfortune and his bouncing back from brokenness gave Cammy a strange sort of hope. Wasn't it F. Scott Fitzgerald who'd famously written, "There are no second acts in American lives"? Well, her dad had proven old F. Scott wrong: He'd found peace and gone on to enjoy three decades with a wife and child he adored. Could his daughter emerge from her own fucked-up first act and follow in his footsteps?

Cammy lifted Honey off her lap. The cat meowed in protest. "I should go, Aunt Miriam."

"Oh. Okay. Do you wanna take any fruit?"

"No, thanks."

"I hope this wasn't too much for you."

"It was a lot. But I needed to know."

"Maybe don't tell your mother I told you? Not yet, anyway."

"I won't." Cammy did have one final question: "So what *were* you and my mom talking about the other night?"

"Whether we should try to track Debra down. To call her up and let her know about your father." Just as Cammy had guessed from the fragment she'd overheard.

"And did you?"

"No. We decided it was better to let sleeping dogs lie." An animal idiom, fittingly.

"You think she's still around, though?"

Miriam shrugged. "I assume she is. I'm really not sure. It's been so long." She followed her niece to the door. "Hey, why don't I give you a ride to the shiva, sweetie?"

"That's all right. I'll see you over there," Cammy fibbed once more, returning the photograph to her backpack—the picture that was the last tangible remnant of Cy and Debra's ill-fated union.

The moment she stepped outside, Cammy opened her phone and googled "Debra Baron Adler." She got goose bumps when the top search result appeared: Whitepages.com. She clicked on the link and found a listing for a Debra B. Adler, age sixty-eight, in, of all places, Portland, Maine. If this were indeed the same person, then she'd apparently fled to the corner of the country, with its lobsters and lighthouses, to get away from *her* fraught first act.

There was a phone number on the page. It seemed to float off the screen like a ghost. Who knew if it was correct or not? Sites like this one could be hit or miss.

Impulsively—because impulsiveness was becoming her brand these days—Cammy decided to find out for herself. She sat down on a sidewalk bench and dialed, without any clear purpose or plan other than to verify Debra's identity and see what the interaction yielded.

Why let sleeping dogs lie when you can wake them up?

After three long rings, an older woman's clipped, wary voice answered. "Hello?"

Cammy started. Should she hang up? No, don't chicken out now. "Hi. Is this—is this Debra?"

"Who's calling?"

"Um—"

"Are you a telemarketer? I'm on the no-call list. You're not supposed to be calling me."

"No, I'm not a—I'm . . . Cammy Adler. Cy Adler's daughter. Are you . . . the Debra he was . . ." She trailed off before saying the superfluous "married to."

A heavy silence, during which Cammy recognized this was yet another spectacularly bad idea.

"Is this a joke?" Debra said in a brittle tone that betrayed a life that had been neither easy nor pleasant.

"No—"

"Why are you calling me?"

"I'm just calling to let you know . . . he passed away Saturday. I—I thought you might wanna know."

More silence. Then Debra said, with a harsh coldness that took Cammy aback, "Why would I want to know that?"

She couldn't believe what she'd heard. The callousness of Debra's response to her dad's death was so startling that she felt instantly on the verge of tears. Angry retorts materialized in her mind: *Why would you want to know? Because he was once your husband? Because he was my father? Because maybe you could have a shred of decency and empathy?* But she didn't have a right to be angry; Debra hadn't asked for this, and Cammy had set herself up by initiating the careless call.

"I told Miriam forty years ago, I didn't want anything more to do with that family," Debra said, her bitterness poking through the speaker like sharp little needles. "You shouldn't have called me." That was evident. "Don't do it again. I'll report you for harassment."

Harassment? Surely a single phone call didn't qualify, and Cammy certainly wasn't about to do it again. She did have something left to say, though. "Look, I'm sorry I bothered you. I know you and my dad had a—a hard time. But he was a good man. He was. And I honestly don't understand how you can still have so much resentment that you'd—"

Beep-beep-beep.

Debra had hung up. Possibly the one living soul who held a grudge against Cy Adler, for the domestic strife of four decades ago. She was gone, along with her festering rancor and, more hauntingly, her side of the story, which Cammy now realized she would never know.

★ ★ ★

Summoned by text, Fran swooped to the rescue in her bright yellow Volkswagen Golf hatchback, whose loud color often drew stares and comments from strangers. She picked Cammy up in Palisades Park and drove to one of their favorite former hangouts, the Tick Tock Diner, a glowing neon temple built in the 1940s. They'd had many a serious conversation here in their day.

Over burgers, gravy-and-cheese-covered disco fries, and milkshakes—heart health be damned—Cammy filled Fran in on all that had transpired since she'd left the deli after lunch: The visit to the Clubhouse. Hearing about Nick's car accident and almost having sex with him. ("What was his dick like?" Fran asked, inevitably. "I didn't get to see it," Cammy said, to her friend's disappointment. "But it felt nice.") The blowout with her mother and her subsequent expulsion from the house.

Cammy chose *not* to mention what Aunt Miriam had just revealed about her father's past, or the tense call with Debra that had followed. This was too fresh, too personal, too complicated to share with anyone yet, even her closest confidant. She would bury it for now, like a relic in the dirt to be retrieved later on.

"Shit," Fran said, shaking some loose gravy off a drenched fry. "Eventful afternoon."

"Yeah."

"Must've felt amazing to make out with Nick."

"It did."

"Sucks about you and your mom, though."

"It does."

"You know, it's like . . . your dad was the glue that held you two together. And without him, you fall apart."

It was a trite metaphor—literary flair wasn't Fran's forte—but accurate nonetheless: Somehow the Adler family unit had worked as a trio, but as a duo, it failed miserably.

Cammy remembered a specific time during her teenage years when she and her mother had had a squabble over something trivial and stopped speaking to each other. Every night for a week, they sat at dinner and didn't say a word. Cy tried to get them talking again, to no avail. Finally, one evening, he stood up from the table, took a piece of notepaper out of his pocket, and started singing (off-key) a humorous song he'd written called "The Silence Is Killing Me." His wife and daughter laughed so hard at his shtick that it shattered the tension between them and ended their standoff then and there.

That was the glue, and now it was gone.

"Can I crash at your place tonight?" Cammy asked.

"For sure. But I'm leaving for A.C. in the morning—" Fran halted midsentence, as if one of those cartoon light bulbs had flashed on above her head. "Wait—you can come with me now, can't you?"

"Yeah . . . I guess I can."

"What do you mean you guess?" Fran said, kicking into gear. "Girls' trip down to A.C.? Have some fun, blow off some steam? Doesn't that sound awesome?"

"It kinda does," Cammy admitted, though she knew that a jaunt to Atlantic City less than a week after your dad's death was unorthodox, to say the least. But who made the rules of "proper" grieving, and who said she had to abide by them?

"It'll be sweet. We'll hit the boardwalk, gamble a little, have some good meals. Check out the strip club—"

"Do we have to check out the strip club?"

"Come on. Don't be lame. The guys who dance there know me. I'm a VIP. I can't go to A.C. without stopping by the club."

"Okay, then."

Fran slurped her chocolate milkshake. She was getting excited. "This is just what you need, you know? Get away, clear your head, breathe in that sea air . . ."

"I'll be breathing in more than sea air on that gross boardwalk."

"It's not gross! It has *character*." Fran added earnestly, "We'll get to spend more time together than we have in a while."

"That's true."

"We'll be like Thelma and Louise on the run."

On the run. It was an apt phrase. Cammy may not have been a fugitive like that iconic pair, but she too was on the run—from her mom, from her grief, and, most of all, from herself.

Day Five: Friday

♦ 14 ♦

In Jersey, you don't "go to the beach." You don't "visit the coast."

You go down the shore.

Cammy had always thought of the Jersey Shore as a state of mind as much as a physical place. Every summer growing up, she'd heard those immortal words—"We're goin' down the shore"—from too many people to count. But what the words signified wasn't just a trip to Asbury Park, Cape May, Ocean City, or one of the other beachy towns that dot the coastline. No, these words evoked a whole world of sensations: warm sand, salt water, boardwalks teeming with bodies, carnival music, ice-cold Coronas, hamburgers and hot dogs sizzling on the grill.

Then, when Cammy was in middle school, the eponymous MTV reality show came on the air and turned the Jersey Shore into a national laughingstock. That was a drag.

But now, years later, she was goin' down the shore again, zipping along the Garden State Parkway in Fran's yellow Volkswagen, fleeing the clusterfuck of grief back home. As they drove, her troubles seemed to recede in the rearview mirror. Which didn't mean they were gone—only that they were temporarily out of sight.

Fran had put on Blondie's *Greatest Hits* on Spotify. Debbie Harry, another of Cammy's punk rock heroes, was lamenting her heart of glass over a disco beat.

"So, uh . . . do you wanna talk about anything?" Fran asked.

"Like what?" Cammy said, deliberately obtuse.

"Like how you're feeling, or . . ."

"I'm fine." Just keep telling yourself that. "I mean, I know this isn't what I *should* be doing right now, but what I should be doing doesn't help, so . . . Anyway, my dad would get it."

"Should you maybe text your mom, at least, to tell her where you're going?"

"My mom doesn't wanna hear from me. She's fed up."

"Okay." Fran took her eyes off the road to glance over with concern. "But if you *do* wanna talk, about your dad or whatever else, I'm here."

"Thanks. I know." Desperate to deflect the conversation from anything raw or painful, Cammy turned up the radio and said, "Hey, who do you think's cooler, Debbie Harry or Patti Smith?" They often quizzed each other with these kinds of pop-culture matchups.

Fran got the message: This wasn't the moment to probe.

So they filled the time in the car by listening to music they loved, gazing out at the open highway, and bantering about nothing, in the way best friends can do.

When they passed exit 82 for Seaside Heights, Fran sat up and smiled. "Shit. There it is."

"Historic landmark," Cammy said, saluting the green sign overhead.

"You remember that weekend?"

"Yes. It was insane."

"It was epic."

The weekend in question was the one after prom, which they'd spent in Seaside with much of their senior class.

Everyone stayed in trashy oceanfront motels and got as drunk and high as humanly possible over the course of two debauched nights. (Cammy was still reeling from her dance-floor confession of love to Nick, so she hit the Bacardi extra hard.) By some divine miracle, nobody succumbed to alcohol poisoning.

Cammy did get a scare at one point, though, when she lost sight of Fran at the Casino Pier amusement park. She wandered around stoned, dizzy from all the garish lights and the pulsing sounds of the arcade, searching in vain for her friend. Fran resurfaced hours later back at their motel, tripping balls. It was difficult to draw a coherent story out of her, but the gist seemed to be that she'd gone off to a house party with a group of strangers and taken ecstasy.

"I can't believe you did that," Cammy said now, shaking her head. "No one knew where you were."

"I went on an adventure."

"You could've gotten killed."

"But I didn't."

"That's your takeaway?"

"Oh, and what about when we saw Snooki?!"

"Oh yeah! I totally forgot about that!"

Yes, it was true: Cammy, Fran, and some of their classmates had actually spotted Nicole "Snooki" Polizzi, at the height of her spray-tanned fame, on the boardwalk at Seaside. (She was shooting the ill-conceived *Jersey Shore* spin-off *Snooki & Jwoww* at the time.) Surrounded by an MTV film crew, she'd stopped to curse out a random guy who'd heckled her. Both appeared extremely inebriated, exchanging creative variations of "Go fuck yourself!" A beefy bodyguard intervened before punches could be thrown.

As they cracked up over the absurd memory, Cammy registered how good it felt to laugh—to really *laugh*—with Fran. Traveling the roads of Jersey together, reminiscing about old times: This was how their decades-long friendship thrived.

They were just sixty miles from A.C., and she was glad she'd agreed to come along. In spite of everything—her dad's absence, her mom's disgust, her own existential confusion—she was going to have some fucking fun this weekend, if it was the last thing she did.

★ ★ ★

"The World's Playground."

This had been Atlantic City's nickname during its heyday in the early twentieth century. Back in that golden age, A.C. boasted grand luxury hotels, the nation's first-ever boardwalk (seven miles long!), and its very own patented candy: saltwater taffy (no actual salt water included). Vacationers arrived by train in droves. Socialites hobnobbed with gangsters. In the swanky nightclubs, jazz bands played and bootleg liquor flowed.

Cammy knew this stuff, incidentally, not because she was a regional historian, but because she'd watched all five seasons of the HBO series *Boardwalk Empire* with her dad in high school. The dynamite combination of a *Sopranos*-pedigreed creator, a Scorsese-directed pilot, and the scintillating Prohibition-era subject matter had made the show must-see viewing for both father and daughter.

In the latter half of the century, tourism to A.C. declined and urban decay set in, so, ingeniously, the state of New Jersey revitalized the city by legalizing gambling within its limits. From the late seventies onward, flashy casinos began popping up along the boardwalk: Caesars, Bally's, Harrah's, the Tropicana. And as hoped, the people returned.

If you build it, they will come.

Cammy had all this colorful background in mind as Fran pulled into a spot in a parking structure next to their hotel.

"We're here," Fran announced with glee. "A.C., baby!"

They climbed out of the car, stretched their legs after the two-hour drive, and fetched their bags from the trunk. It was drafty in the garage, and the sky outside was gray and overcast. October was a very strange time to be here. Cammy smelled the salty ocean. She heard the squawk of seagulls. And she saw at her feet a pinkish puddle of vomit that made her retch.

"Someone had a good time," Fran noted approvingly.

They rode down a narrow elevator that reeked of cigarette smoke, crammed next to a squat middle-aged couple who looked as if they came here way too often. A long corridor led them to the hotel's large, marble-floored lobby. Busy geometric patterns covered every surface, screaming imitation art deco.

"God, I love this place," Fran said as they headed to the front desk to check in. "I always stay here."

"What's it called again?"

"Resorts."

"What?"

"Resorts Casino Hotel."

Cammy thought she might be mishearing. "Resorts plural?"

"Yeah."

"That's a stupid name. That's like calling a place Hotels."

"I didn't make it up," Fran shrugged. "Hey, you know the theme here is 'Roaring Twenties'?"

"I kinda noticed."

"It's like that show . . ."

"*Boardwalk Empire.*"

"Pretty cool, right?"

Fran was clearly in hog heaven. For her part, Cammy wasn't sure whether she was in heaven or hell, but she resolved right there in the lobby to surrender herself to the gloriously gaudy atmosphere of Resorts [sic], to let it overtake her, to become one with it.

And what an atmosphere it was. On the way to the elevator bank, they had to pass through the casino floor, and Cammy could barely process all the sensory input: the psychedelic carpeting, the flashing lights and electronic bleats of the slot machines, the green felt tables piled with cards and chips, the spinning roulette wheels, the flying dice, the frigid air-conditioning being piped in to keep people awake, the skimpily outfitted servers (What year was this?), and, of course, the gamblers themselves—the glassy-eyed, chain-smoking, cocktail-sipping crowd planted in their chairs, waiting to hit that big jackpot.

This was the World's Playground, and Cammy felt like running amok.

But first, they went up to their surprisingly ample room (Fran had upgraded to the "Coral Junior Suite" to accommodate her friend), flopped down on their respective queen beds, and crashed for an hour. When they awoke, fresh and full of energy, they took turns showering and got ready. Cammy put on a little black dress she'd thrown in her backpack in Astoria, along with a light denim jacket to guard against the cold. Fran, who hated dresses with a passion, opted for tight black jeans, a white tank top, and a vintage leather jacket.

Hair done and makeup applied, they inspected themselves in the brightly lit bathroom mirror. They looked good.

"Rock and roll," Fran said.

★ ★ ★

Cammy's problems began at Five O'Clock Somewhere, a circular bar in the middle of the casino inspired by Jimmy Buffett's song of the same name. (The hotel also housed one of his trademark Margaritaville restaurants. The late tropical troubadour had built a brand empire.) She and Fran had decided to stop off to have a drink and figure out their itinerary.

Well, one drink quickly became two, and now they were both on their third "Loaded Landshark," which consisted of a bottle of Landshark Lager enhanced with a shot of tequila and topped with a slice of lime. They were smoking Marlboro Reds that Fran had brought with her, because, yes, you could smoke here.

The afternoon scene at the bar was what you'd expect: a rogues' gallery of A.C. diehards licking salt off the rims of their glasses as they licked the wounds of their losses at the tables. "*Wastin' away again in Margaritaville . . .*"

"I wanna play some cards," Cammy declared, sucking on a beer-and-tequila-soaked lime.

"We could play blackjack," Fran suggested.

"Blackjack's boring. I wanna play poker."

"Do you know *how* to play poker?"

"What do you mean? Of course I do. My dad taught me. He played every week for twenty years."

It was no exaggeration: Whatever else was going on, come rain or come shine, Cy had attended his Tuesday-night poker game with near-religious devotion. Cammy remembered the excitement she'd felt as a kid when he returned home after a victorious evening and let her count up his cash. She'd smooth out and neatly stack the singles, the tens and twenties, the fifties, and the coveted hundred-dollar bills, then tally them and sing out the sum. He usually had a few new dirty jokes to share too, which made Cammy double over with laughter while Beth shook her head in disapproval.

"Okay," Fran said, "but are you sure you wanna like sit down at a poker table at a casino? It takes strategy and stuff. Some of these people are pros."

"My dad was basically a pro. He even played here a few times. Maybe it's in my blood."

"I don't think that's how it works."

In her Landshark-loaded state, Cammy really did have the boozy conviction that she'd somehow inherited her father's poker skills. Never mind that this made absolutely no sense. "I wanna play," she repeated, scooting off her stool. "As a tribute to him. And you know what? My life's been so shitty lately, I'm due for some luck."

Fran didn't bother to argue. "Hey, you do you. I'm gonna go hit the blackjack table. I'll catch up with you in a little bit."

"Sounds like a plan, Fran." Cammy was buzzed enough to think this rhyme was funny.

Left alone, she opened the Bank of America app on her phone and found that she had exactly $1,944.04 in her checking account. She pretty much lived paycheck to paycheck, or temp gig to temp gig, with most of her funds going to her Greek landlady, Tina, in whose dungeon-like Queens basement she dwelled. How much, then, could she afford to spend on gambling? "Nothing" was the responsible answer, but that was no fun, so she settled on two hundred dollars—roughly ten percent of her current net worth.

Cammy went to a window and bought chips from an ornery cashier, then roamed the room in search of a low-stakes game with an open seat. And there it was, calling to her like a gleaming oasis: a Texas Hold'em table with a fifteen-dollar minimum bet. Its present occupants included a tough old bird who resembled Bea Arthur in *The Golden Girls*; a bulky, mustached man in a cowboy hat; a young dude with multiple piercings and full-arm tattoos; and a blinged-out girl in a Juicy velour tracksuit. They were a motley bunch.

She sat down among them, laid her chips on the table, and said, more dramatically than necessary, "Deal me in." The unimpressed dealer, clad in red vest and bow tie, just nodded.

Now, here's the thing: To Cammy's startled delight—and the annoyance of her opponents—she actually won her very first hand, thanks to a pair of hidden aces, or "pocket rockets," as her father had called them. (This also sounded like a slang term for penises.) As the dealer slid over her winnings, she felt a surge of confidence. Hey, look at me, she thought, placing the chips in their proper piles. I can do this. How 'bout that, Dad?

Unfortunately, this beginner's luck didn't last long.

The reality, as soon became apparent, was that Cammy didn't have a clue what she was doing. Because, no, poker ability isn't passed on genetically, and there's a vast difference between playing for pennies at the kitchen table with your dad and gambling for real. She didn't know the mathematics of the game. She didn't know how much to bet, or when to call or raise or fold or bluff. She couldn't even remember which hands were better than others. Did a straight beat a flush or vice versa? Was there a cheat sheet handy?

Still, despite losing hand after hand, despite the arched eyebrows of her fellow players (their subtext: "What the hell is this girl doing?"), she didn't quit. Her judgment may have been somewhat impaired by the free Landsharks a friendly-faced server kept bringing her. But there was also something perversely exhilarating—liberating, even—about blowing through her money this way.

So when Cammy ran out of chips, she hurried to the same cranky cashier, got another two hundred dollars' worth, and beelined back to the table. "Deal me in." And when *those* chips disappeared, she did it again.

Then, finally, her fortunes seemed on the verge of changing. She had her best hand yet: a flush in hearts—two in the hole and three on the table. At last, her father was smiling down on her, blessing her with the cards she needed. Okay, be smart, Cammy. She bet high but not too high, so as not to scare anyone off, maintaining a studiedly neutral expression all the while. She let the pot grow nice and big and prime for the taking.

"Turn 'em over," the dealer intoned once all bets had been made.

Everybody flipped their cards, and Cammy couldn't believe what she saw: The tough old bird, the Bea Arthur doppelganger, had a full house. Two queens and three nines. A fucking full house. Which even *she* knew beat a flush. Wow. Was this God punishing her for abandoning the shiva?

"Close one, kid," the lady rasped in sympathy. "Them's the breaks, huh?"

"Damn. Tough hand." Cammy heard Fran's voice and spun around to find her standing there. "How's it going?"

"I'm losing."

"You still have some chips left."

"I've already gone through a bunch."

Fran looked alarmed. "What do you mean? How much have you lost?"

Cammy examined her remaining chips and did the mental arithmetic. "Probably about five hundred dollars," she said with drunken nonchalance. (Yes, it was fair to say she was drunk by this point.) "Aka a quarter of my checking account."

"Five hundred dollars?! It hasn't even been two hours!"

"Really? Man, time is weird in casinos. That's why they don't have clocks on the walls, right?"

"Are you in or out?" the dealer prodded. Cammy's muzzy musings were holding up the game.

"She's out," Fran said, scooping up her chips and leading her away.

"Hey, what're you doing?"

"I'm keeping you from burning through any more money."

"Maybe I could've won it back."

"No, you definitely could not have."

"How'd you do at blackjack?"

"Fine. I broke even." Fran stopped by a row of blinking slot machines and stared at her friend, incredulous. "Dude, what were you *thinking*? I wouldn't have let you go off and play if I thought you were gonna drop half a grand."

"I don't know." Cammy glanced back at the table and tried to formulate a response. "I guess . . . while I was playing, I felt connected to him."

"To your dad?"

"To his spirit. Doing something that he did. Is that stupid?"

Fran softened. "It's not stupid. But it might've been smart to stop a little sooner."

"Yeah. You're right."

"Come on," Fran said, draping an arm around Cammy's shoulder. For all her feistiness, she could be tender when she wanted to be. "Let's cash you out, and you can walk it off. Oh, also, I made us a dinner reservation for later."

"Where?"

"Dock's Oyster House. Best restaurant in A.C. Their oysters are killer. You like oysters, don't you?"

"Sure."

★ ★ ★

The Atlantic City boardwalk, late on a fall afternoon.

Among the towering casino hotels, there were tacky souvenir stands, tattoo shops, and massage parlors. Places with "Famous" in their names offering every conceivable kind of junk food: pizza, gyros, cheesesteaks, ice cream, frozen custard, funnel cakes, candy. (They couldn't *all* be famous.) There were kids chasing each other and stomping on the wooden planks, couples engaged in heavy PDAs, elderly folks ambling by with walkers, addicts nodding off on benches, people riding along in rolling chairs, guys selling orb toys that levitated in the air. A veritable cross section of humanity.

In the distance, the wind blew trash around the beach, like the plastic bag in *American Beauty*, and the ocean waves ebbed and flowed. The Steel Pier amusement park was visible too, with its gigantic Ferris wheel and roller coaster and slingshot that catapulted thrill seekers straight up into the sky.

"What's on your mind?" Fran asked as they passed Ripley's Believe It or Not!, a kitschy "museum" dedicated to bizarre oddities. Cammy had been silent for most of their walk. "You bummed about the money?"

"No, I'm over it. I start a new temp gig on Monday. I'll make it back." She paused. "I was actually just thinking about the first time my parents ever took me down the shore."

"You remember that?"

"I think so. Or maybe it's 'cause I've seen photos. They rented a bungalow in Belmar for a month. And I do have this one memory of being on the beach with my dad. I was a toddler, and I'd never been in the ocean before. I was scared to death of it. It was so huge, I thought it would swallow me up. I thought Ursula from *The Little Mermaid* was down there, waiting to get me."

"Oh yeah, Ursula gave me nightmares."

"My dad promised he'd protect me, though. So I held his hand, and he led me out into the water, and I felt it running over my feet. It was the most amazing thing. My fears went away in a second. I wanted to stay there all day with him. Then he took me to a soft-serve stand and got me a swirl cone for being so brave. There's a picture of me covered in ice cream."

"That's a good memory," Fran said.

"He just had this way of making me not afraid of stuff. Like I knew I'd be okay as long as he was around . . ."

How ironic: Cammy had absconded to A.C. to escape her grief, yet even here, bleary-eyed on the boardwalk, she'd met with another bittersweet reminder of her father.

Some things follow you wherever you go.

♦ 15 ♦

At Dock's—"SINCE 1897," the sign out front proudly stated—they feasted as if it were their Last Supper.

First of all, their buff, man-bunned waiter, Marcus, was young and hot and seemed to be openly flirting with them, which added some extra zest to the dining experience. Every word out of the guy's sensual mouth sounded like a double entendre. When he made smiling mention of "jumbo shrimp," Cammy was convinced he was alluding to his member.

"I think he wants to have a threesome with us," Fran said. This was after he'd brought over their Palomas with the winking warning, "Now don't get too crazy on me, ladies."

"Usually I'd say you were imagining it, but this time I don't disagree."

Their appetites whetted by Marcus's coy teasing, they went to town, ordering a dozen oysters ("dealer's choice," so he could pick them), clams casino, Maine chowder—and these were just the starters. For her main dish, Cammy got the crab meat au gratin, while Fran splurged on the sixty-three-dollar lobster tail.

"Whoa," Cammy said. "You're really goin' for it."

"Don't worry. Dinner's on me. So's the hotel room."

"What? No. Why?"

"'Cause your dad passed away last weekend, your mom threw you out of the house, and you just lost five hundred dollars at poker."

"Yeah, but—"

"Please don't argue. I'm trying to enjoy my meal."

"Fine. Thank you. I appreciate it."

Fran swallowed an oyster and smiled. "Anything for my girl."

They dipped and slurped and chewed and drank, maintaining a steady buzz with the help of Marcus, who kept the cocktails coming. The restaurant was packed, the ambience was classy but alive, and someone was playing tinkly jazz piano in the other room. Cammy felt herself getting a second wind. She ignored the bloated fullness of her stomach and asked for crème brûlée off the dessert menu. After some deliberation, Fran settled on chocolate cake.

Who said a little gluttony can't heal an ailing soul?

"So," Cammy said, biting into crunchy caramelized sugar, "what's the deal with this strip club you're obsessed with?"

"Oh, it's awesome. You're gonna love it."

"What's it called?"

Fran took a theatrical beat. "Savage Men."

Cammy's fork clanged against her plate. "You're joking."

"I am not."

"We're going to a place called . . . Savage Men?"

"Yes. And it might just change your life."

"What's it like? *Magic Mike*?"

"Kind of, if *Magic Mike* was rated NC-17."

"Oh boy."

"Hey, don't be such a prude."

"I'm not being a prude. I just—I've never really gotten the whole strip club thing."

"What's not to get? Ripped guys dancing around practically naked?"

"It's so impersonal, though."

"That's the point. It's not about making a deep connection."

"What's it about?"

"Ogling and touching and having fun. It's feminist too, if you think about it."

"How is it feminist?"

"'Cause *we're* looking at *them*."

Cammy supposed this was true: There was a legitimate social value in reversing the male gaze. And she wasn't prudish about strip clubs or sex work or anything of the kind. For her, the issue was simply that, unlike Fran, she'd never found the spectacle of hunky bodies divorced from their possessors' personalities very enticing. She needed something more. Even her massive crush on Nick—Beautiful Dancer Boy himself—had been based on his talent and character as much as on his sculpted physique. (Although the physique didn't hurt matters.)

She'd visited a strip joint once before, for the bachelorette party of her loudmouth Long Island cousin Hailey, and the occasion had wound up feeling forced. Everyone in the group made a big show of themselves, hooting and hollering as if to say, "Ooh, look at us! We're being naughty!" But ultimately, it was just boring and dumb.

"Stop judging," Fran said, finishing off her cake. "I can see you judging. Keep an open mind. Savage Men is different."

"Okay, okay. My mind is open."

"Can I get you lovely ladies anything else?" Marcus had returned. From the tone of his sultry voice, he may as well have been propositioning them.

"No, thank you, Marcus," Fran cooed. "We'll take the check, please."

"Coming right up." And he sashayed away.

"Did you hear the way he said 'coming'?" Cammy asked.

"I did, and I liked it."

He reappeared moments later with the bill. Laying it gently on the table, he purred, "It's been such a pleasure serving you."

Fran was loving the innuendo. "The pleasure's all ours."

It came as no great shock that Marcus had written his phone number on the check, along with a small, childlike drawing of a heart containing a smiley face. The only question was whether the number was intended for use by Fran or Cammy or both of them. Cammy generously gave her friend dibs on calling him. After all, Fran was a regular in A.C., and she was paying for dinner.

When they stood up, Cammy realized she was so stuffed she could hardly move. "I think I overate."

"No shit," Fran said, cupping her own bursting belly. "That's what you do at Dock's."

They waddled outside with seafood and tequila sloshing around their tummies. The sun had set, and the air had grown chillier. They headed back toward the boardwalk, into the subterranean nightworld of Atlantic City.

★ ★ ★

Standing under the bright red awning of Savage Men, Cammy wondered, like David Byrne in the Talking Heads classic "Once in a Lifetime," "How did I get here?"

Just four days ago, she'd been at Star of David Cemetery in Saddle Brook, reciting the Kaddish over her father's grave. And now she was on a shadowy side street in A.C., waiting in line with a bunch of drunk women (herself included) to enter a male strip club. Quite a journey.

She'd gotten here because she'd misbehaved. Acted out. Offended the rabbi and outraged her mother. Why had she done it? Why had she caused so much trouble? Why hadn't she been able to mourn her dad in a respectable, respectful way? She couldn't come up with a clear answer, except that losing her favorite person so suddenly had filled her with an indescribable anger, and this anger had led her to raise hell.

It was an explanation, not an excuse. Cammy still had enough self-awareness to know that she'd fucked up at every opportunity this week and, worst of all, further broken her mom's already fractured heart. But that didn't mean she was ready or able to redeem herself.

And where was Beth right now? Probably at the Friday-night service at the synagogue, listening to Rabbi Wiener deliver his pseudo-eloquent sermon on—what a coincidence!—redemption. (Shiva technically gets paused during the Sabbath, Cammy recalled from Hebrew school, so you can go to services.) Was her mother finding comfort there as she spoke the prayers and sang the songs? Did it help to cling to her late husband's religion, which she'd adopted and embraced as a convert? Or was she too preoccupied thinking about her derelict daughter?

The derelict daughter could only guess, as Beth hadn't reached out to her since yesterday's ultimatum.

"Hello? ID?" A gruff voice snapped her out of her soul-searching. It belonged to a hulking security guard in a black shirt with white letters that read, um, "SECURITY." Cammy hadn't even noticed that she and Fran had reached the front of the line. How long had he been trying to get her attention?

"Sorry—"

"I need your ID."

"Right. ID. Got it."

As Cammy dug through her purse for her wallet, the guard looked at Fran. "Is your friend okay?"

"Yeah, she's good."

He rubbed his shaved head. "She's not tripping, is she? If she's tripping, she ain't comin' inside."

"I'm not tripping," Cammy averred, producing her New Jersey driver's license. She'd never bothered to get a New York one. "I was just deep in thought."

Unamused, the guard flashed an ultraviolet light on the license. Handing it back, he said, "Lift your arms up."

"Why?"

"I need to pat you down."

"Pat me down?" Was this for real? "What, you think I have a weapon?"

"It's policy."

"Do I look like I'm trying to sneak a gun into the strip club?"

"It's policy." He reminded her of one of those talking action figures that, when you press a button, can utter only a few stock phrases.

Indignant, Cammy turned to Fran, who sighed and said, "Don't make a scene, dude."

"I'm not making a—" But she was, and it wasn't worth it, and she didn't want to ruin Savage Men for her friend, so Cammy bit the bullet and flung her arms up. The oaf performed a quick, cursory frisk, then gave Fran the same royal treatment. Why exactly ladies would show up at this place packing pistols remained a mystery.

Fran swung open the black front door, and they stepped into a dimly lit foyer, where a thickly painted, gum-chewing woman shook them down for a forty-dollar-per-person cover charge.

"Forty dollars? Just to get in?" Cammy had to shout over the pounding music coming from inside the club.

"That's the weekend rate."

"Jesus."

"Relax," Fran interjected, attempting to avoid yet another scene. "I got this, too."

"No—"

"Yes. But can you stop mouthing off to everyone? You're gonna get us kicked out before we even get inside."

"Sorry."

Fran extracted a wad of cash from her wallet and stuck it in Cammy's palm, like a real Italian gangster diva. "Here. This should be enough for everything."

"Fran—"

"No arguing! I wanna see some bulges!"

And bulges they did see.

Well, first they saw nothing, because the club's main room was pitch-dark and their eyes needed a second to adjust. But then the lit-up, runway-like stage became visible, and they were face-to-face with a parade of muscle-bound dancers in barely-there thongs. Oiled up and glistening, the he-men bumped and humped and grinded to the thunderous throb of a techno bass, waving their junk in the air like X-rated hula hoopers. Together they formed a kind of moving cubist painting—fragments of protruding pecs, hard nipples, cut abs, tight asses. And their gyrating pelvises had a hypnotic effect.

All around the stage, clusters of plastered women whistled and laughed, tossing dollar bills at the dancers or inserting them in the waistbands of their wedgied thongs. One girl in the cheap tiara of a bride-to-be appeared to have entered a state of euphoric delirium, and was making it rain on an eager hunk's twerking behind.

Perhaps this *was* some sort of wayward postfeminist utopia, Cammy mused. Or just a really down and dirty spot.

"What do you think?!" Fran yelled, nudging her ribs. Yelling was the only way to be heard above the earsplitting soundtrack.

"I think . . . it's something."

"It sure fuckin' is."

They ordered Heinekens from a smiling server in torn tighty-whities. Cammy remembered the funny New Jersey law by which strip clubs that offered partial nudity could sell alcohol, while their full-nude counterparts could not. If the liquor were flowing *and* the genitals were out, things would apparently get too crazy.

They'd hardly sipped their beers when a long-haired Samson in leopard-print underwear ran up to Fran and bear-hugged her. He bore a striking resemblance to that brawny model from the romance novel covers and the I Can't Believe It's Not Butter commercials. What was his name? Fabian? No, Fabio! "Francesca!" he cried in an indeterminate European accent.

"Hey, Dima!" Fran beamed.

"I missed you, girl."

"I missed *you*."

"Who's your friend?"

"Oh, this is Cammy. She's my BFF. My sister from another mister."

"Hi." Cammy held out her hand, but Dima—short for Dmitri, if that was even his real name?—hugged her too. He was an affectionate fellow.

"Very nice to meet you, Kimmy," he grinned. She chose not to correct him. "You been here before?"

"Never. This is my first time."

"Then welcome to Savage Men, where we blow your mind." Was that a tagline? "Why you girls come to A.C.? You celebrate something?"

"Nope, we're not celebrating anything," Cammy said. "Fran's just trying to cheer me up 'cause my dad—" She felt Fran step on her foot to shut her up, and she realized it was probably unnecessary to tell Dima about her father's death. "We're just here to have fun."

"If you want fun, you're in the right place," he said, running a hand through his wavy locks. His cologne was overpowering.

Fran whispered in Cammy's ear, "Dima's my favorite one here. We've hooked up a couple times."

"You've—"

"You want lap dance, Francesca?" The pleasantries were over now, and Dima was getting down to business. The man had to earn a living.

"I would love one." Fran checked with Cammy: "You mind if I—"

"Go ahead. Knock yourself out. I'll stand here and leer at the beefcake."

Dima took Fran's hand and began to lead her off to an area in the back of the club separated by a tall partition. He called over his broad shoulder, "I send someone for you, Kimmy!"

"No, you don't have to—"

"You will like him! He's very handsome!"

And they disappeared behind the divider. Cammy inched toward a wall and stood awkwardly next to it with her Heineken, watching the antics onstage. The ecstatic bride-to-be was currently riding a dancer in assless chaps as if he were a horse and howling "Yeehaw!" while her bachelorette buddies cheered. A last premarital hurrah.

Cammy hoped Dima wouldn't actually "send someone" for her. It was enough to be here in the den of sin without having to engage a dancer in empty small talk and get badgered for a lap dance. But when she saw the someone approaching from across the room, she changed her tune.

This man *was* handsome, and muscular, but not in an outsize, cartoonish way, like most of the other performers. He had a dark crew cut, and the lights of the club lent a sheen to his smooth copper skin. Instead of a thong, he wore far less ridiculous black briefs. Kudos to Dima, who'd done a remarkable job guessing Cammy's type.

The dancer sauntered up to her and said in a silky voice, "Dima told me you might need some company."

"Did he?"

"My name's Valentino." Sure, it was.

"Like the silent movie star?"

"Who?"

"Never mind."

"What's your name?"

"Cammy."

"Cammy," he repeated breathily. "That's cute."

"Thanks."

He gave her a sly once-over. "You don't look like you come to places like this too often."

"I don't."

"So you're a good girl."

"I'm not that good. But yeah, my friend brought me. She's a big fan."

"Your friend who's in the back with Dima."

"Right."

"Well, I'm glad you came. You're beautiful."

"I bet you say that to all the ladies."

"I do. But this time, I mean it."

Cammy knew, of course, that this whole thing was a well-rehearsed act, that Valentino's job was to flirt with her and flatter her and get her to give him money. Boy, was he good at it, though. In spite of her better judgment, she felt the familiar tingle of arousal.

"You two need anything?" the tighty-whitied server asked as he made his rounds.

Valentino batted his eyes at Cammy. "Buy a guy a drink?"

"Sure. Whatever you want."

"I'll take a G and T. Or should I make it two?"

Cammy saw that she had only a drop left of her Heineken. "You can make it two."

"That's what I like to hear."

They got their drinks, which Cammy paid for with Fran's cash. "Bottoms up," Valentino said provocatively. Bringing the straw to her lips, she took a mental inventory of all the alcohol she'd imbibed over the past few hours: lager, tequila, and now gin. This in addition to devouring an aquarium's worth of seafood.

With a salesman's suavity, Valentino asked, "How 'bout a dance?"

"How did I know you were gonna suggest that?"

"You ever have a private lap dance before?"

"Actually, no, I haven't."

"You've gotta try it, then. I'll rock your world." He lingered on these last three words, accentuating every syllable.

"How much does it cost to have my world rocked?"

"Forty dollars."

"Same as the cover charge."

"For you I'll make it thirty."

"That's very generous."

As she considered this bargain, he ran his fingers lightly over her back. She had her denim jacket on, but she got chills anyway. "I can feel your energy, Cammy. Lots of tension." True. "Let Valentino relieve some of that stress for you."

Yes, he'd referred to himself in the third person—normally an egregious offense—but Cammy didn't care. She'd been searching for relief all week, hence the weed and the booze and the hookups, yet nothing had truly done the trick. Nothing had taken her out of herself. Maybe this Savage Man with the made-up name of Valentino held the key.

"Okay," she said. "Let's go."

He guided her through the throng of thonged dudes and thirsty gals toward the hidden section in the back. En route, they passed Fran and Dima, fresh off their own dance. Thrilled to see her friend indulging too, Fran gave Cammy two thumbs up and mouthed, "Fuck yeah."

As it turned out, the area for "private" dances wasn't particularly private. It was a dark, narrow space lined with black, vinyl-cushioned folding chairs, on which women sat receiving lap dances in full view of one another. Cammy had assumed she and Valentino would at least have their own little romantic cubicle or something. Nope.

He led her to a chair in the corner, straddled her, and went to work like the professional he was. To the thumping beat of a rap song with incredibly raunchy lyrics (Cammy heard *"My coochie pink, my booty hole brown"*), Valentino thrust his hips, shook his butt, and breathed hot and heavy on her neck. She didn't know what to do with her hands until he grabbed them and placed them on his ass. "Touching's allowed," he quipped. "Squeezing too." Good to know.

At first Cammy felt uncomfortable—she'd never had a man perform for her like this—but as Valentino practiced his magic, she let herself loosen up and enjoy it. After all she'd been through since Saturday, she deserved to have her world rocked for a few fleeting minutes.

Her face was buried in his firm chest when he put his mouth to her ear and said, "Do you party, Cammy?"

"What do you mean?"

"I'll show you." Swiveling his body so that his back was to the other dancers and customers, he reached into his briefs and pulled out a small baggie of white powder.

"Oh."

"You want some? It's good shit. My treat. But we gotta be quick."

Cocaine. Cammy had limited experience with the drug, having done a line here and there at a handful of parties over the years. But from the scare stories she'd seen in the news, coke had grown more dangerous recently. A bad dose laced with fentanyl could kill you. Valentino claimed to have "good shit," though. And why not trust a dancer you met in a strip club fifteen minutes ago?

Whatever. None of this mattered now. Grief was still gnawing away at her insides, and she wanted the numbing oblivion of a narcotic.

Self-destructively, she nodded yes. What Valentino did next was an awesome feat: He stretched his torso back at an almost ninety-degree angle, poured a little line of powder onto his abdomen, plucked a dollar bill from his waistband, and rolled it up and handed it to Cammy. The sheer gymnastics of this were Olympics-worthy, if you forgot about the illegal substance.

She bent down and snorted the coke off his abs.

Yes, she really did that.

Was this rock bottom or a new kind of peak?

"Nice," Valentino said with admiration. He dipped a finger inside the baggie and rubbed some coke on his gums before stuffing it back in his briefs.

Soon the raunchy rap track ended, which meant the dance was done. "Oh no," he pouted as a reggaeton number began blasting. "I want more time with you. Another song?"

"Thirty?"

"Uh-huh."

"Okay. One more." Cammy went to pick up her purse, but before she could fetch the cash, she felt a terrible rumbling in her gut. The rumbling of multiple varieties of liquor and seafood. And she remembered one of the inglorious side effects of cocaine: It can make you shit.

She had to do just that. Urgently. All at once, her night of hedonistic gorging and guzzling had caught up with her.

"I'm sorry," she said, pushing Valentino off her and standing up.

"What's wrong?"

"I don't feel well."

"Is it the coke?" he whispered.

"No, it's my—I have to use the bathroom."

He grimaced at the unsexiness of this admission. "Oh."

"Where is it?"

"Back by the entrance. Good luck . . ."

Cammy muttered, "I'm sorry," again and rushed out of the dance area, clutching her stomach. She wove through the orgy of bacchants to the opposite side of the club, only to discover—Lord, no—a line of several women waiting to use one single-occupancy restroom! She couldn't wait that long, and neither could her cramping bowels.

She found Fran and Dima and ran up to them.

"There you are," Fran said in a satisfied tone. "How was your dance? Was it super hot?"

"You like Valentino, yes?" Dima added. "He's very handsome."

Cammy had no time to waste. "I've gotta go."

"What? Go where?"

"Back to the hotel."

Fran was baffled. "Back to the—What're you talking about? We just got here. Did something happen?"

Cammy leaned closer so Dima couldn't hear. "I need to use the bathroom."

"You mean you have to—"

"Yes."

"Okay. Why can't you use it here?"

"Look! There's a huge line!"

"You can't hold it a little?"

"You don't understand. I just did coke back there with that dancer—"

"You did?!" Fran sounded impressed.

"Yeah, and on top of all the food and the drinks, I'm about to explode."

"You think you can make it to the hotel?"

"If I sprint." Resorts was just a couple of minutes away on the boardwalk. "It's either that or shit myself here in the club."

"Don't do that, or I'll be blacklisted here forever."

Cammy raced out of the club like a track star. (She'd actually played tennis in high school. Track seemed too exhausting.) As she emerged onto the street, brushing past the brusque security guard, she noticed it had begun to rain. No, rain was too mild a word; this was a full-on, out-of-the-blue downpour. Fantastic.

She dashed down the puddly boardwalk, pelted by freezing droplets, her stomach churning and gurgling. This had to be her biblical comeuppance for snorting cocaine off a dancer's body on the first Jewish Sabbath after her father's passing. If she could only get to a toilet, she'd repent for everything.

Soaked and shivering, Cammy burst into Resorts and bolted to the nearest elevator. The ride up to the sixteenth floor took eons. She bounded through the hall to her and Fran's Coral Junior Suite, fumbled with the glitchy card reader, and finally made it in at the very last second before Armageddon. She didn't even bother to shut the bathroom door behind her.

Oh, sweet relief.

Once the ghastly deed was done and flushed away, she staggered out into the suite, a soldier returned from battle. Instantly she sensed something was askew. Her backpack was lying open on the carpeted floor. Hadn't she left it on the bed earlier? Had it fallen? Was the room haunted by ghosts of A.C.'s scandalous past?

Cammy went over to pick up the bag. It felt lighter than it should have. She looked inside and gasped audibly: "What the fuck!" Her mess of clothes was still there, but the laptop compartment was empty.

Her MacBook was gone.

16

It wasn't about the computer. Cammy didn't give a shit about tech or hardware or Apple's latest hyped-up releases. She cared about what was *on* the damn thing.

She'd bought the MacBook years ago, in college, and it contained all the writing she'd done since. The old, scuffed laptop was a trove of her past work, her manifold attempts (key word) at literary creation, her own intellectual history. Most crucially, it housed the draft of the all-important grief play she'd started earlier this week.

Now the machine was missing. And thanks to her own stupendous lack of foresight, none of its contents were backed up anywhere.

"I need your help," Cammy bawled to Fran on the phone. She was breathing fast, slumped in a pitiful pile on the hotel room floor, tapping the back of her head against the wall.

"You sound like you're having a panic attack!" Fran yelled over the cacophony of the club.

"I think I am. All my stuff was on it. Literally everything I've—I don't believe this. I don't know what to do."

"Okay, hold on. I'll be right there. I'll tell Dima I'll catch him next time."

"I'm sorry . . ."

"Don't be. Hoes before bros."

Twenty minutes later, they were seated at a desk in the fluorescent-lit, bare-bones office of Resorts' hotel security, across from a wiry, bug-eyed security officer—a "rent-a-cop," if you will—whose uniform might've been purchased at Party City. His name tag read "Nibs." Presumably, this was his last name.

"Are you sure the laptop was in your backpack when you left the room?" Nibs asked in a nasal voice of utter apathy. He was jotting notes in chicken scratch on a clipboard, or maybe he was just doodling.

"Yes, I'm sure," Cammy said, her anxiety exacerbated by the alcohol and cocaine surging through her system. "And when I got back a little while ago, it was gone."

"Was anything else taken?"

"I don't think so. There was nothing else valuable to take."

"Was the door open?"

"No. It was closed."

Nibs frowned. "Mm."

"Mm?"

"Might've been an inside job, then."

"An *inside job*? You mean like someone who works here stole my laptop?"

"Not a current employee, no. But we've had some, uh, incidents lately—"

"What kind of incidents?"

"Well, a few staff members who've been fired have, uh, duplicated master room cards, and then they've come back and stolen things from guests' rooms."

"What?!"

"Yeah, it's an issue," Nibs reflected.

"So a disgruntled ex-employee broke into our room and took my MacBook?"

"Unfortunately, yes, probably."

"And you don't have any way of preventing that?"

"Unfortunately, no, we don't."

Cammy looked at Fran for moral support. "Sucks, dude," Fran said.

"Where were you tonight, by the way?" Nibs queried.

"Why does that matter?" Cammy shot back.

"I just wanna put it in my report."

"That stuff you're scrawling—that's a *report*?"

"I'm gonna type it up later."

"We went to Dock's Oyster House for dinner. And then . . . we were at Savage Men. The strip club. You got a problem with that?"

"Nope," he said, scribbling. "No problem at all."

Cammy felt Fran step on her foot again, as she'd done at the club. The tacit message: Pipe down. But Cammy was too desperate (and high) to keep from being combative. "So what happens now?"

"Well, I'm gonna file my report—"

"Good for you, but how do I get my laptop back?"

"We'll have to wait and see if it turns up."

"Huh? Why would it 'turn up'? If whoever stole it has a crisis of conscience?"

Nibs ignored this rhetorical question. "Is the laptop insured?"

"No, it's not insured. I've had it for like ten years."

"Oh. At least it's not new."

"That's not the point." Cammy grabbed the edge of the desk and leaned forward, like a woman in a Lifetime movie demanding that a detective find her missing child. "The point is: It has important stuff on it. It has my *work*."

"I'm sure your company will understand—"

"No, not *that* kind of work. I'm talking about my writing. My art. My cathartic new play about my dad dying!"

Nibs appeared uncomprehending. Fran said, "Sorry, she's in an emotional place right now. And she's had a few."

"I'm stone-cold sober," Cammy lied. "Can we call the police?"

"You could try," Nibs said, "but I doubt they'd do anything."

"Why not?"

"'Cause the Atlantic City Police Department has a lot more to deal with than stolen laptops."

"Like what?"

"Assaults and murders."

"So I'm just fucked, then, is what you're saying."

"I wouldn't put it like that."

"How would you put it?"

Nibs scratched his wispy chin beard. "You're not getting that computer back."

Cammy leapt from her seat and banged her fist down on the fake wood. Fran jumped up, ready to restrain her.

"Ma'am, please—"

"I'm gonna sue this place!" She sounded like her mom at the rehab facility.

"I guess you didn't read the fine print when you checked in."

"No, I didn't. Why?"

"We're not responsible for lost or stolen items."

Cammy groaned in exasperation. "I hate this dump! 'Resorts'! Who the fuck gives a hotel a plural name? It's one hotel! It should be called 'Resort'! And even *that's* stupid!"

Nibs graciously let this slide.

★ ★ ★

Drunk and coked up and blind with rage, Cammy fled from the hotel back onto the rain-slick boardwalk, nearly colliding with a posse of popped-collar assholes.

"Hey, watch where you're goin'!" one of them shouted.

"Suck my dick!" she shouted in response.

The biblical deluge had turned to a cold, steady drizzle. She didn't know where to go, so she ran straight ahead, down some wooden steps, and onto the sodden sand of the darkened beach. She could hear Fran behind her, calling her name.

Standing at the ocean's edge, with the black waves crashing in the night, Cammy felt as though she'd reached the end of the earth. Thanks to a clever room-card scam perpetrated by resentful former Resorts employees, she'd just lost years' worth of her writing, including the new, deeply personal play she had such high hopes for. (Could she attempt to rewrite the partial draft from scratch? What an awful prospect.) But that wasn't all she'd lost this week.

She'd lost her dad. She'd lost any semblance of a functional relationship with her mom. And somehow, she'd also lost her sense of self, which had been slipping away even before her father's death.

What the hell was she doing here, anyway? Why was she in Atlantic City, blowing money at poker and doing blow with a dancer named Valentino? What was wrong with her?

Cammy tilted her face up to the falling rain, wishing it would wash her clean.

There was no doubt about it: She'd bottomed out.

"What're you doing? You're gonna get sick." Fran was next to her now, holding her leather jacket above her own head in a futile effort to stay dry.

"I shouldn't have come here," Cammy said. "This was a horrible idea."

"Why? I thought you wanted to get away."

"I did, but I *can't*. My dad's still dead. My mom still despises me. And debauchery in A.C. doesn't help anything. It's just depressing."

"Even Savage Men?"

"Especially Savage Men."

"Sorry," Fran said, wounded. "I've been trying to cheer you up . . ."

"I know you have. But I'm not you. Hanging out with exotic dancers doesn't make me feel better. I wish it did, but it doesn't."

Fran shook wet sand off her shoes. "Look, I get that you're upset about the laptop—"

"Of course I'm upset about the laptop! While I was busy snorting coke off Valentino, someone stole, like, the last decade of my thoughts!"

"But don't you hate most of your old writing?"

"Yeah, but I still want it! And there's this new thing I started this week—this play about losing my dad—and now that's gone, too. And it's all my fault."

"How is it your fault you got robbed?"

"Because it wouldn't have happened if I hadn't been here. If I hadn't been such a fuckup that my own mother kicked me out of the shiva for my father."

"You didn't *wanna* be at the shiva, though, remember?"

"I know! I'm a walking contradiction!"

"Isn't that a Green Day song?"

Cammy threw her hands up. She trudged along the soggy shoreline, toward the phantasmagoric lights of the Steel Pier, which was still going strong past ten o'clock. The distant, jaunty carnival music seemed to be mocking her and her pathetic plight. She couldn't even tell if she were crying or if it was just the rain.

"Well, hey," Fran said, jogging up to her side, "maybe this is an omen, you know?"

Cammy stopped. "An omen? What's an omen? Me getting my shit stolen?"

"No, like . . . maybe this means you're ready for a fresh start."

"I have no idea what you're talking about."

"I'm talking about you moving back home to Jersey and helping me turn the deli into a restaurant—"

"I don't wanna do that!" Cammy said with startling force.

Fran flinched, taken aback. "You said you'd think about it."

"I don't need to. Fran, seriously, can you imagine me living in Jersey again?"

"Sure, why not?"

"'Cause I'd feel stuck. I'd be miserable."

"As opposed to how happy you are in New York?"

"That's beside the point."

"You'd be working with me. We'd be building something together."

"Sorry, but I'm not ready to, like, give up on all my dreams and work in the *food service* industry." Cammy spat this out with more disdain than she meant to, but she couldn't take it back.

For a rare moment, Fran was too stung to speak. "Oh, I get it," she said at last. "So working with food is beneath you."

"That's not what I—"

"Unlike your amazing temping or whatever."

"The temping's just a side gig—"

"A side gig to *what*? What else do you do, Cammy?"

She wanted to proclaim, "I write! I'm a writer!" But how could she? Nothing she'd written had ever seen the light of day. The harsh truth was that being a writer was merely an illusory idea she had about herself—an idea that didn't mean shit to the rest of the world. She was a fraud.

"God," Fran said, "I didn't know you'd become such a snob."

"I'm not a—"

"Yeah, you are. I've been your best friend for twenty years, but you look down on me 'cause I still live in our hometown and I work at my dad's deli and I'm not some pretentious New York asshole. Well, guess what? I'm cool with who I am. I fuckin' *like* Jersey. I like feeding people good food. And one day soon, I'm gonna open an awesome restaurant, even if you don't wanna be a part of it."

"Fran—"

"You know, this whole week, I've just been trying to be here for you. And I'm so sorry about your dad, I really am, but that doesn't give you a pass to be shitty to me."

Cammy opened her mouth to speak. She didn't know what to say, though. Fran was right.

She remembered a weekend several years ago when Fran had come to stay with her in Astoria. They'd gone to a party on the Lower East Side thrown by some people Cammy knew from one of her fruitless writing workshops. The whole evening, she'd engaged in substanceless literary repartee with her fellow posers while Fran stood around uncomfortably, drinking whiskey. Cammy had made zero effort to include her in these conversations, except when she'd told a couple of insulting Jersey jokes that Fran had no choice but to laugh along with.

They'd never discussed this night since then, yet it had been the last time Cammy had invited Fran into her city life, and Fran had never asked to return. They hung out together only when Cammy was back on the safe terrain of Bergen County.

Why? Because, yes, on some ugly, unreckoned-with level, Cammy did look down her nose at her oldest, closest friend, for all the superficial reasons Fran had mentioned. Which, when she considered Fran's unconditional loyalty and love, was pretty despicable.

"I'm going back to the casino," Fran said. "I'm gonna play some slots or something. I'm done standing out here in the fuckin' rain. Are you coming with me?" Cammy didn't answer. "Okay, whatever." And Fran turned and strode off toward the boardwalk.

Her clothes and hair sopping, Cammy sank down to the squishy sand and stared out at the dark expanse of the sea. She'd now managed to alienate Francesca, the sole person left in her corner. What next? Maybe she could catch pneumonia, as her dad had at the hospital; die alone on the beach at A.C.; and reunite with him in heaven.

No, she thought. That would be too easy.

★ ★ ★

Here's what Cammy did instead:

She went back to the room at Resorts, took a hot shower, and changed into dry clothes. Then she wrote a note on hotel stationery and placed it on Fran's bed: "Going home. I'm sorry." At the concierge desk, she learned that a Greyhound bus to New York City—to her favorite place, the Port Authority Bus Terminal—would be leaving in a few minutes, at eleven o'clock. She bought a ticket for $29.99, bid farewell to the casino with the inexplicably plural name, and waited out front for the bus.

The nice thing about riding a Greyhound from Atlantic City to New York at eleven PM was that no matter how badly you were doing, everyone else on board seemed to be equally down and out.

This was the only nice thing. Jammed into a window seat at the rear of the bus, her oversize backpack balanced on her lap, Cammy was subjected to an array of unpleasantness: the putrid smell emanating from the bathroom (she had to pee, but she dared not go inside), the stale heat blasting on her head, the passengers carrying on loud phone conversations and blaring music from portable speakers—not to mention the large, mutton-chopped guy with sleep apnea manspreading right next to her, whose snores sounded like death throes. Help.

At some point during the two-and-a-half-hour-long journey, she began to think of David. Her betrayed ex-boyfriend, with whom she'd once thought she was in love, with whom she'd once imagined a future. And she realized that he *still* didn't know her dad had died. In fact, she'd been drunk-dialing him outside the Williamsburg beer hall last Saturday night when Rabbi Wiener called with the terrible news.

Should she tell him? Not to garner sympathy—she'd cheated on him with a rando actor, and he was done with her; she understood that. But just to, like, let him know? David had met her father, had dinner with him, laughed at his jokes. They'd gotten along well. He didn't deserve to be kept in the dark, right?

So Cammy called him. She turned her face to the window, holding her phone up to her right ear and plugging her left ear with her index finger to block out the snores and clamor. She didn't think David would answer, especially after the rambling voicemail she'd left him last weekend, in which she'd absurdly proposed that they take a hike together to patch things up. (What?) But to her shock, he did.

"Hello?" There was that soft librarian's voice of his.

"David. You picked up."

"Hi, Cammy."

"Sorry, I wasn't expecting you to—Hi. How are you?"

"I'm all right."

"What're you—um—what're you up to?"

"Well, it's midnight, so I'm in bed." David wasn't a partier.

"Did I wake you up?"

"No, I was reading."

"Tolstoy still?"

"*War and Peace.* Still muddling through."

She missed him. She missed being with a sweet man who read nineteenth-century Russian literature in bed on a Friday night. But that ship had sailed, or, rather, she'd wrecked it. "Listen, I'm sorry for that ridiculous message I left you—"

"It's okay."

"I was drunk, if you couldn't tell."

"I assumed."

"This isn't another please-take-me-back call, I promise. I just, uh, I wanted to tell you—"

"Hey, I can't hear you that well. There's a lot of background noise."

"Sorry, I'm on a bus." This was her third "sorry" in the past minute. Maybe she could set a record.

"A bus to where?"

"Back to the city. I was in Atlantic City with Fran."

"Atlantic City?"

"Don't ask. Anyway, I wanted to tell you . . ." She hesitated, unsure how to proceed. As usual, she opted for bluntness. "My dad died last Saturday."

A beat. "What?"

"Yeah."

"Oh my God."

"I know."

"How . . ."

"You remember he was having surgery to have that tumor removed from his kidney?"

"Uh-huh . . ."

"Well, it ended up being benign. But he got pneumonia in the hospital, and then they moved him to a rehab place, and he died there. We still don't really understand what happened. My mom wanted to sue."

"Cammy . . . I'm so sorry." Now *he* was the sorry one.

"Thanks."

"I can't believe that."

"Neither can I, really."

"Your dad was a great guy. He loved you so much."

"He liked you, too. He said, 'David's a good one.' I never told him why we broke up." When reporting the split to her parents, she'd conveniently omitted the fact that her infidelity was the cause. "But yeah, I thought you'd wanna know, so . . ."

"Of course. Thank you for telling me. Is there a shiva or something I can come to?" Though a lapsed Catholic himself, David was familiar with the Jewish ways.

"There is a shiva, but, um, my mom and I are kind of on the outs right now, so you can probably skip it."

"You're on the outs with your mom?" he said, clearly bewildered by the idea that Cammy and her mother could be at odds so soon after Cy's death.

"It's a long story. That's why I was in Atlantic City."

He didn't probe any further. "Okay. Well, I'll send a card to the house, then. And let me know if you need anything."

She felt like saying, "How about a second chance?" What she actually said was, "Thanks, David. I hope, you know, you're doing well and everything."

"I'm fine." Did he sound choked up? It was hard to discern over the din of the bus. "I'll be thinking of you and your mom. Take care of yourself, Cammy."

"You too. Bye." She hung up and gazed at the window, where the faint outline of her reflection was superimposed over the nighttime highway whooshing past.

She was glad she'd told David about her dad, yet there was something achingly sad about it, too. If they'd still been together, he could've held her, comforted her, stood by her side through all the grief and pain. But thanks to her own destructive actions, they *weren't* together, and the best she could get was a brief phone call on a crowded Greyhound.

The snoring man's head lolled and landed on Cammy's shoulder. She didn't push it away. At least she had him.

* * *

"I'm not here to hook up with you again," Cammy announced to Sugar Shane after stepping into the Dirty Bird at two thirty in the morning. (The dive closed at three on Fridays and Saturdays.)

"That's cool," Shane said magnanimously. "Want a drink?"

"No. I can't drink any more. Can I just have some seltzer?"

"Sure can."

She'd arrived at the Port Authority at one thirty, with just enough time to hustle through the horror-show terminal and catch the last local NJ Transit bus back to Bergen County. She couldn't go home to her mom, though. Not like this. Not in the middle of the night. So she sought refuge here in the grimy bar with Shane O'Leary, the backward-capped Jersey bro from high school.

As much as Cammy had enjoyed their previous encounter, she wasn't in the market for another alley make-out now. No, all she wanted from Shane at this moment was a sympathetic ear. That and a place to sit and nurse her seltzer. Both of which the humbled former jock was more than happy to provide.

"Rough night?" he said, spraying soda water into a nicked glass.

"You wouldn't believe it."

"Try me."

In the tradition of great barstool monologues, Cammy recounted the sordid saga of the past thirty-six hours: getting booted from the house by her mom, going on a spree in A.C., losing her laptop and lashing out at her best friend. (She conveniently left out the part about her coitus interruptus with Nick, so as not to hurt Shane's feelings.) As she spoke, Shane listened patiently and attentively. This bro was full of surprises.

When she'd finished her tale, he said, "Damn."

"Damn indeed."

"You know, I get what you're going through."

"You do?"

"Yeah. My mom died a few years back."

Cammy sat upright. "Wait—what?"

"Cancer. Took a long time."

"I'm sorry." She paused. "But... why didn't you tell me that when I first came in this week? When I mentioned my dad?"

He shrugged. "I don't usually bring it up." Wiping a rag along the counter, he said, "I went kinda crazy after it happened. Lots of fucking and drinking and drugs. And then one day I woke up on the floor of some random party house, and I was like, 'You've gotta stop, man. You're gonna kill yourself.' And I realized what I needed to do."

"Which was?"

"I needed to go talk to her."

"To your mom?"

"Yeah."

"I don't—How?"

"What do you mean how? I went to the cemetery and talked to her. And she straightened me out. You should try it with your dad."

Cammy nodded, still adjusting to the sudden shift in her perception of Sugar Shane. He wasn't a fratty fuckboy anymore. He'd lost a parent, too, and he was offering her hard-won life advice. Who would've thought?

"You look exhausted," he said.

"Do I?"

"You got bags under your eyes."

"You know how to flatter a girl."

"You can crash here if you want. If you can't go home."

"In the bar?"

"I do it sometimes, when I've got an early shift at the body shop. There's an office in the back with a cot. Gus doesn't know the difference."

"Who's Gus?"

"The dude who owns this dump."

"So you'll just lock me in here?"

"Nah, I'll stay with you. I'll snooze in a booth. They're pretty comfortable, actually."

"Um. Okay. Thanks."

The place was empty save for the two of them, so there were no customers to kick out. Shane cleaned up, took out the garbage, and locked the doors. Then he ushered Cammy down a dingy hall to a cramped, cluttered "office" that contained a flimsy cot with a scratchy-looking blanket. Well, it was better than sleeping on Main Street.

"I appreciate the hospitality," she said sincerely.

"No probs." He lingered in the doorway, a vision in his blue Mets hat. "Look, I know we were just messing around that night, and it's not gonna go anywhere"—correct—"but . . . it's been fun catching up with you, Cammy."

"It has. And for the record, I don't think you're a dick, like you were in high school. I think you've turned into a nice guy."

"Thanks," Shane said, pleased. Before heading back to the barroom to doze on a ragged red vinyl booth, he added, "Hey. You're gonna be all right."

That remained to be seen.

Day Six: Saturday

♦ 17 ♦

Dawn. Saturday morning.

Cammy grabbed her backpack and stepped out of Shane's Nissan Sentra in front of Star of David Cemetery. She'd slept for a few hours on the creaky cot, then roused her gallant host to ask him for one final favor: a ride. On the way over, they'd picked up coffee and breakfast sandwiches at Dunkin' Donuts. Her treat.

"Sure you don't want me to wait for you?" he asked from the driver's seat.

"No, I'm good. Thanks for everything."

"Anytime."

She shut the car door, tapped a goodbye on the window, and watched Shane drive off into the sunrise like a cowboy who's saved a dusty town from thugs and is on to his next adventure. Happy trails, Sugar.

Cammy turned to face the cemetery's wrought-iron gate, with its imposing Star of David design. She'd been here on Monday to bury her father, and now she'd returned. She was taking Shane's advice, as superstitious as it seemed: She was coming to "talk" to her dad, to get "straightened out." What did that actually mean? She didn't know. But she'd exhausted all her other options and still hadn't found any peace, so it was worth a shot.

There was, of course, a problem, though: The gate was closed. Like *closed* closed, with a padlocked chain looped through its bars. And a sign posted next to it revealed that the cemetery didn't open until ten AM on Saturdays.

She checked the time on her phone: 7:13.

Fuck! The universe was laughing at her again. She couldn't even visit her dad's grave in search of spiritual clarity without some stupid obstacle being thrown in her way.

Cammy tried to see if she could squeeze her body through a gap in the bars, but she'd been drinking too much beer lately, and her belly wouldn't allow it. In a fit of fury, she seized the gate and began to shake it like a caged animal.

The rational part of her knew what an insane sight this must've been: a young woman rattling the gate of a cemetery, huffing and puffing with exertion, early on a quiet weekend morning. Needless to say, the rational part wasn't currently in control.

"Excuse me! Excuse me!" Cammy heard the croaky voice and froze. "Please stop that!" Wheeling around, she saw a small, hunched old lady in a thick wool coat and a babushka doddering toward her. Framed by the patterned headscarf, the lady's face resembled a pale, wrinkled bean. When she reached Cammy, she sized her up and said, "What do you think you're doing?"

"I—I was trying to get in."

"The cemetery isn't open yet."

"I know, but—"

"You scared me half to death. I thought you were a bad guy."

"A bad guy?"

"Sometimes bad guys come here and make trouble."

Oh yeah—there'd been a spate of vandalism at Jewish cemeteries in the past few years, here in Jersey and elsewhere. Cammy hadn't thought of that before acting like a lunatic. Now she felt guilty. "I'm sorry. I didn't mean to scare you. So you, um, you work here?"

The lady looked offended by the question. "I'm Eva. I'm the caretaker here. Have been for forty years. I look after the dead."

"You look after the—"

"I live there." Eva pointed a bony finger at a tiny cottage in the distance. Wow, she actually resided on the cemetery grounds. Had Cammy just wandered into a Stephen King novel? "Now, why do you need to get in so badly?"

"My father's buried here."

"So are lots of people's fathers." Touché.

"He was *just* buried. On Monday."

Eva squinted in concentration. "Adler, right?"

"Right," Cammy said, impressed. "How'd you know that?"

"I know everyone here."

"There are hundreds of graves—"

"I know them all."

"Okay, I believe you."

"So you want to see your father?"

"I *need* to see him. Now."

"Why?"

"Because—I don't know, I can't put it into words. But it's important. Can you please let me in?"

Eva studied Cammy with crinkled eyes. She'd no doubt come across countless grief-stricken strangers in her four decades as caretaker—unsettled souls who flocked to the cemetery in moments of crisis to commune with their departed loved ones. Cammy was only the latest specimen. "Fine," she said after some consideration. "I'll let you in."

"Oh, thank you *so* much—"

"If you don't do any more crazy stuff."

"I won't. No more crazy stuff. I swear."

"Good. Then follow me."

With a slightly quivering hand, Eva removed a long key from her coat pocket, unlocked the gate, and pushed it open in what seemed like slow motion.

"Can I help you?" Cammy asked.

"No." Fair enough.

Eva led her through the cemetery's labyrinthine paved paths—the same ones Cammy and her mom had embarrassingly gotten lost on the morning of the burial. But this was Eva's domain, and she knew exactly where she was going. As they walked, Cammy took in the ethereal atmosphere: the fog rising up from the leaf-strewn ground, the whisper of wind in the trees, the stillness of the gray headstones bearing Jewish names and Hebrew letters. Was that an autumn nip in the air, or the cold presence of the dead?

For a hallucinatory second, Cammy dreamed that Eva wasn't even real, that she was a figment of her addled imagination. Then she felt the wizened old woman grip her forearm.

"Here we are."

Yes, here they were, standing over the unmarked rectangle of dirt under which her dad lay in his pinewood coffin. Back at the scene of the crime, where this wild week had begun. Without warning, Cammy's knees weakened, and she thought she might collapse, but the caretaker held her up with surprising strength.

"Are you all right?"

"Yeah. Sorry. It's just intense being here again."

Eva let go of Cammy's arm and peered down at the dirt. "What was your father's first name?"

"Cy."

"Cy Adler. That's a good name. He was a good man, wasn't he?"

"He was."

"I can tell."

"How?"

"I can feel it."

"You mean you can sense if someone was a good person by being near their grave?"

"Mm-hmm. Or if they were a son of a bitch."

"That's quite a skill."

"It's not a skill, it's a power," Eva said with certainty. It wasn't that far-fetched: After forty years spent among the unliving, she probably *had* developed a metaphysical intuition. "And what's your name?"

"Cammy."

"I'll leave you with your father now, Cammy." She rubbed her tissue-paper hands together to warm them. "I hope you find what you need."

"Thank you."

"Shut the gate behind you when you leave."

"I will."

Eva tightened her babushka, turned up her coat collar, and shuffled off in the direction of her cottage. She struck Cammy as less a caretaker than a kind of mystical watchwoman, a protector of the cemetery and its inhabitants. And she'd been generous enough to guide her here, to bring her to her dad.

Cammy dropped her backpack on the grass and rooted around for a stone to place on the grave. This was another Jewish custom whose origin and meaning she was ignorant of, but she liked it anyway. There was something solid—no pun intended—about putting a rock on a person's resting place. It was a way of showing you'd been there, you'd paid your respects, you'd borne witness. (Also, on a shallower level, you could gauge the popularity of the deceased by how many pebbles had been left for them by loyal visitors.)

She found a smooth, round, good-sized rock; wiped it off; and, since her father didn't have a headstone yet, set it directly on the dirt. His dirt. There you go.

Then she sat down on a rickety wooden bench beneath the nearest tree, suspended her disbelief, and spoke to him: "Hi, Dad."

"Hiya, Cam," he answered. He was the only one who ever called her that. And his mellow voice wasn't drifting up from the ground, nor was it floating down from the heavens. No, it was coming from next to her.

He was next to her.

Cammy's father, Cy Adler, dead for a week now, was sitting beside her on the rickety bench in the empty cemetery on this brisk fall morning. He wasn't translucent and spectral, like in the movie *Ghost*. He didn't have a glowing halo encircling his head. No cheesy CGI effects on display. He was himself—salt-and-pepper beard, impressive nose, playful eyes—and wore the brown corduroys and beige sweater he'd been buried in. She could smell his Head & Shoulders shampoo.

Well, what do you know? Shane had been right.

Oddly, Cammy didn't feel stunned by her dad's appearance, though it defied all the laws of time and space. Sitting by his side seemed like the most natural thing in the world.

"You're here," she said.

"Of course I'm here," he chuckled. "Where else would I be? At Disneyland?" Even in the beyond, he remained a jokester.

She had so much to ask him, so much she needed to understand. First things first. "Dad, you were *married* before?"

"Miriam spilled the beans, huh?"

"I found that picture of you and Debra. Why didn't you ever tell me?"

"Why didn't I?" Cy mused. "Superstition, maybe. That was my bad old life. Now I had my good new life. I didn't wanna jinx it." He looked sheepish. "You aren't mad at me, are ya?"

"No, I'm not mad, but I was hurt. I didn't think we had secrets from each other."

"It wasn't about you, Cam. Really. It was about me moving forward. Leaving the past in the past. Having my second act." She could understand the desire to blot out one's mistakes, turn the page, start again. "I always figured I would tell you the story someday. But then I died."

"*How*, Dad? How did you—You were healthy. You were only sixty-eight—"

"The pneumonia. It hit me hard. My body gave out on me. Bum luck, I guess."

"Mom blames the rehab place."

"They probably could've done a better job keeping me alive."

"She went back there and screamed at them."

Cy smiled. "I don't envy them that. Mom can be fearsome."

Cammy glanced at her dad's grave and wondered if he were still under the dirt, or if he'd magically teleported to the bench when she'd addressed him, or if he were in both places at once. Physics had never been her strong suit. "So . . . what was it like?"

"What? Dying?"

"Yeah."

"Well, I'll tell ya, I was lying in bed at that rehab place, watching TCM. They were showing *Casablanca*. And I wasn't in great shape, you know. I was weak. I kept coughing. I mean, I didn't think I was at *death's door*, but—Anyway, the movie was a nice distraction. I was enjoying it, even though I'd seen it a hundred times. It was the last scene with Bogart and Bergman, before she gets on the plane to Lisbon. And just when he said, 'Here's lookin' at you, kid,' I had this heavy feeling, like I needed to sleep. I didn't want to miss the end of the movie, but I was so tired all of a sudden, I couldn't keep my eyes open. So I closed them. I heard the music swell. 'As Time Goes By.' And that was it."

"You died to the end of *Casablanca*?"

"There are a lot worse ways to go."

"Then what?"

"Then nothing."

"What happens after?"

Cy shook his head coyly. "I can't tell you that."

"Why not?"

"It's a secret." Perhaps this was an oath the dead had to take once they'd reached the afterlife: They could return to earth to visit those they'd left behind, but they couldn't divulge any details of what lay in store in the next world. If there *were* a next world.

"I—I'm sorry, Dad," Cammy said, her voice cracking.

"For what?"

"For not coming to see you after your surgery. I never got to say goodbye."

"It's okay. It was supposed to be 'routine.' How could you have known?"

"Mom guilt-tripped me for not being there."

"I'm sure she didn't mean it. She's upset."

"She's devastated. So am I." Cammy looked into her father's softly lined face, which was an uncanny mirror image of her own. "Honestly, Dad . . . I don't know what to do without you. I feel like you're the only person who ever really got me." Cy nodded. "I've been a total train wreck this week. I've like dodged the shiva—"

"I don't blame you. I never liked sitting shiva. All that endless mourning."

"See, you get it!" Divided by death, they were as simpatico as always. "But yeah, I've been awful to pretty much everyone. I've been rude to the rabbi—"

"Ah, Rabbi Wiener," Cy laughed. "I won't miss his sermons, that's for sure."

"I even got arrested—"

"Arrested?"

"Well, sort of." Cammy took a breath of cool air. "The worst part, though, is that I feel this . . . this enormous sense of shame."

"Shame? Why?"

"'Cause of the state of my life: I'm alone. I live in a basement. I temp. And you died without getting to see me *do* anything."

"I saw you do lots of things."

"I mean anything of *value*. Like, when I was a kid, isn't that why you took me on all those 'adventures' into the city? Isn't that why you exposed me to plays and movies and museums? Isn't that why you gave me Roald Dahl books and got me into reading? 'Cause you believed in me, and you wanted me to grow up to be a writer or an artist or someone who does something *important*?"

"No," Cy said simply.

"What?"

"I did that stuff with you because it was fun. Because I loved sharing it with you. Not because I wanted you to become a certain kind of person." Oh. "From the day you were born, Cam, all I ever hoped was that you'd be healthy and happy. I didn't have any other expectations. You could work at a gas station or win a Pulitzer Prize, and it wouldn't change how I felt about you. So whatever this shame is, you're putting it on yourself, and you should let it go."

Blam! Mind blown. For years, Cammy had carried the leaden weight of needing to make her dad proud of her, through literary achievement or some other standout success. And when he died, she thought she'd lost that opportunity for good. But now she realized the whole complex—the pressure she'd put on herself, the consequent self-loathing—had been in her head.

He just wanted her to be happy. Imagine that.

"How's it going between you and Mom?" Cy asked.

Cammy kicked at a pile of yellow-orange leaves, like the guilty child she was. "Not so well. She asked me to leave the house the other day. She said I was making the shiva 'impossible' for her."

"That's not good," he frowned.

"I know it's not."

"What's the problem?"

"We can't seem to get along. We push each other's buttons. I'm grieving, and she's grieving, and our grief, like, collides or something. And now you're not there to play peacemaker like you used to."

"So you need to figure out how to fix that."

"What if we can't? What if we just become this estranged mother and daughter?"

"Then I'll haunt you from the grave," Cy said in a spooky tone that made Cammy laugh. He stroked the underside of his chin: his signature thinking gesture. "You know, Cam, you do take Mom for granted. You always have."

"Take her for granted?"

"Yes. And it's partially my fault. I got to be your *pal*, but she had to be your *parent*. She was in charge of the essentials: food and clothes and doctors' appointments and do-this-and-don't-do-that. Meanwhile I was bringing you to Broadway shows and taking you to John's for pizza. No wonder I became your favorite. She got stuck with the unglamorous job."

"But—"

"And don't forget: When you were born, *Mom* was the one who quit real estate to take care of you. She made that sacrifice. I was off in the city every day, at the ad agency, and she was home changing your diapers. In those early years, *she* was the one who spent all the time with you. Not me. But you don't remember that, do you?"

Cammy contemplated this. "No, I don't really."

"What about when you were afraid to go to school?"

"God, I haven't thought about that in forever."

"Mom was the one who helped you get through it."

What her dad was referring to—what Cammy had virtually blocked out of her memory—was the horrendous case of separation anxiety that had plagued her from pre-K well into elementary school. Sure, plenty of children experience some mild version of this affliction, but for Cammy, it was different. It was extreme. It was ugly.

As a little girl, she'd felt an all-consuming dread, an overwhelming panic, at the prospect of being away from her parents—ironically, her mom in particular. This irrational fear produced daily morning tantrums during which she had to be led kicking and screaming to the car. At the drop-off spot in front of River Hill Elementary, she created mortifying scenes by chasing after her mother's vehicle, sobbing and begging Beth to come back and get her.

Once, in first grade, a boy innocently asked her, "Why are you always crying?" In reply, she shoved him and cried even harder.

Special accommodations were made. Beth was allowed to spend one day a week in Cammy's classroom to help her sensitive daughter acclimate. She brought her to Dr. Sugarman, a benevolent child psychologist in town who let Cammy feed the rabbits in her backyard. And each morning, over a breakfast of blueberry Eggo waffles, Beth gave Cammy a gentle pep talk: "You're going to be okay. You'll be so busy at school, the day will be over before you even know it. And I'll be right there at three o'clock to pick you up."

Eventually, by second or third grade, Cammy got past the worst of the anxiety. She still missed her mom and sniffled sometimes, but, thankfully, the parking-lot meltdowns were over.

Thinking back now on the entire ordeal—and it *had* been an exhausting ordeal—she saw that her mother had handled it with remarkable patience and understanding. As a matter of fact, Beth had done a lot that Cammy had forgotten about: She'd played dolls with her, made her snacks, put Band-Aids on her boo-boos, sang her lullabies, tucked her in at night. The unglamorous essentials.

And where had her dad been "in those early years," as he'd called them?

Not there. Somewhere else. Working.

He was right. She did take her mom for granted. Mind blown again.

"I should've said all this to you when I was alive," Cy continued, "but I selfishly liked being your number one. You should be nicer to Mom, though. Cut her some slack. If she seems less 'fun' than me, it's because she had to be. You can't have *two* fun parents." He paused meaningfully. "She loves you more than anything, Cam. And now that I'm not around, she needs you more than ever."

Cammy let this sink in. Her father's words were prompting her to revise her own well-worn narrative: No more Dad-as-good-cop, Mom-as-bad-cop. They were *both* good cops; Beth's police work was just less flashy.

Yes, it was long past time for Cammy to grow up and give her mother her due. She silently resolved to make things right with her, somehow.

To make things right with everyone.

"I have to be going soon," Cy said.

"No. Don't."

"I have to."

Cammy clung to her dad's arm and rested her head on his shoulder, on the familiar fabric of his mothball-scented sweater. A light breeze blew. Leaves danced. A chirping sparrow landed on the tree branch above them. As tears welled in her eyes, she said the most commonplace, most true thing possible, which she hadn't gotten the chance to say one final time: "I love you so much, Dad."

He leaned over and kissed her forehead. "I love you, too." They sat for a while without speaking. Then a sly grin crept across his face, and his mischievous eyes lit up. "Wanna hear a joke?"

"A joke?"

"It's a great one. I don't think I've told it to you." Her dad had a habit of prefacing his jokes this way, whether or not they were great, whether or not he'd told them before.

"Okay . . ."

"So two old Jewish guys run into each other on the street." A promising start. "And the first guy says, 'Excuse me. Can I ask you a question?' And the second guy says, 'Sure, go ahead.'" He was imitating their thick Lower East Side accents. "The first guy asks, 'Is it pronounced Ha*w*aii or Ha*v*aii?' 'Ha*v*aii,' says the second guy. The first guy says, 'Thank you.' The second guy says, 'You're *v*elcome,' and walks away." Cy uttered the punchline and cracked up immediately, as was his wont. When it came to dumb jokes, he was his own best audience.

Cammy couldn't help but laugh too, not so much at the bit as at her dad's contagious enjoyment of it. Lifting her head off his shoulder, she said, "I don't know if that's a *great* one, but . . ."

When she looked over again, though, he was gone. She was alone on the bench.

This was how her father had chosen to conclude his otherworldly visitation? With a dose of Borscht Belt shtick?

Of course it was.

Always leave 'em laughing.

♦ 18 ♦

CAMMY LEFT THE CEMETERY, but not before lying down in a fetal position on the hardened dirt of her dad's grave. She stayed like this for a couple of minutes, or maybe five, or, fine, a legit twenty. Then she got up, brushed herself off, and found her way out, making sure to shut the gate behind her, as per Eva the caretaker's instructions.

After her heart-to-heart with her father, Cammy felt like a new woman. A better woman. And a woman who had a shit ton of amends to make before the day was through.

The shiva would end tomorrow morning, Sunday, and then she'd be returning to the city to resume her life (such as it was), her temping, etc. Which meant she had roughly the next twenty-four hours to right the various wrongs she'd perpetrated over the course of the week, to mend the riven relationships—to, well, redeem herself.

Ladies and gents, welcome to the Official Cammy Adler Redemption Tour.

Like the North Jersey nomad she'd become, she walked to the nearest bus stop and hopped the next ride back to River Hill. As the bus bumped along, she reflected proudly on how she was really mastering the art of Bergen County public transportation.

And her fellow travelers, the senior citizens with grocery bags, were feeling more and more like old friends.

Cammy alighted outside the River Hill Public Library at a quarter past nine AM. She was here, somewhat humiliatingly, because she wanted to use a computer to send an email. She also needed to charge her phone, which she'd neglected to do while sleeping on the cot in the office of the Dirty Bird. Such are the ways of the nomad.

Modest though it was, even by the standards of small-town libraries, this place held great sentimental value for her. She'd hurried to it almost every day after middle school to escape from the *Mean-Girls*-meets-*Lord-of-the-Flies* social climate and do her homework in peace. Usually, however, she wound up wandering out of the kids' section into the adult stacks, where she picked up strange books and marveled at their mysterious contents. (For example, eleven-year-old Cammy expected Erica Jong's *Fear of Flying* to be about nervousness on airplanes. Instead it was loaded with graphic sex.) Her love affair with literature had blossomed within this building's brick walls.

Now she stepped inside and snuck over to the computer area, hoping to go unrecognized. The library, which still boasted an eighties aesthetic (e.g., orange carpeting), was mostly empty at this early Saturday hour. A few elderly locals sat at the boxy desktop PCs, checking their AOL email accounts, surfing the net, and playing political YouTube videos at full volume.

An old soul herself, Cammy joined them. She plopped down at a workstation, plugged in her dying phone, and logged on to a computer. She opened her Gmail and addressed a message to the Drama Collective group list. What should the subject line be? Something simple, sincere. Aha: "An apology."

Dear Drama Collective,

   I hope you guys are doing well.
   I'm writing to apologize for my behavior at the meeting Wednesday night, and for telling you all to "go fuck yourselves." That was obviously rude and inappropriate, and I'm sorry for any offense I may have caused.
   As I mentioned before I stormed out, my dad died last Saturday, so I haven't exactly been at my best this week. And I was clearly extra sensitive about the pages I brought in, since they were so personal. Still, that doesn't excuse my deranged reaction to your feedback. I know the workshop is supposed to be a "safe space," and you probably didn't feel very safe while I was shitting on you.
   (FYI, that play I was working on is a moot point now anyway. My laptop got stolen in Atlantic City, and I lost the document, along with a ton of my old writing. Karma's a bitch.)
   So, in addition to being an apology, this email is also a humble request. Believe it or not, I would still like to be a part of the Drama Collective and meet with you folks every Wednesday. You're a cool group of talented people, and I'd love to keep hanging out with you. I totally understand, however, if you don't want me back. I probably wouldn't either if *I'd* been told to go fuck *my*self.
   But if you are gracious enough to let me return, I promise not to throw out any more negative energy. Positive vibes only, as Gretchen might say. And one day, hopefully, I'll bring in some better pages. ☺
   Thanks for reading this. Have a great weekend.

Yours truly (and repentantly),
Cammy

Reviewing what she'd written, Cammy was satisfied that it struck the proper balance between earnest contrition and wry humor. She did genuinely feel bad about her outburst, and even if the theater kids wished to have nothing more to do with her, she wanted them to know she was sorry.

She hit "Send." The Redemption Tour had begun.

By chance, a new email had appeared in Cammy's inbox while she was composing her missive. It came from Dr. Strum and had no subject.

Dear Cammy,

    Sorry to write you on such short notice, but you're not still in town, are you? I couldn't recall how long you were staying, or whether the shiva for your father had already ended. If you do happen to be around and not otherwise occupied, would you care to join me for lunch this afternoon? That bakery on Main Street—I forget what it's called—serves tasty soups and breads. There's something I've been thinking about since I saw you that I'd like to talk over. Or we can do it some other time. Let me know before noon. Ciao.

RS

This was interesting. What could Dr. Strum want to "talk over" with her? Cammy had visited her beloved former teacher at the high school just a few days ago; they'd chatted, Cammy had had a minor breakdown, and Dr. Strum had bucked her up in her no-nonsense style. So what did her mentor have to say now?

There was only one way to find out. Cammy quickly wrote her back to confirm that, yes, she was still in town and available for lunch at noon at Song Bakery (this was its name). She'd see her then.

"Young lady, can you help me?" The grizzled man at the neighboring workstation was asking for Cammy's assistance. He wore a camouflage jacket and a black baseball cap with yellow letters that read "U.S. Army Veteran." He was the one who'd been watching the political clips. YouTube was open on his screen.

"Sure. What do you need?"

"Well, I'm looking for a video, but I don't know how to find the darned thing."

"See the search bar there at the top? You can use that."

"Can you do it for me? My eyesight ain't too hot."

"No problem." Meet the new and improved Cammy, who apologized for her misdeeds and was always ready to help out her elders. "What should I search for?"

"Tucker Carlson," he wheezed.

★ ★ ★

Having charged her phone and killed some time skimming the *New York Times* website—a left-wing antidote to the alt-right propaganda playing next to her—Cammy departed the library. She'd barely set foot outside when she felt the phone vibrating in her pocket.

It was Gretchen.

Oh God. She hadn't expected to hear from anyone in the Drama Collective so soon after sending her message—if at all—and she wasn't sure she wanted to answer. But she had to face the music. "Hello?"

"Hi, Cammy." Gretchen's voice, normally so upbeat and energetic, sounded more low-key, less performative.

"Hi, Gretchen . . ."

"I just saw your email to the group."

Cammy sat down on the library's cold concrete front steps. "Oh. Okay."

"Thanks for sending that."

"Yeah. It seemed like the decent thing to do."

"Well, just so you know"—here came the blowback—"none of us are mad at you."

Cammy did an internal double take. "What?"

"We're not. Really."

"Wait, *why*? I like lost my shit at the meeting and told you all—"

"To go fuck ourselves, yes," Gretchen giggled. "That was a first. But come on. Your dad just passed. We get it. We're theater people. We're emotional. When you ran out, we were worried about you."

"You were?"

"Of course. I thought about texting you, but I didn't wanna make things worse. I figured you needed some space."

"I—I appreciate that," Cammy said, absorbing all this. So the drama crew whom she'd judged for their big personalities and artsy affectations also happened to be concerned, caring people. Another eureka moment.

"Everyone wouldn't have been so hard on your pages if we knew about your dad. Why didn't you just tell us to begin with?"

"I guess I wanted the pages to stand on their own. But that massively backfired."

Gretchen sighed. "You know how it goes in workshops sometimes. One annoying person gives negative feedback"—she meant Hunter, the pompous Sam Shepard wannabe with the patchy ginger beard—"and then everybody else jumps on board. It's not fair. But by the way: *I* liked your scene. I should've spoken up."

"You don't have to say that."

"I know I don't. I mean it. The mother-son relationship felt super real to me. And it's brave of you to write about something so vulnerable."

"All right, all right, you're gonna give me a big head," Cammy said with a self-deprecating lilt. She wasn't great at accepting compliments.

"Seriously, you should stick with the play. You might have something there. A mom and a son trying to move forward after the dad is gone, and hurting each other in the process. That's a strong story."

"I lost the whole thing, though. Like I said in my email. My laptop—"

"Why can't you just rewrite what you had?"

"From memory?" Cammy whined.

"How far along were you?"

"Like forty pages?"

Gretchen snorted. "Oh, gimme a break! You can redo forty pages!"

"Ugh. Yeah. I probably can."

"And once you finish a draft, maybe we can put together a reading of it."

"'We'?"

"You and me. I'm a director, remember?"

"You'd wanna direct it?"

"Yeah! It would be awesome to work on it with you. We could get some actors, find a good space, invite some people . . ."

"That sounds amazing."

"But first you need to *write the play!*"

"Right. Yes. That makes sense." Cammy could hardly believe the turn this call had taken. She'd been anticipating a stern rebuke on behalf of the Collective ("Please don't ever contact us again."), but instead Gretchen had extended kindness, empathy, and, now, an invitation to collaborate. Why did she constantly expect the worst from others? "So . . . does this mean I can come back to the group?"

"I'm sure everyone'll be fine with that. But out of respect, I'll bring it up at our meeting next week and get their definite okay. Then I'll let you know. Is that fair?"

"That's more than fair. It's democratic."

Gretchen chortled. "And Cammy, if you ever wanna grab a drink sometime, like just the two of us, and shoot the shit about theater or life or whatever, I'd be down."

"So would I, Gretchen."

"Way cool. And hey—I'm sorry for your loss."

Cammy hung up and remained on the steps, watching the children navigate the multicolored jungle gym at Wood Park, which abutted the library. She'd slid down that same curving slide a quarter century ago (!), while her mom supervised from a nearby bench.

She felt grateful for Gretchen's compassion, and excited to possibly work with her. She felt stupid for underestimating the members of the Drama Collective, who'd actually been *worried* about her well-being. And she wondered if perhaps there were some truth to that hackneyed adage she'd always scoffed at: When you put good out into the universe, you often get it back.

★ ★ ★

Cammy loved the musty, papery smell of a stationery store. On her walk to the bakery to meet Dr. Strum, she'd swung into the old one on Main Street, which had been around since she was a kid buying school supplies. Given the sad fate of her laptop, she thought it might be wise to purchase a nice notebook and a good pen for first-drafting. These items tended to be less attractive to thieves.

She picked out a narrow-ruled National Brand notebook with green-tinted "eye-ease" paper and a Pilot pen with black gel ink. They would be her tools as she set about reconstructing her grief play. Gretchen's investment in the piece had lit a blazing fire under her ass to hunker down and do the work.

Cammy's next stop was Song Bakery, a Korean-run spot a few blocks away that did, as Dr. Strum had said, offer a tantalizing array of soups and breads. The shop was airy, brightly lit, decorated in pastels. She ordered a black coffee from the aproned girl behind the counter and sat at a crumb-speckled table by the window to wait for her teacher.

Outside, it was a sleepy autumn Saturday. Across the street stood the Heads Only hair salon and Maxwell's Hardware and DeCicco Jewelers. An octogenarian couple strolled past. Then some teens in soccer uniforms. Then a young family with toddlers in tow.

Cammy felt a sudden flood of warmth toward her hometown. Even if she didn't want to live here, how could she hate it? She'd spent her whole life scorning River Hill as dull and provincial, comparing it to the world-class city on the other side of the river. But in reality, it had been a perfectly fine place to grow up. It was safe. It was pleasant. It was liberal enough. And all the memories of her first eighteen years were woven into its texture. Why not embrace that?

The epiphanies kept coming today.

Dr. Strum appeared in the window. In her pleated skirt, tweed coat, and bucket hat—each in a different shade of brown—she called to mind Miss Marple from those Agatha Christie mysteries on BBC America. She entered the bakery, found her former student, and took a seat opposite her.

"Hello again, Cammy," she said, brushing crumbs off the tabletop with an efficient hand. "I'm glad you could meet me."

"So am I. I go back to the city tomorrow."

"Ah. Then I caught you just in time."

"You did. The shiva ends in the morning."

"How are you managing? How have the past few days been?"

"Eventful," Cammy said, choosing to leave it at that.

"Mm." Dr. Strum didn't pry. "Well, shall we go up and grab some food before we get down to business?" What business? What was this about?

"Sure."

They both got the soup of the day—wild mushroom and farro—which came with half a crisp, freshly baked baguette. Dr. Strum asked for her preferred Yorkshire Tea but had to settle for a hot cup of Lipton. She paid for lunch. Once they'd returned to the table with their trays, she said, "I imagine you're wondering why I summoned you here."

"I really am."

"I won't keep you in suspense any longer, then." Dr. Strum blew on a steaming spoonful of soup. "After our tête-à-tête on Wednesday, it occurred to me that you may be able to help me with a little project of mine. If you're interested, that is."

Cammy broke off a piece of baguette. "What's the project?"

"I've decided to write a book."

"A book?"

"Yes. A sort of tell-all memoir about my three decades as an English instructor in the wilderness of American public education. What I've seen, what I've learned, what I believe. I certainly have enough colorful stories to fill a volume or two. An old friend of mine from graduate school at Buffalo is an editor at a university press. She's intrigued by the premise, which has finally spurred me to write the thing after years of idle musing."

"That's—that's wonderful, Dr. Strum. You should do it. But . . . how can *I* help?"

"I need an assistant," she said, taking a sip of tea. "An amanuensis. A right hand, if you will. Someone to read my chapters and discuss them with me. To research and fact-check. To hold me accountable. Otherwise I'll end up getting distracted with my teaching duties and let this opportunity fall by the wayside."

"And you want me to be that person?"

"Who else but my favorite pupil?" Dr. Strum formed her restrained version of a smile. She wasn't one for broad displays.

Touched, Cammy looked down at her bowl. "I'm honored that you'd ask me."

"Oh, let's not get sentimental now. This is a job I'm talking about. I'd compensate you for your labor."

"You don't need to pay me—"

"Of course I do. Your time is valuable. We'll come to an appropriate arrangement." She spoke like a BBC character, too. Cammy adored it. "There's one caveat, however."

"Yes?"

"I'd like to do our work together in person. Not over the phone or, God forbid, on *Zoom*." Dr. Strum grimaced, as if the notion of videoconferencing made her ill. "We could convene at my home once a month, say." She lived alone in a small, antique-filled Tudor house Cammy had visited back in high school. "I'd offer to travel to the city, but my middle-aged nerves can't abide the frenzy. Would meeting here in town be too much of a burden for you?"

"No, not at all." Quite the contrary: Cammy relished the idea of monthly sessions spent poring over Dr. Strum's pages, Yorkshire Tea in hand. Providing feedback to her mentor might be intimidating at first, but she'd get past that. It would be a thrill to serve as the "amanuensis" (she'd check the dictionary later) of such a brilliant woman, and to have her in her life again.

"Good. Then that's settled. Shall I share a few of my initial thoughts with you?"

"Please. I'd love to hear them."

As Dr. Strum laid out her plans for the book—in elegant complete sentences, naturally—Cammy ate her flavorful soup and listened. She found herself thinking of how lucky she was to have had a teacher like this: a literary lioness, a high priestess of the written word, who stuck to her intellectual guns despite the numbing onslaught of technology and social media and all the rest of this century's vacuous bullshit. Even luckier, Dr. Strum had singled her out at a pivotal age, seen something special in her—a spark of potential.

Maybe that spark was still there.

♦ 19 ♦

To see Nick, or not to see Nick. That was the question.
Cammy hadn't spoken to Beautiful Dancer Boy—er, Man—since Thursday afternoon, when her mom had walked in on them in her bedroom and perpetrated a cockblock of epic proportions. "Call me, okay?" he'd said before slinking off in shame. But she hadn't called him. She'd had a falling-out with her mother and fled to Atlantic City, where she'd gotten grinded on (ground?) by Valentino at Savage Men. Nick didn't need to know about that last part.

What he *did* need to know—and what Cammy needed to figure out quick—was what the hell was going on between them.

It should've been a no-brainer, right? You bump into your high school crush after a decade. He's still as hot as ever. Life has dealt him some blows, yet he's bounced back and helped to build a thriving community center for at-risk youth. So he's basically a hero. Oh, and one more thing: He's into you now.

What do you do in this situation, according to every rom-com currently streaming on Netflix? You run straight into his toned arms.

Not so fast, though.

Cammy knew that the key to her capital-R Redemption lay not within a dude's embrace—ideal as that dude might seem—but within herself. Nick couldn't fix her life for her. Only she could do that, by heeding her dad's guidance and being a better human, or at least trying to be one. And was it really a smart move to dive into a romantic attachment the week of his death, and so soon after her last breakup?

No. It was not. Sorry, Netflix.

On the other hand: What if she were missing out? Denying the power of serendipity? Throwing away her shot, as the Founding Fathers rap in *Hamilton*? Cammy had done enough dating in the city to determine that most of the guys there were assholes. (And when she'd unearthed a non-asshole in David, *she'd* been the asshole and cheated on him. Nice.) Nick, however, seemed like an amazing person, and he'd emerged from her past as if sent by Providence, or Nora Ephron. Could she afford to pass that up?

She wouldn't be able to decide until she saw him again.

Hey, Cammy texted, sitting at the bakery after Dr. Strum had bid her farewell. *Sorry for the radio silence. What're you up to?* She drank the cold dregs of her coffee and waited for a reply. In a few minutes, it came, with correct spelling and grammar. Nick was a man after her own heart.

Hey! No worries. I'm at the Clubhouse.

On a Saturday?

Yeah, we have stuff on the weekends.

Could I stop by and see you?

Like right now?

Sorry, is that crazy? I don't have a lot of time.

I'm only in Jersey one more day.

Oh. I didn't realize that . . .

Yeah, shiva ends tomorrow, so . . .

But if it's not a good time, I get it.

No, it's cool. Come by. I'll be here.

Okay. Thanks. See you soon.

Cammy carried her tray to the front and emptied its contents into a trash bin. Yes, she'd effectively invited herself to Nick's workplace, but it felt important that she talk to him face-to-face. The old Cammy would've probably just said "fuck it" and avoided the awkwardness of dealing with the situation. She would've gone back to New York, ghosted him, and turned the episode into a funny story to tell at parties, about how she'd almost banged her teenage fantasy figure.

She didn't want to be like that anymore. She wanted to have some goddamn integrity.

So, out on Main Street, she boarded her second bus of the day. This one was headed to Hackensack, where, inside his Clubhouse, Beautiful Dancer Man awaited.

★ ★ ★

The kids were doing arts and crafts. Specifically, they were making collages out of magazine cutouts on construction paper, embellished with watercolors, glitter, fabric, buttons, and various other materials. Supplies were spread across the long tables in the Clubhouse's art studio: scissors, tape, paintbrushes, markers, bottles of glue. The room looked as though it had been hit by a tornado of childhood creativity. One of Nick's colleagues, a bubbly young woman in a spattered smock, was roaming around, doing her best to control the chaos. "That's enough glitter!" she implored after a girl dumped the sparkly stuff onto her masterpiece.

"I didn't know kids were here on the weekend too," Cammy said. She was standing by the doorway with Nick, who had on jeans and a puffer vest over a long-sleeved shirt. Everything he wore flattered his slim figure.

"A lot of their parents work on Saturdays, so they leave them here. We try to keep them occupied."

"They look occupied all right," Cammy laughed, watching a ten-year-old Jackson Pollock in a Spiderman T-shirt hurl paint at his collage.

"Should we go to my office?"

They slipped out of the studio and made their way through the halls to Nick's neat office space, where Cammy had first kissed him the other day. She planted her behind on the blue stability ball in the corner. She needed some stability now.

"So," he said, sitting down in his ergonomic chair, "we left things in a pretty weird place."

"I know. I'm so sorry about that. If I'd known my mom was gonna show up, I never would've—"

"It's okay. I've had a couple days to regain my self-respect."

Cammy clasped her cheeks. "God, that was bad."

"Was your mom angry?"

"Yes. Very. Especially when she found a stray condom on the floor."

"Oh no."

"We had a pretty nasty argument, actually. She told me to leave the premises."

Nick's eyes got large. "Because of *me*?"

"No, no, it had been building all week. Me bringing a guy home was just the last straw."

"So where have you been staying?"

"I crashed with Fran one night. And last night . . ." She elected not to mention her lodging at the Dirty Bird, courtesy of Sugar Shane. "Never mind."

"Are you okay, Cammy?" Nick said. She could see why he'd be concerned: Her dad had died, and her mom had cast her out. By any reasonable metric, she was a mess.

"I *wasn't* okay, but I think I'm starting to be. I'm—I'm turning over a new leaf. Or something. Apologies for the cliché."

She exhaled. "Anyway, that's why I'm here. To do the right thing."

"Which is . . . ?"

Cammy stared into Nick's handsome, astonishingly well-proportioned face—the one she'd lain awake picturing as a moony teen. He'd seemed so unattainable then, like a shooting star. Now he was on the same earthly plane as her, mere feet away. She'd already kissed him, undressed him, and she could have more of that if she wanted. More of all of him. But she knew better. "I don't think we should see each other, Nick."

"Oh," he said after a beat, not hiding his disappointment.

"Believe me, with how obsessed I used to be with you, I'm shocked to be saying this too."

Nick shifted in his chair. "Can I ask why? 'Cause, honestly, I kind of thought us running into each other again was, I don't know—"

"Kismet?"

"Yeah. As cheesy as that sounds. And I thought it was at least worth seeing where it could go . . ."

Had she lost her marbles? Why was she rejecting Nick Ramos, the dancing dreamboat, her first-ever love? "It's not you," Cammy said, realizing she'd uttered another clunky cliché. "Sorry, I know people always say that, but in this case, it's really true. As far as I can tell, you're like a flawless man—"

"I'm *not* flawless."

"You could've fooled me. You're gorgeous and sweet and altruistic"—he blushed—"and you've been through rough shit and come out the other side." She put a hand on her chest. "*I*, however, am full of flaws. And grief. And I have a lot of hard work to do on myself before I'm ready for a relationship, or anything *resembling* a relationship. I mean, I could sleep with you, which would definitely be enjoyable for me, but you're too good for a meaningless fuck."

"Well, thanks." Nick nodded. He got it. "I respect that."

"Thank you."

"I've been there. If I'd tried to date someone after the car accident, it would've been a disaster."

"Exactly."

He twirled a pen with the Clubhouse logo on it between his fingers. "This doesn't rule out a friendship, though, does it?"

"A friendship?"

"Unless," he teased, "you can't handle being friends with 'Beautiful Dancer Boy.'"

"Hm. I don't know. It might be tough. I guess we'll just have to see." Having made her mature decision (what?!), Cammy wanted to keep the doors of possibility open a crack. So she added, "FYI—just because I'm not ready for something now doesn't mean I won't *ever* be."

Nick smiled. "Are you telling me to wait for you?"

"Maybe."

"How long? Another ten years?"

"I waited for *you* for eleven."

"We'll be forty then."

"Forty? Impossible." As they bantered, Cammy's body relaxed. In putting the brakes on their dalliance, she'd acted like an adult for once. It was a new, nice feeling. She rolled up to Nick on the stability ball and gently kissed his cheek, as she'd done at the senior prom.

"What was that for?"

"For being a mensch."

"You know," he said, "you're not off the hook yet. You still owe me one after making me do the walk of shame in front of your mom."

"Fair. What can I do to atone?"

"Well, as a matter of fact, we've been talking about adding some creative writing classes here for the kids . . ."

Cammy stiffened. "Hold on. You're not suggesting *I* could, like, teach these kids about writing?"

"Just throwing it out there." Nick play-coughed. "I've been meaning to mention it."

"Sneaky. But yeah, no, I'd be terrible at that."

"Why?"

"First of all, I'm not really a writer, so I shouldn't be teaching creative writing, even to ten-year-olds—"

"What do you mean you're not a writer? You've been writing since high school. I still remember those depressing lit mag stories."

"Don't remind me," Cammy winced. "But no, a writer is someone whose stuff gets like published or produced, which mine has *not* thus far—"

"Says who?"

"Says . . . the world."

"The world says a lot of stupid things." A legitimate point.

"Also, I'm sure if I taught a class, I'd fuck it up and the kids would hate me."

"How would you fuck it up?"

"Oh, I'd find a way. I always seem to."

"I don't buy that." He stood up and held out his hand. "Come on."

"Where are we going?"

"I wanna introduce you to them."

"Nick—"

"You *owe* me."

Against Cammy's sputtering protests, Nick led her to a cozy lounge where the kids were recovering from their artistic explosion with a nutritious repast of fruits and veggies.

"Guys," he announced, "I'd like you to meet my friend Miss Cammy." Friend. They were friends.

"Hi, Miss Cammy!" the children sang out in unison.

"Miss Cammy is a *writer*—"

"Sort of," she mumbled under her breath.

"—and she's gonna come back one day soon and help you all write your *own* stories." He turned to her for confirmation. "Isn't that right?"

Nick's emotional blackmail was masterful. Now how could she let these adorable youngsters down? "Yep," she said. "That's right."

"Cool!" "Sweet!" "Yeah!" Her potential future students were psyched.

She felt Nick nudge her, as if to say, "See? It'll be fun."

Who knew? Maybe it would be. Maybe, despite her own resounding lack of success as a writer, Cammy could get these elementary schoolers excited about writing, about self-expression, about the power of putting their thoughts into words. Maybe she could take the lessons she'd learned from Dr. Strum and try to pay them forward.

Hey. Stranger things had happened.

★ ★ ★

She'd been so caught up in her grief this week, she'd barely noticed that Halloween was fast approaching.

On the bus (number three!) back to River Hill, Cammy saw the holiday decorations that had started to pop up on people's lawns: the carved pumpkins and plastic skeletons and cheesecloth spiderwebs, the inflatable ghouls and goblins, the cardboard gravestones that read "RIP." (These had a different meaning for her now.) She remembered one year when she and Fran had trick-or-treated as Daphne and Velma from *Scooby-Doo*. They'd inhaled candy corn and chocolate bars until their sugar high made them jittery, laughing their asses off all the while.

Fran.

Was she still in Atlantic City? That's where Cammy had left her bestie after their bitter fight on the rainswept beach. Fran had accused her, rightfully, of being a snob, of shitting on the idea of living in Jersey and working in the food industry. And rather than own it and apologize, Cammy had pulled her usual cowardly stunt and peaced out.

But now she was on the Redemption Tour. Now she needed to salvage the most important bond she had with anyone outside of her dad.

She took out her phone and dialed.

Fran answered after several rings, sounding scratchy and shot. "Hello?"

"Hi." Cammy wasn't sure where to begin. She was still getting used to this penitence thing. "Um, are you in A.C. still?"

"Nah. I drove back this morning. I was too bummed to stick around."

"Didn't you have the hotel room for two nights?"

"I ate the cost. Whatever."

"I can pay you for it."

"Forget it. You already lost enough money." Fran cleared her throat. "I found your note on the bed last night. Where'd you go?"

"I took a Greyhound to the city, then a bus home."

"Where'd you sleep?"

"At the, uh, at the Dirty Bird."

"What? You mean you fucked Shane?"

"*No.* He put me up on a cot in the back."

"Wow. What a gentleman."

Cammy didn't want to do this on the phone. She wanted to talk to Fran in person. "Are you at your place?"

"Yeah. I've got a raging hangover. I feel like crap."

"Can I come over?"

Fran hesitated. "I don't know. Maybe we could like . . . use some time apart." In two decades of friendship, she'd never said no to hanging out before. It felt like a tiny Halloween stake had been driven through Cammy's heart.

"I leave tomorrow, though. I wanna see you before I go."

"I mean—"

"Please?"

"Jesus. Fine. If you're gonna fuckin' beg me."

Cammy got off in town and realized she should probably show up at Fran's with a peace offering of some sort—a tangible token of her remorse. The options on Main Street were limited, to put it mildly, but then she hit upon the perfect solution: a pizza.

A simple gift, yes. Yet who doesn't feel a surge of happiness at being presented with a surprise pie, particularly when they're battling a bad hangover?

Sonny's, River Hill's one and only pizzeria, was just down the block, and, fortunately, it had the goods. Everyone said New York was the pizza capital of the world; still, New Jersey didn't lag far behind.

Cammy had a rich history of patronizing Sonny's with Fran (it was their go-to whenever they smoked weed), so she knew precisely what to order. She walked into the joint—a narrow, unadorned hole in the wall with cracked white tiling—and up to the burly guy at the counter. He looked like Robert DeNiro at the end of *Raging Bull*, after he'd gained sixty pounds to play the aging boxer Jake LaMotta. She recognized him from days gone by. What was his name? Angelo?

"How ya doin'?" Angelo (?) bellowed. "What can I getcha?"

"I'd like a large Monster, please. With extra cheese. Plus a side of garlic knots."

"Gimme fifteen minutes."

The Monster was as monstrous as one might imagine: a pie topped with pepperoni, ham, spicy sausage, mushrooms, onions, green peppers, and black olives. Oh, also, for absolutely no reason, bacon. It should've come in a special box with the phone number of a local cardiologist printed on the front. Greasy excess and all, the pizza had long been Cammy and Fran's guiltiest pleasure, and if any edible item could help bring them together, this was it.

While she waited for her food, Cammy sat on the frayed cushion of a wobbly stool and thought about her mom. Beth would be at the house now, preparing to welcome guests for the final night of shiva. The stragglers who'd put off paying their respects until the very last minute. Cammy could've easily gone over and joined them, but she wasn't ready for that yet.

No, the reunion with her mother was the ultimate destination on her Tour. She was building up to it. Or stalling.

First came her friend.

"Here you go," Angelo said after the promised fifteen minutes, banging the pizza box down on the counter. He placed a white paper bag full of garlic knots next to it. The grease was already seeping through. "You need anythin' else?"

"I'll take one of those big bottles of Coke. Thanks." Coke, not Pepsi: the gourmet choice. Cammy was splurging.

He punched the keys of the analog cash register. "Thirty-two fifty."

Thirty-two fifty?! The prices here had practically doubled since her pot-smoking youth. No wonder she'd been hearing so much about inflation lately.

★ ★ ★

Fran lived in a nondescript apartment complex on the edge of town. Cammy walked there like a wayfarer, backpack on her back, pizza in her hands, garlic knots and soda in a plastic bag slung around her shoulder. Could she get any classier?

She arrived as the late-afternoon sun was casting a reddish glow on the fall foliage. She knocked on the door with her elbow, and Fran opened it and let her in.

Although she wasn't a bachelor, Fran's place had the appearance of a stereotypical bachelor pad: spartan furniture (including the obligatory black leather couch), mostly bare walls, empty refrigerator (save for a six-pack or two). She just couldn't be bothered to decorate. "I go to work, I come home and crash, then I go out and party," she'd once explained. "I don't need to be fuckin' Martha Stewart over here." A valid defense.

Fran herself looked the worse for wear, with dark circles under her eyes. The bender in Atlantic City had taken a toll on her, too. She had on baggy sweatpants and her gray cross-country hoodie. "Hey," she said. "You got a pizza?"

"The Monster from Sonny's. And garlic knots."

"No shit. Clutch."

They sat down in the living room, Fran on the couch, Cammy in a brown La-Z-Boy. There was a half-drunk bottle of lemon-lime Gatorade on the coffee table, along with a packet of Alka-Seltzer Hangover Relief tablets. An episode of *Hoarders* was paused on the TV.

Cammy cut straight to the chase. "Okay, so, for starters, I'm an asshole, and I'm sorry."

"Uh-huh," Fran agreed.

"I didn't mean to like condescend to you for living here. Or for what you do. I don't look down on it. I'm actually jealous of it."

"Jealous?"

"Yeah. You know who you are. You know where you belong. You have a business—a deli that people love. You're gonna have a restaurant. While I'm just . . . flapping in the wind."

"Then why don't you wanna come back here and work with me?"

"'Cause I don't think it would be right for me. But it's right for you. And I respect the hell out of it, I do."

Fran popped a tablet and swigged it down with some Gatorade. "I appreciate that."

"And the day the restaurant opens, I'll be the first one in line to eat there."

"You better be."

"You're my best friend in the world, Fran," Cammy said, feeling unexpectedly emotional as the sentence left her mouth. "You've been there for me this week. You've *always* been there for me. I don't want you to think I'm not grateful for that, or that I have some stupid, snobby opinion of your life. I was just being a shithead last night."

With a forgiving shrug, Fran said, "You're allowed to be a shithead the week your dad dies."

"Am I?"

"I think so. But it's cool of you to apologize."

"Does the pizza score me any extra points?"

"Oh, hell yeah. Major points."

"I was hoping it would."

Cammy moved over to the couch and gave Fran a firm hug. Neither of them were touchy-feely types, but this seemed like a good moment to make an exception. The beauty of a lifelong friendship like theirs, Cammy thought, was that an apology didn't require a big, dramatic display. A few honest words were enough to do the job.

Fran brought in paper plates from the kitchen, and they dug into the food with gusto, as if they'd never quarreled. Cammy told her about the day's events: the trip to the cemetery, lunch with Dr. Strum, cooling it with Nick at the Clubhouse. ("If I were you," Fran noted, "I woulda fucked him once before you became friends.") They made plans for Fran to come spend a weekend in the city next month, when Bikini Kill, the iconic nineties riot grrrl band they'd idolized as kids, would be playing a reunion show at Irving Plaza.

Halfway through the pizza, they decided to put on a movie. In their high school days, they'd always binged horror flicks in October to celebrate the spooky season. After some discussion (*The Exorcist? Halloween?*), they settled on their most-viewed favorite: *Carrie*. Not the blasphemous recent remake, of course, but the classic 1976 original. Nothing gave them more of a kick than Sissy Spacek drenched in pig's blood, telekinetically transforming her prom into a fiery inferno. You go, girl.

They vegged on the couch, eating and watching and scream-laughing, until they eventually passed out. Later, Cammy felt her friend get up. Opening her eyes a sliver, she saw Fran return with a fluffy comforter, which she draped over Cammy before stumbling off to her bedroom for the night.

She didn't have a sister, but she had the next closest thing.

Day Seven: Sunday

♦ 20 ♦

THE BEST WEEK CAMMY had ever had with her mom was when she was twelve years old and they went to visit Beth's mother, Patricia, in California. It was winter break of seventh grade. Cy couldn't make the trip because he had to work. No Dad this time.

Cammy felt such excitement sitting in the window seat of the Continental Airlines jet as the crew performed their safety demonstration dance. She'd never traveled across the country before; Grandma Patty had always come to see them in Jersey. During the flight, she and her mom watched *The Princess Diaries* and ate ham-and-cheese sandwiches Beth had packed in advance. Cammy had brought along a paperback copy of *A Wrinkle in Time* from the school library, but she was too amped to read. California!

They flew into San Francisco, rented a vehicle, and drove down the scenic 101 to Morgan Hill, the small, pretty city where Grandma Patty lived. Almost immediately upon their arrival in the Golden State, Cammy noticed something different about her mother. Bopping her head to a soft rock station in the rental car, Beth seemed younger somehow, more relaxed, less high-strung. Maybe because this was her home terrain. Or maybe because this trip meant a reprieve from all her usual responsibilities: real estate, PTA meetings, managing the household.

Whatever the reasons, Beth was in fine, carefree form, and she and Cammy had a wonderful week together. Grandma Patty, whose snug apartment was crowded with Christmas ornaments—including a mechanical Santa that crooned Elvis songs—fed them and doted on them in grandmotherly fashion. They spent a day cruising around sunny San Jose, where Beth had grown up. Cammy got to check out her mom's old stomping grounds: her schools, her hangouts, the frontier-themed amusement park where she'd worked in the summers.

Another day, they drove back up to San Francisco to attend a matinee of *The Nutcracker* at the grand War Memorial Opera House. The ballet was beguiling. Afterward, they rode a cable car through the hilly metropolis, and Cammy stuffed her face with premium chocolate at Ghirardelli Square. Then came the breathtaking Golden Gate Bridge and a meal with Beth's hippie college friend Janine, who resided on a houseboat in Sausalito. Cammy was enamored of the houseboat concept. "I want one of these one day," she proclaimed to the laughter of the adults.

Cammy cried on the flight home. Beth asked her what was wrong. "I just had so much fun with you, Mom," she said. "I don't want it to end."

★ ★ ★

Cammy recalled this memory as she trekked from Fran's place to her mother's house on Sunday morning. She wondered what Beth would do when she got there. Would she let her in? Would she block the door? Would she call the cops?

Passing by St. Paul's, she saw folks filing into church for the ten o'clock mass. She had an urge to sneak in and ask Jesus to make things go smoothly with her mom. So what if she wasn't Catholic? He was a Jew, too, wasn't he?

Cammy thought better of this and kept moving. Turning onto Hill Avenue, she felt her stomach lurch. Her nerves weren't only about seeing her mother, whom she'd had zero contact with since their conflagration on Thursday. ("If you leave again now," Beth had warned, "don't bother coming back.") They were also about the fact that today was the last day of shiva.

This should've been a relief, no? The official weeklong mourning period, with its visitors and rituals—which Cammy had found so suffocating and unhelpful—was finally at an end. Okay, great. But now what? What were the guidelines for grief going forward? Were you just supposed to snap your fingers and be fine again?

She stopped across the street from the house and ducked behind a tree, observing it like a spy. Was her mom in there alone, or did she have company? Cammy hoped she was alone. She didn't want an audience for the scene that was about to unfold, whether it turned out to be a tearful reunion or another turbulent clash.

Working up her courage, flimsy as it was, she emerged from her hiding place and approached her childhood home. She climbed the front steps and stood frozen at the door.

Come on, Cammy. What're you waiting for? Some deus ex machina to swoop down and solve your problems for you? Grow up. It's your mom in there. The person who gave birth to you. If you can't face her, whom can you face? Ring the fucking doorbell.

She rang it.

But Beth didn't answer. Rabbi Wiener did.

"Cammy," he said sagely, as if he'd been expecting her. In his khakis, cardigan, and knit yarmulke, he looked like a goateed, Jewish Mister Rogers.

"Rabbi."

"I knew you'd show up."

"What do you mean?"

"I knew you'd see the light."

"How do you know I've seen the light?"

"It's in your eyes." Cammy was about to counter this, but then it occurred to her that perhaps the rabbi was right. If, as the saying went, the eyes were the windows to the soul, did hers reflect the change of heart she'd undergone at the cemetery? And did the clergyman possess a special ability to detect such subtle spiritual shifts? Or was he merely full of it? "Your mother and I were just sitting in the living room. Would you like to join us?"

"Would she be okay with that?"

"I think she would be, yes."

Rabbi Wiener ushered her into the room, where Beth was seated on the sectional, dressed in widow's black.

"Hi, Mom," Cammy said in a repentant voice that was almost a whisper. "I'm back."

Beth rose. "Hi, babe."

Then they both promptly fell to pieces. They rushed forward and held each other while the rabbi hung back at a respectful distance. Cammy felt all her years of built-up resistance flow out of her, like liquid through a sieve. She realized she hadn't been wrapped tightly in her mother's arms for a very long time. Why had she deprived herself of their warmth and comfort?

"I'm sorry," she stammered, wiping away tears. "I'm sorry for everything. For this week. For how I've been. For how I've been to *you*."

"It's okay, it's okay . . ."

"I just—I miss him so much."

"I miss him, too."

"I'm gonna be better, Mom. I promise. I'm gonna be better now."

"Shh, shh . . ."

And this, quite simply, was how it happened. This was how the hard layer of ice was broken at last. Not with lengthy speeches and explanations—those could come later—but with the pure, unassailable power of a mother and daughter's embrace.

★ ★ ★

"*Shtey oyf,*" Rabbi Wiener said in a funny accent.

They were still in the living room. Cammy and Beth sat on the sofa; the rabbi occupied Cy's worn tan easy chair. Coffee had been set out, but nobody was really drinking it.

"What does *shtey oyf* mean?" Cammy asked.

"It's Yiddish," he explained. "It means 'get up.'"

"You're telling us to get up?"

"It's a custom. The bereaved *sit* shiva, and then, on the final morning, they get up and take a walk around the block."

Yet another tradition Cammy had never heard of. Her Jewish bona fides were sorely lacking. "Why?"

"It's meant to symbolize coming out of the first stage of mourning. Returning to the world. Beginning to move on." He gave them a searching rabbinical gaze. "Are you ready? Shall we walk?"

Cammy and her mom looked at one another. Were they ready? Would they ever be ready?

"Yes," Beth said.

So they walked.

Rabbi Wiener led them out of the house and onto the leaf-covered street. The sun had appeared, warming the cool autumn air. If any nosy neighbors were watching from their windows, they would've seen a curious group: the yarmulked Mister Rogers a few strides ahead of the middle-aged woman and her millennial offspring as they strolled silently down the sidewalk at a leisurely pace, going nowhere in particular.

But they *were* going somewhere, Cammy thought. Step by steady step, she and her mother were venturing into the new, alien, post-Dad phase of their existence. Into the great unknown.

As they circled the block, images of their life as a family unit flashed through Cammy's mind, like a rapid-cut movie montage: Sunday pancake breakfasts. Birthday celebrations in the backyard. Cy helping Cammy with her math homework at the kitchen table while Beth listened to Lite FM and cooked bow tie pasta for dinner. Thanksgiving-weekend road trips to Boston, Baltimore, D.C., Quebec. Petty arguments. Silly jokes. Snow days. Passover Seders and Hanukkah parties. Staying up late, past Cammy's bedtime, to watch *Saturday Night Live*. Brunches in the Village when she was at NYU. Thousands of three-way conversations.

All of it history now. Past tense. And the future uncertain.

When their brief circuit was nearly complete, Cammy reached out to grip her mom's hand. Beth squeezed back in acknowledgment. The rabbi halted in front of the house and placed his own hands on their shoulders. "*Yehi zichro baruch*," he said. The age-old Hebrew benediction. "May his memory be a blessing."

There was a quick rush of wind. And just like that, shiva was over.

★ ★ ★

Before he left, Rabbi Wiener cornered Cammy in the foyer and did a bit of proselytizing. Beth was in the bathroom, rinsing her face.

"So," he said, with a tug at his goatee, "can I expect to see you at synagogue anytime soon?"

"Doubtful," Cammy replied.

"Still not your thing, is it?"

"Not so much." She figured she should throw him a bone. "But, uh, thanks for all your help this week. Even if I didn't appreciate it. I know it's meant a lot to my mom."

"That's my job."

"Oh, and I'm sorry my dad and I used to crack jokes during your sermons."

"Water under the bridge. I kind of miss it, actually. Kept me on my toes." All things considered, the rabbi wasn't a bad guy. Though Cammy didn't buy into the brand he was a spokesman for, he carried out his pastoral duties with care and compassion. And he'd been by her mother's side when she wasn't. Zipping up his windbreaker, he said, "May I ask you one more question?"

"Shoot."

"What brought you back here? What made you come around?"

She hedged. "I, um—I went to the cemetery yesterday morning. And I . . . I spoke to my dad. I mean, not literally. Or maybe literally. I don't know. Does that sound nuts?"

"Nope," the rabbi said. "I hear it all the time."

"You do?"

"You know, Cammy, you can always do that. At any point in your life when you need to. You can go and speak to him and hear his voice in your ear. This is the gift our loved ones give to us when they leave." Corny? Yes. True? Also yes.

Cammy heard the bathroom door open. Her mom would be back in a second. "Rabbi," she said, "I have a question for *you*, if you don't mind."

"Go ahead."

"What's the Jewish take on the afterlife? I've never really been clear on that."

"Well, do you want the short version or the long version?"

"The short version."

Rabbi Wiener turned his palms up in a pose of cosmic humility. "We don't really know."

★ ★ ★

Cammy and Beth nibbled on crackers and cheese at the kitchen table. It was just the two of them now. No friends or relations would be arriving later with provisions and pity. The public performance was done.

The Berlin Wall between them seemed to have crumbled with their initial embrace, or it was in the process of crumbling. They were talking to each other more easily, without that old edge of tension.

What better moment to broach a sensitive subject?

"By the way," Cammy said, deliberately nonchalant, "I know about Dad and Debra."

"Debra?" Her mother blinked. "You mean . . ."

"Yeah, I know her name, and that she wasn't just Dad's college girlfriend. I know they were married. I went to Aunt Miriam's the other day. I showed her the Polaroid, and she told me everything." Beth sighed, presumably at the thought of her sister-in-law's big mouth. "Don't worry, Mom. I'm not upset about it. I was at first, but I'm not now." A beat. "Also, I called her."

"What?"

"I found Debra's number online. I thought I would tell her—I don't know *what* I thought. It was dumb. She definitely didn't wanna talk to me, though. She hung up. She's still angry."

"I'm not surprised. There was a lot of bad blood there." Her mother was quiet for a bit. "I'm sorry I lied," she said, abashed.

"Why did you?"

"Dad told me about his first marriage on our third date. I remember the conversation. I saw how hard it was for him to talk about. How sad it made him. The wounds were still raw. And we barely ever discussed it again. So, until he wanted to bring it up with you himself, I didn't think it was my place to. But I probably should have."

"It's fine. I get it. I forgive you." Cammy felt good taking the high road, showing her mom some grace, doing the forgiving for once. "Everyone has a secret or two, right?"

"I suppose they do." Beth turned her head and surveyed the homey kitchen. Then she took a breath and said, as much to herself as her daughter, "I think I'm gonna sell this house."

"What?"

"I'll be too depressed if I stay here by myself. All the memories. I should downsize to an apartment anyway. Dad and I had already thought about it."

"Where would you go?"

"Somewhere local. Maybe one of those high-rises in Fort Lee, with the other old ladies."

"You're not an old lady, Mom."

"I'm getting there. I'm sixty-five." Cammy frequently forgot this fact. Beth looked terrific for her age, which boded well for her own genetics. "I'm thinking about retiring, too."

"No more real estate? That's like your mojo."

"It's wearing me out. Has been for the past couple of years."

"What would you do instead?"

"Collect social security. Volunteer at the temple. Have lunches with Toby Goldfarb and the crew. Smell the roses."

"You're such a go-getter, though. I can't imagine that."

"Me neither, to tell you the truth. But it's time for a change." Beth placed a cheddar cheese square on a Club cracker and bit into it. "What about you, babe? What's your plan?"

"My plan? I guess . . . I'm just gonna keep trying to figure things out."

"Wanna move in with me?"

"Um—"

"I'm kidding," Beth chuckled.

"Good one. No, but I—I have some irons in the fire. Things I'm excited about." She did: her play, her potential collaboration with Gretchen, her role as "amanuensis" to Dr. Strum. Hell, even teaching writing to the kids at Nick's Clubhouse. "It's the first time I can say that in a while."

"I'm glad."

"Me too."

"When do you have to go back to the city?"

"Tonight? This new temp job starts tomorrow." At the Midtown office of a software company with the disturbingly nebulous name of InfoTech.

"Could you stay here and commute in the morning?"

Seeing the naked need in her mom's eyes, Cammy said, "Oh. Sure. I can make that work."

"Thanks, babe. I'd rather not be alone tonight."

"Can I borrow one of your outfits, though? I don't have any office clothes with me."

"You can have your pick."

Cammy stood up and carried their plates to the sink. "So what should we do now?"

"I might lie down this afternoon. I'm still not sleeping very well." Beth smiled. "But I have a suggestion for later, if you're up for it."

"Yeah?"

"Dad and I have had a Sunday-night ritual lately. Chinese food and Scrabble. How does that sound?"

"That sounds *perfect*."

After they both napped—Cammy was drained, too—Beth called Fun Lum, the takeout place around the corner. She asked for egg rolls and wonton soup and chicken with broccoli and shrimp in lobster sauce and a side of pork fried rice. The staples.

For some reason, Chinese cuisine held an exalted status as the chosen comfort food of the Chosen People. It's what American Jews ate on Christmas.

Cammy went out to pick up the order. When she handed the older woman at the register her debit card, the woman glanced at it and said, "Adler. Is your father Cy?"

"Yes."

"He didn't come last Sunday. He comes every Sunday. Is he all right?"

Oh boy. She had to break the news to someone else. "He, um, he passed away. Last Saturday."

The woman let out an involuntary gasp and covered her mouth. "Passed away? Was he sick?"

"No. He had a surgery. There were complications." The perennial euphemism.

"I'm so sorry."

"Thank you."

"He was a very nice man. He always had funny jokes."

"That was my dad." The woman gave Cammy back her card without swiping it. "Oh, you didn't—"

"No charge this time."

"What? No—"

"Please. Please. Take care."

Cammy nodded, moved by the kind gesture. How many people had her father affected in small ways she had no idea about? She dropped a five-dollar bill in the tip jar and left, the door chiming behind her.

Beth beat her daughter handily in Scrabble. Cammy had a relatively solid vocabulary, but she hadn't played in years and lacked a coherent strategy. Her mom, meanwhile, had sharpened her skills through weekly battles with Cy, a savant-like master of the game.

Once they'd finished competing and eating, they made lemon tea and drifted into the living room. They sat together under a fleece throw blanket, flipping through family albums Beth had brought up from the basement. Each page, each picture, was a time machine.

"Mom," Cammy said, studying a soft-focus portrait the Adlers had taken at a mall studio in the nineties.

"Mm?"

"I just want you to know, when I'm in the city, I'm gonna call you every night. To check in. Okay?"

"Okay."

"And I'm gonna come home more often. I'll be here for you. I won't go AWOL again."

Beth traced invisible patterns on the back of Cammy's neck—something she'd done to soothe her when she was an anxious little girl. "I know, babe."

EPILOGUE

Monday

Cammy awoke to the ding of her alarm at seven the next morning. She showered, dried her hair, applied her makeup, and put on a charcoal pantsuit she'd found in Beth's closet, which fit surprisingly well. Looking in the mirror, she felt confident that nobody at InfoTech would have the slightest inkling of the wringer she'd been through the past week. To them, she'd be just another anonymous temporary copywriter. And that was more than fine with her.

In the kitchen, she brewed a pot of coffee, warmed herself with a piping hot cup, and poured the rest into the carafe. She stuck a Post-it note on it for her mother, who was still asleep: "Have a good day. Love you. Call you tonight."

Before heading out to catch the bus to New York—to the "busy city life" that awaited her—Cammy stopped by the mantel above the unused fireplace. Here were the photographs her mom had arranged for the shiva: Cy as a boy, as a high school grad, as an adman, as a newlywed. She stared at the last one, of her father lifting her up in the air against the backdrop of a bright, cloudless blue sky.

Lifting her up.

When she was a toddler, she'd always wanted to be picked up. Relatives still laughed about how she would cry, "Upsies!"—that was the expressive word she'd invented—and demand that her parents cart her around. Well, why not? The ground was so treacherous; being a bundle in their arms seemed like a much safer alternative. Apparently, one day her mother had put her foot down: "We can't just carry her every time she asks to be carried." "Sure, we can," her father had said, as if it were the most obvious no-brainer in the world. "She wants 'upsies.'"

Beth liked to tell this story as an example of how Cy had indulged his daughter. And yes, undeniably, he had. But to Cammy, the story also signified something else, something about the way he'd held and protected her.

Lifting her up.

Whenever she'd experienced one of those minor childhood setbacks that feel dauntingly major at the time—being treated meanly by girls at school, getting a bad grade on an exam, losing a key tennis match—she would, without fail, find a card in a small white envelope lying on her bed later that day.

Dear Cam,

You'll get 'em next time.

Love,
Your biggest fan,
Dad

"You'll get 'em next time." The Cy Adler ethos. Ever optimistic. Now the trick was to figure out how to hang on to that spirit in his absence. How to keep going without her biggest fan.

Then again, Cammy thought as she eyed the photo, he wasn't really absent, was he? Her dad was still present, not in the vague, platitudinous sense of, "He'll always be with you," but in a very real one. Because, after all, she *was* him. Genetically, chromosomally, and in so many ways beyond what the science could ever explain. The ridiculous jokes, the classic-movie nights, the poker games at the kitchen table, the thrilling adventures in the city—every single second she'd been lucky enough to spend with him had shaped her ineluctably into the person she'd become.

"We're going to follow our noses," he'd said as they crossed the bridge into Manhattan, not revealing their final destination until the last possible instant. The sweet flourish of a surprise. The satisfied grin on his face when they arrived. She would've followed him anywhere, to the ends of the earth and back. She was following him even now, with each breath she drew, with each clumsy step she took in her unsettled life.

Lifting her up.

It was time to go. Time to leave the house and get back to the grind. Cammy stood at the mantel a moment longer, struggling to pull herself away from the picture of her and her father. She knew that to walk out the door would mean a kind of ending. But maybe a beginning, too.

She kissed her hand and touched it to the glass frame.

Goodbye, Dad.

ACKNOWLEDGMENTS

Thank you to my incredible literary agent, Maria Whelan at InkWell Management, for your friendship, for being the first one to believe in me as a fiction writer, and for reading this book in staggered installments and offering your enthusiastic encouragement and insightful feedback along the way. None of this would have happened without you, and I'm forever grateful.

Thank you to my brilliant editor, Holly Ingraham, for instantly understanding the humor and heart of this story; for your sharp, perceptive guidance; and for spurring me to lean into the Jersey love. I feel so fortunate that this novel fell into the hands of a fellow Bergen County kid who got all the inside jokes. Thanks also to the fantastic team at Alcove Press—Monica Manzo, Rebecca Nelson, and Thaisheemarie Fantauzzi Pérez—for your hard work in making this book a reality. To Chelsy Escalona for the gorgeous cover design. And to Becca Rodriguez at Untitled Entertainment for coming on board with an exciting vision for the future.

I'm grateful to Joe Brancato, Andrew Horn, and the board and staff of Penguin Rep Theatre in Stony Point, New York, for giving me an artistic home as a playwright and being such tireless supporters of my work. And to my terrific theatrical agent, Susan Gurman, and Reilly Conlon and Patryce Williams Belvius at the Gurman Agency.

I wrote part of this novel at the beautiful James Stevenson Lost and Found Lab in Cos Cob, Connecticut, where I had the privilege of being an artist-in-residence in March 2023. I'm thankful to co-directors Josie Merck and Janine St. Germain for graciously hosting me and providing me with invaluable time and space to work.

Thank you to Ivan Anderson and Erica Moretti, Frank Macri, Brian Raucci, Nico Benedetti-Fang, and Matt Bastar for your decades of friendship and for all the endless hours we spent hanging out in Jersey together, creating the memories that inform this book. A special shout-out to the late, great deli Park Italian Gourmet, the inspiration for DeMarco's. And to my dear longtime friends from my days at the 92nd Street Y, Carrie Oman and Serena Robbins, for the camaraderie and the happy hours.

I'm grateful to Dr. Michael Pinker, my English teacher and mentor at Leonia High School, for deepening my understanding of literature and challenging me to think critically and write with greater care and precision. I've been bolstered by your belief in me, and I continue to relish our twenty-year-long email correspondence. And to Amy Feltman, my fellow LHS Poets in Progress member, for setting an example as an accomplished novelist from Leonia and for kindly sharing your candid wisdom about the process.

Thank you to the VanArsdalens and the Rebers, the warmest and most generous in-laws anyone could ask for. To my loving extended family: on the West Coast, the Baldwins and the Goldens, and on the East Coast, the Aigottis and the Cutrones. And to my wonderful sister, Donna Gitter, and the Gitter-Dentz family, whose company and conversation I cherish.

I never got to meet my grandfathers, but both of my late grandmothers shaped me indelibly. Teresa Golden, née Cutrone, had a blunt Brooklyn Italian sense of humor, a colorful vocabulary, and zero tolerance for bullshit, and Eva Gitter had a distinctly Eastern European Jewish combination of seriousness and wit, along with a strong love of learning that she took pains to pass down.

My mother, Virginia Gitter, has always been a dazzling dynamo. Thank you for taking care of me, for showing me what boundless energy looks like, and for being my biggest champion and flying across the country on red-eyes to see my plays. Our weekly phone calls anchor me. I owe you more than I can ever repay.

I have so much to say about my late father, Sidney Gitter, and I tried to say it in these pages. I wrote this novel because of him. I am who I am because of him. He gave me everything and exposed me to the things I love most: plays, movies, literature, art. This book is my attempt at a thank-you, my way of keeping his memory alive. I hope it does him justice.

Finally, to my wife, Meghan VanArsdalen. This novel is dedicated to you because you've given me a life that made its writing possible—a life full of love, support, and creativity. You encourage me day in and day out, and you inspire me with your own committed artistry as an actor, director, and teacher. I feel wildly lucky to have you by my side as we navigate all the thrilling rewards and anxious uncertainties that come with pursuing our passions. I love you.